THE GRID 3

CATHARSIS

PAUL TEAGUE

ALSO BY PAUL TEAGUE

Sci-Fi Starter Book - Phase 6

The Secret Bunker Trilogy

Book 1 - Darkness Falls

Books 2 - The Four Quadrants

Books 3 - Regeneration

With Jon Evans

Book 1 - Incursion

Book 2 - Armada

Book 3 - Devastation

CHAPTER ONE

Before the Plague

The young doctor studied the viral modelling data on his computer screen, desperately trying to figure out why his attempts at creating a cure had accelerated the death toll. The information didn't make sense. It was supposed to save lives, not take them. They had created two new strains of the disease, and the virus had mutated with a devastating impact. The deployment of a cure had just made the situation worse.

The pandemic had come out of nowhere and was sweeping through urban populations at a rate faster than had ever been seen before. They knew it was airborne, it was infecting just over nine out of ten people and it was spreading like a bushfire across the planet. With two new strains now wreaking fresh havoc, even those who had survived the first wave were in danger once again.

International travel had been stopped too late – they'd grounded the planes several weeks after they should have done. The advisory teams had warned the President at the briefing sessions but he'd ignored them. The Government always assumed the problem would be solved before it became necessary to pull the plug on the airlines.

The protocols were in place, but world governments were always reluctant to shut down cross-border controls. They waited and waited, then acted too late. The plague was going to have to burn itself out, but it would wipe out most of the world's population in the process.

Gripped by a sense of guilt and anxiety, he stayed up into the night when the facility was deserted. They'd all been working ridiculous hours for weeks on end, and the team was beginning to tire. The problem with humans is they need rest, they have to take breaks, however severe the crisis.

He needed to understand what he'd overlooked. He'd been sure he'd got the cure at last, but it had all gone so wrong. He tested and refined the data then started the process all over again to prove and then re-prove his theory. Every time it pointed to the same thing. There was a reason for the mutations, but so far nobody in his team had seen what was staring them in the face. Even the pooled information-sharing across the world had not spotted this. A single database updated 24/7 with the findings of the best scientific minds across the globe, yet nobody had seen what he'd seen. This was sabotage, and it had taken place at the highest level of government. They'd made him and his team the fall guys. They hadn't even used his cure, they'd gone ahead and substituted the NiVac3 option. It had been hurriedly released and they'd been warned of the consequences. His own solution was more difficult to manufacture at speed, but it would have worked. Now they'd messed up, and they were pointing the finger of blame at him.

The doctor sat in his chair and considered the world

they were about to bequeath to the next generation. Towering walls were being built around major cities on the orders of President James Morgan. Those who'd survived each strain of the plague were being herded into segregated concrete fortresses. The voice of the President was broadcast constantly across all media, issuing instructions calmly and authoritatively. Armed checkpoints were being set up where those who'd survived the plague were to report for sanctuary, barricading themselves in infection-free ghettos, packed with Immunes and survivors. They were all that would be left – humanity was hanging on by a thread.

The Government would struggle to maintain control after this. The existing world order would disappear. Too many people had died, and it was still far from over. But here was the secret, and nobody had seen it yet. This global catastrophe had been accelerated by the Government. President Morgan had overruled the advice of his advisory panel, rushed through NiVac3, and now the entire world was paying the price.

Significant power resided in this information – he cursed that he hadn't seen it earlier, before it had reached the endgame. It might have been useful then, but there was no longer the infrastructure to deliver a cure globally, not with three deadly strains harvesting so many lives. The plague would have to burn itself out as it would have done in the Middle Ages.

As a doctor, he was accustomed to healing and curing, but that world of compassion no longer existed. Everything was simplified: you survived or you died. What was happening would divide mankind. Those with the contagion would be left to die and the survivors would cling together, desperate to grasp whatever scraps of humanity they could salvage. He could see it already as the cities were beginning to fall and huge fortresses were being built.

He decided to keep the evidence to himself, removing it from his computer and securely encrypting it on a data card. He had no status now. He'd been shamed and it would take him some time to recover his reputation after such a disaster. The data card would be his free pass – with this knowledge he could wield massive power in the new world that would rise from the ashes of the plague. He had damning evidence against President Morgan and his senior team. Their negligence had caused the Earth to burn. One day, Morgan would be held to account.

He took off his lab coat and placed the data card in the pocket of his trousers. As he was about to walk away, something sentimental in him made him step back. His name badge was still attached to the lab coat. He unpinned it and examined it, recalling the life and career that had once held so much promise for him. That world no longer existed. There was no need for these laboratories anymore, since the plague was unstoppable. They were being hurriedly relocated to a new and secure facility where they would make their final stand against the disease. It was all about the survivors now and the world that would arise from the ashes once the plague had burned itself out. He turned the badge over and put it in his pocket. There was no more need for Doctor Josh Delman. He would have to become something very different in this new world.

Crisis

Joe was stunned to see his father standing in front of him as the elevator doors opened. His heart was still pounding furiously and painfully from the events that had just taken place in The Grid. Matt hugged him hard, then surveyed his son.

'You've done well to get here in time, Joe, but we have to move on straight away. Your entire Sector is going to be destroyed, and we've got to do something about it. The City will be wiped out in a matter of hours.'

'What about the others?' Lucy said. 'We can't just leave them there!'

'You have to, for now. You can't protect them in The Grid. In any case, you need urgent medical attention. Come with me, we must leave The TriPlex now. We have to get you patched up and fully briefed.'

Joe was overwhelmed by these events. Over the past six years, he'd gone through all the stages of grief: anger, resentment and acceptance. He'd vowed to seek revenge for Matt's death, yet here he was, alive and well. There was no conversation as Matt ushered them away from the elevator entrance towards a circular platform in the middle of the vast rotunda. He was serious and focused, there were no pleasantries. The place he called The TriPlex was deep underground, but high above them at the top of the structure was a massive glass dome through which the sky was just about visible.

Joe looked around, taking in as much as he could while he struggled to process what was going on. He thought of his friends in The Grid and how they would be fighting for their lives. He wanted to run and help them, but he also needed to know more.

They were in an empty triangular hall with three featureless elevator entrances situated equidistantly at the edges. They were marked 'Sector 1', 'Sector 2' and 'Sector 3'. The only other object in the area was the central platform, which looked very similar to the one the Justice

Seekers had been standing on at the beginning of their trial.

Matt was flanked by two armed guards. They were not Centuria, and Joe had never seen anything like them before. Their weaponry too was much more sophisticated than anything he'd ever come across.

Without warning, Lucy made a move for one of the weapons, pushing the butt into the guard's face and making him stumble.

'I'm going back up there to help them!'

'Lucy, stop!' called Matt.

Lucy paid no attention. She was running towards the elevator entrance, intent on returning to The Grid. She placed her hand on the red panel outside the elevator in the Sector 2 area.

'If you return to The Grid you will place all of your friends in immediate peril,' Matt shouted. 'Your actions could also lead to the annihilation of the entire population of your city. Please, Lucy, I know you're desperate to help your friends, but you can only do that with our help.'

Lucy stopped dead in her tracks and removed her hand from the activation panel. Joe looked on, unsure what to do next. The second guard pointed her weapon directly in Lucy's direction.

'The only reason you could enter that elevator is because you're Immunes. Both of you are. If anybody tries to enter this area as a plague carrier, they'll be eliminated before they get here. That applies to your friends too. If they're carriers, they'll be killed before they ever step into the elevator.'

Lucy hesitated, looking from Joe to Matt. Her finger moved to the trigger of her weapon but she'd begun to doubt herself.

'I'll explain to you both when we enter Centrum. We need to run some urgent tests on you straight away. You have to trust me, Lucy. You'll get the chance to enter your city again very soon, but I have to brief you both before you do that.'

The elevator door opened, but Lucy let it close once again without stepping inside.

'Joe, what do you think?'

'We've come this far, Lucy. We set out to discover what happened to Dad ...'

Joe corrected himself.

'We wanted to find out what happened to *our* dads ... We're getting close to the truth now, we need to find out what's going on. Everybody gains if we succeed, Lucy. We've come this far – we have to carry on now.'

Matt nodded. Lucy held out her weapon so it could be retrieved by the guard. His face was bloodied, but he took hold of the firearm carefully without any sign of threat to Lucy.

'I'm sorry,' she said. 'Things were getting really stressful up there.'

The guard indicated that she should step back onto the platform. When all five people were standing within the circular area, Matt activated a small device he'd been holding in his hand. The platform was surrounded by a bright red grid which passed over their bodies like a virtual net.

'It's alright,' Matt tried to reassure Lucy. 'This is just to make sure you're not carrying anything that could contaminate Centrum. You're about to enter a contamination-neutral zone – this is called a BioSweep.'

Lucy was not consoled by this, but whatever scanning process had just taken place was now over. The platform was surrounded by a shimmering haze of light which ended after a few seconds. They had now left The TriPlex and were in a completely different location.

'Welcome to Centrum,' Matt announced. 'I'll be happy to answer all of your questions here. First, though, we need to run tests on both of you. Lucy, you're in a bad way. We must get those wounds looked at.'

Lucy nodded. She'd been impetuous only minutes before but now she felt exhausted. Her mind was going crazy with thoughts of her friends, and she felt guilty for finding this sanctuary when her companions were still fighting for their lives in The Grid. The guard she'd just assaulted took her arm and escorted her away from the platform.

'Joe, stay with me for a while. We need to talk.'

Joe looked towards Lucy.

'Will she be okay?'

'They'll take good care of her. I want you to be checked out too; you don't look much better.'

oe scanned the area. It was lie nothing he'd ever seen before. Compared to The Climbs, Silk Road was technologically advanced, clean and well-maintained, but Centrum was something else.

It was modern, antiseptic, calm and extremely hi-tech. There were consoles everywhere, vast arrays of flashing lights, information screens and data displays. Joe noticed how few people were around, but those who were operating the consoles were dressed simply in clean tunics and trousers. It seemed focused, purposeful and well ordered.

There were huge digitized screens placed all along the corridors. They were counting down to zero with fewer than nine hours to go. What was going to happen? There was no indication of what the displays might be for, but Joe guessed the countdown was the reason for Matt's urgency.

'Joe, I'm so sorry I couldn't tell you I was alive. It was impossible – I might have got you killed, and I couldn't get a direct message to you anyway.'

Joe's eyes began to moisten with tears. Things had happened so fast, he'd barely had time to register what was going on. Now he was out of immediate danger and had made his escape from the prospect of a terrible death, he needed to let it all out. He was overwhelmed by the situation. One minute he'd been moments from death, the next he'd been reunited with the father he'd thought to be dead.

Matt hugged him tight. It felt good to Joe to have someone taking care of him again. He'd been the strong one for six years, having to grow up fast and help his family survive. At last he'd got someone to take that weight off his shoulders.

'What happened, Dad? How did you get out of The Grid?'

'Similar to you, Joe. I thought it was all over for me, but then from nowhere I got a chance to get out.'

'But how? I don't even know how Lucy and I got out of there alive.'

Matt seemed reluctant to give more detail. He was keen to move on with his own agenda.

'We're under a lot of pressure, Joe. There's so much happening all at once. You got here just in time – you've given us all a chance. What's going on in your Sector is the least of our worries.'

Joe had never heard The City referred to as a Sector, though he'd noticed that three Sectors were marked when he and Lucy had descended to The TriPlex in the elevator.

He couldn't recall ever having been in a working elevator before. Everything was completely alien to him at Centrum.

'In just under nine hours, Catharsis will begin. What's going on in The Grid is insignificant in comparison to this. I know you're desperate to help your friends, but there are many more lives in danger. Hundreds of thousands of people could die.'

There was a lot to take in. Joe placed his hand on his chest which was tight and uncomfortable, but he put it down to the stress of the situation. It would pass, just like the pain from all of the cuts and bruises he had sustained.

'Catharsis was set in motion a hundred years ago, before any of us were born. It was agreed as part of The Pact, after the plague had driven what was left of humanity into three separate cities. We call them Sectors here.'

'So there is something else beyond these walls?'

'There's a lot beyond the walls of The City, Joe. It's what Tom and I had discovered when we were arrested.'

'I thought there had to be more. Delman was speaking to somebody outside The City. He's part of this, isn't he?'

'Delman has a lot to answer for, Joe, and yes he's in this up to his neck. There are three Sectors – or cities – in all, and ours is just one of them. But there's a problem, and that's why The Pact was created in the first place. The three cities were our last hope. Each one housed survivors from a different strain of the disease. Catharsis was created to choose who would take humanity forward. If the disease remained uncured, the Sectors would be destroyed and Centrum would have to rebuild from the ashes.'

'Where are we now? How come we're all safe here?'

'We're all Immunes in Centrum, Joe. There aren't that many of us in existence. As well as Immunes, there is a smaller group of people out there we call Conduits who have survived the plague and now carry the disease. They could spread it to other people who've never had the disease. It's how Tom Slater and I were drawn together. Lucy is an Immune too. We can survive among the Conduits, but we're not immune to all three strains of the virus. This entire unit at Centrum houses just over one thousand Immunes, made up of scientists, doctors, tech experts and their families.'

'This is incredible. Are we in a Sector now?'

'No, this is something different. Centrum is isolated – it's located below ground at the centre of the three Sectors. The only way in and out of each Sector is via what you call The Grid. It's there to serve as a barrier, a defence mechanism, it protects each Sector from entry, exit, attack or invasion. In our city it's been abused and adapted as a system of punishment. It was never meant for that purpose – it was built as a neutral zone.'

Joe's mind was creating more questions every time Matt told him something new. It was amazing that all of this could be going on. None of them had had any idea.

'Centrum is a contained area, the one thing that links the Sectors and preserves continuity. It was populated with just enough Immunes to give humanity a fighting chance if the Sectors ever failed. It's worked well for a hundred years, but now the designated time is over. It all ends tomorrow morning with Catharsis.'

Joe didn't like the sound of what was coming. He'd survived The Grid to walk into this?

'What's Catharsis? I'm guessing that's what this is all leading to.'

'Yes, Joe. At 08:00 tomorrow morning our Sector will be destroyed. The countdown timers you can see all around Centrum show how long we have remaining.'

'Does anybody else know about this? In the Sectors, I mean?'

'There's only one person outside Centrum who knows what's going to happen, and that's Josh Delman.'

Joe stared at his father, waiting for an explanation. Delman was rumoured to have made it out of The Grid alive, so it might make sense if he knew about Catharsis. But what made him unique?

'Delman is the problem and the solution,' Matt picked up. 'Delman is the only person who can stop Catharsis.'

'So what is the problem? What has Delman done and how can he fix it?'

'The Pact was an agreement made a hundred years ago to allow humanity to survive. It had to be that way or all of the Sectors would have perished over time anyway. But the plan was sabotaged, and the man we know as Delman is responsible. Centrum was supposed to survive but in just over eight hours everybody here will die. The walls and buildings of the three Sectors will implode and Centrum will collapse soon afterwards. We'll all perish in a concrete grave.'

Hunted

The new Justice Seekers were dazed and confused. Clay beckoned them over to the huge concrete pillar which they were using for cover. It had happened so fast. One minute they'd been in a labyrinth, the next their environment had changed to a bleak cityscape. It was not unlike The Climbs, but it was in a far greater state of decay.

Clay had seen Joe and Lucy vanish into the elevator. He'd encouraged them to go, it was their only chance of walking out of The Grid alive. If there was something beyond that deathly arena, Joe and Lucy had to press on and find it. There had to be some way of escaping and Joe and Lucy had seized their chance, a new opportunity for them all to survive.

Clay had barely had time to question what had happened. The bot had approached an area which at first appeared to be a water butt. However, as the bot moved closer, the water butt fragmented into a pixelated form then faded completely to reveal the elevator doorway. Joe and Lucy had disappeared inside and the water butt had rematerialized.

All of the remaining Justice Seekers had been shocked to see a holographic image of President Josh Delman appearing before them. Normally it was Damien Hunter who presided over the trials. Things must have really been kicked off by Joe and Lucy if he'd been forced to intervene.

Then there were the five new Justice Seekers to accommodate. Fortrillium would top up the numbers on the rare occasions a trial had gone to nearly ten Modes and there was virtually nobody left standing, throwing some new victims in just to sustain the action on the screens a little longer. Clay suspected they were trying to make up for the loss of Joe and Lucy, perhaps even diverting attention away from their disappearance. Had their exit been seen on the screens? It would cause a great stir in The Climbs if it had. If there was any suspicion that there was a way out of The Grid, it would have fuelled a new hope.

The bot had become the immediate focus of the snipers who were shooting heavily in order to disable it. It seemed intent on completing its task, despite the physical damage it had sustained from the weapon fire.

As Clay was welcoming the new Justice Seekers and making sure they were sufficiently protected by the concrete barricade, the water butt pixelated once again and the elevator door opened. Joe and Lucy had gone. Whatever had happened, they were out of The Grid. They might be facing something even worse than The Grid wherever they'd gone to, there was no way of knowing.

As the weapon fire continued, the bot sustained more damage and sparks began to fly out of its circuit boards. Clay was distracted, but he saw something – someone – moving at speed behind him. He turned around, it was Miron, running for the elevator door. The weapon fire sounded around him, miraculously missing as he criss-crossed the gap between the barricade and The Core.

'Stay back!' shouted Clay. 'Miron, don't risk it!'

It was too late, Miron was committed. He evaded the gunfire, though he caught a flesh wound on his right arm. It rattled him but he kept on running. As Miron was about to enter the elevator, a bright red matrix appeared and covered his entire body. He froze while the matrix appeared to scan him from top to bottom.

There was a white flash of light and Miron's body exploded. One second Miron was there, the next he was gone, his bloody remains spread where he had been standing.

Clay gasped. There were cries of shocked disbelief. At first they'd thought this was a new torture being deployed by Fortrillium to torment them, but it appeared that Miron's death was connected to the elevator, it seemed to have nothing to do with the trial itself.

The weapon fire targeted at the bot increased until its circuitry failed and, at last, it took the final hit. As the bot's power faded, the water butt pixelated and the elevator entrance disappeared. The sniper fire stopped and there was quiet once again.

It was a few minutes before anybody spoke. The new city landscape had not yet fully rendered, there were still traces of the labyrinth, but these swiftly disappeared. Clay wasn't even certain that this was the third Mode since there had been no formal announcement from Damien Hunter and the Law Lords. It was as if they'd been caught out – whatever had happened with the bot and Joe and Lucy's sudden escape, Fortrillium didn't appear to have been ready for it.

The gunfire had stopped, and it seemed to be safe once again. The water butt had gone and that entire area had been rendered beyond recognition. Clay wasn't entirely sure what he was looking at. Their surroundings seemed to change seamlessly from time to time, and it was difficult to stay oriented.

'What's that Lucy threw towards us?' came Ross's voice from the silence. 'Is it safe to get it, do you think?'

'You're in too bad a way, Ross. Leave it for now. Let's just give it a few minutes to make sure the coast is clear.'

Clay took charge once again, and for the first time surveyed the new Justice Seekers. There was a male there, the same sort of age as Joe. He was bloodied, bruised and completely out of it. He needed urgent medical attention.

Then there was a woman. Again, she'd been beaten, but she was still strong, she could walk and she was alert.

Clay noticed the older man. His hand was heavily bandaged and there was a small blood stain beginning to work its way through the covering.

There was a young woman there too, dressed as a Centuria, but she'd been stripped of her weaponry and protective gear. Clay had never seen a Centuria without a helmet before, and it was shocking to him. There was a human being underneath the helmets. He'd always considered them to be part machine. Something as ruthless as a Centuria had to have been stripped of all humanity, he'd figured.

Finally, there was another young woman who seemed to be in good health, but was clearly terrified. Clay needed to reassure them. It seemed they'd been herded up rapidly and thrown into The Grid with very little ceremony.

'I'm Clay,' he began. 'You're in The Grid now, but I think we're safe for the time being. The weapon fire seems to have stopped.'

There was a palpable sigh of relief from the new Justice Seekers. They seemed glad to have somebody to guide them through their ordeal.

'This is Ross and Chris. We're all that's left of the original prisoners.'

'Where is Joe? What happened to Joe?' the woman said.

'And Lucy, where did Lucy go?' asked the younger woman.

'They made their escape just as you arrived. We don't know where they are now, but they made it out alive.'

Clay looked over to where Miron had tried to make his dash for freedom. The area was now unrecognizable, it had been re-rendered to orientate them away from The Core.

Clay went around the group finding out the new names. He was surprised to discover that three of the new Justice Seekers knew each other already. There was Joe's mother, Jena, and his friends, Mitchell and Hannah. It emerged that the older man's wound had been inflicted by Talya Slater. The pieces soon began to come together as the questions flowed.

Fortrillium was under siege and was closing down the aftershocks left by Joe and Lucy's activities. There had been a team of people outside fighting to keep Joe and Lucy alive, but Fortrillium was onto them, and they'd been hastily rounded up and thrown into The Grid.

Max had revealed that the bot was his doing. He didn't know where Joe and Lucy were heading, but he thought it was to safety. Why else would the bots have been sent to maintain that area so thoroughly during their routine inspections? He could also tell Clay what the object was that Lucy had thrown from the entrance to the elevator.

'That'll be a WristCom. We've been trying to get it to you all along. Turns out I could have just brought it in myself.'

Clay laughed at that. It seemed a crazy thing to do bearing in mind what had just happened, but Max was right. The WristCom was another glimmer of hope, though, one more chance of escape. Clay had spent a lifetime in The Climbs reconfiguring those devices, he was certain he'd be able to nurse it back to life.

Max had a theory about what had happened to Miron. He'd seen a rat following the maintenance bots up the long tunnel to The Grid once, and exactly the same thing had happened to the creature. A bright red lattice had enveloped it and incinerated it on the spot. Max had always wondered if it had been staged by Fortrillium to make sure he didn't get any bright ideas about heading up the tunnels. His theory was that anything living got destroyed in them, and he reckoned the same had happened to Miron.

Clay suspected there was more to it. Joe and Lucy had stepped into the elevator with no challenge, so there had to be something else Max wasn't seeing.

Piece by piece the bedraggled group of survivors put together their stories. Only Julia Levett remained silent, listening and taking it all in. Clay figured she'd expect to receive a hostile reaction as a Centuria, and he let her lie low for a while as he worked out what had been going on outside The Grid.

Hannah had broken down in tears when she began to explain what she'd been doing and how she'd helped to create the very environment they found themselves in at that moment. She told the group how she'd worked to save them from the beasts in the labyrinth, but that something or *somebody* seemed to be fighting her all the way. She became distraught when she heard what had happened from the Justice Seekers' point of view. For her it had all been pixelated gameplay, but for Clay, Chris, Ross – and those who had lost their lives – every moment had been real.

'Nobody in The City is without guilt,' Clay consoled her. 'You gave Joe and Lucy a chance, Hannah. You gave us all a chance. Remember that. We all do what we have to do to stay alive.'

There were existing relationships within this new group of Justice Seekers. Jena attended to Mitchell's wounds. He was weak and silent. Nobody was able to find out what had happened to him, but whatever it was he'd lost a lot of blood and been badly hurt in the process.

By the time everybody had made their introductions, Clay felt that at last they might all have a fighting chance. Jena confirmed that Wiz and Dillon had escaped. If they weren't in The Grid, she assumed they'd got out alive. They had tech and they might still have access to whatever was going on beyond The City's walls. They spoke conspiratorially, unsure if their conversations could be heard, and unwilling to give any incriminating information about their friends on the outside. Max and Jena had confirmed that Talya was still working hard to save them. Julia Levett had shifted uncomfortably at that revelation, but Clay decided to wait a while before challenging her.

Finally, Hannah had been reluctant to share that they still had an ally at Fortrillium. Linwood had gone undetected, and she hoped he would still be looking out for them. Clay had to tease that information from her since she'd been scared to speak, afraid the conversation might be monitored. She didn't want to place her friend in any more danger. Eventually, Clay had got the other Justice Seekers to talk loudly while they discussed the matter in whispers, masking the highly sensitive information.

'You did everything you could at Fortrillium,' Clay reassured Hannah. 'I'm grateful for your help, we'd all be dead by now if you hadn't intervened.'

Hannah wasn't so sure, but she was relieved Clay was around. He seemed to know what he was doing – at least they had a leader. It was Chris who got hold of the WristCom that they'd been aware of for some time, still taking cover in case of snipers.

'Chris, come back!' Ross had shouted, but he made the short journey there and back without mishap. The snipers seemed to have disappeared. Clay was relieved to see it was a standard WristCom and it still had charge. It was an older model, but he was more familiar with those. In The Climbs it was easier to obtain obsolete models than it was to procure the latest devices. He'd look at it later. He would definitely be able to do something with the WristCom, especially if Wiz and Dillon were still out there somewhere. He'd make sure it was switched on at the very least.

Mitchell and Ross were in urgent need of medical attention, and Clay didn't think either would be in any condition to survive the next Mode, if and when it came. He surveyed the area.

'What did you create here, Hannah?' he asked, hoping she might give some clues.

'It's a ruined cityscape. We took The Climbs and moved it fifty years into the future. It's older, more ruined, and a lot more dangerous. This version is different, though. We created pathways so we could get to Joe and Lucy, but it's been reconfigured now and the layout is unfamiliar.'

'Will there be anything useful here?'

'It's difficult to tell,' Hannah continued. 'I only partially rendered the environment, so there was no detail at that time. The Gridders have taken what I started and finished it off. I don't even know if this is your next Mode, but if it is they should have placed food and weapons nearby.'

'Okay, we need to look around. Mitchell and Ross need to get patched up as soon as possible. We don't know when the new Mode will start.'

There were murmurs of agreement. Clay was tired, he'd been hurt in the fighting too, but he could see the Justice Seekers looked to him for leadership.

'I'll explore this area with Julia,' he indicated with his hand. 'Jena and Max, you take a look over there. Chris and Hannah, you stay with Ross and Mitchell. Hannah, I'm putting you in charge here, okay?'

Hannah nodded. Clay figured that if she and Lucy were friends, Hannah would be good with Chris. Meanwhile, he'd separated off Julia which would give him some time to find out why she'd been thrown into The Grid. She'd been quiet so far, she was obviously holding back, and he'd need to find out what she could offer to help the group to survive.

Clay and Julia and Jena and Max split off in their separate directions, leaving Hannah with Chris, Ross and Mitchell.

Clay and Julia walked on without speaking, alert and attentive in case there should be a new attack from an as yet unknown enemy. It seemed safe, this did not appear to be a new Mode. Julia was expecting Clay to start asking questions – she could sense there were things he wanted to know as they moved on in uncomfortable silence. Then, out of nowhere, there was a loud buzzing, a rude interruption in the stillness.

Clay was confused at first, he couldn't work out the source of the noise. It was persistent and demanding, and Clay soon discovered it was the WristCom. He took it out of his pocket and looked at the screen. It was a video call. The caller was President Josh Delman.

CHAPTER TWO

Escape

Wiz felt as if the next ten seconds took place in slow motion. He knew what the sound was the minute he'd thrust upwards in the elevator. The car had sunk a little, and he'd heard something break, followed by a whirring noise, the sound of a heavy cable falling at great speed through the air.

He knew exactly what it was and he understood what was about to happen. Dillon was in terrible danger. The cable suspending the elevator car had snapped and at any moment they would begin hurtle towards the basement below, tearing his companion's body into two parts as it did so. They had seconds. How many floors did the cable have to fall, fifty maybe? Or was Harry's apartment lower than Joe's? He couldn't remember. He thought maybe thirty – they had no time at all.

The elevator car dropped. For a moment Wiz thought he wouldn't be able to save Dillon, but at the same instant an old braking system kicked in, stopping the car shooting straight to the ground. Wiz heard a metallic groan, then a snapping sound as whatever had tried to break their fall failed and faltered, but it gained them valuable seconds.

Wiz sank to his knees. Dillon was whisked immediately out of the doorway, his head entering the elevator car just as it began to plunge to the ground. He fell off Wiz's shoulders, tumbling hard onto the floor. Wiz crashed beside him, pushing him powerfully back down when he tried to raise his head to see what was going on.

'Stay flat!' Wiz called in the darkness. They couldn't see a thing now. There was just the sound of the cable falling and the elevator car clicking past the floors as it hurtled towards the ground. Wiz tried to keep count, but the levels passed by too fast. It didn't take long. They came to a jarring halt with a violent slam against the floor. The very cable which had created their problem served to cushion the impact of the fall when they reached the ground.

They were sore and bruised, but as both raised their heads from the floor, they were astonished to find they were still alive. Dillon was dazed, he'd taken quite a blow to his head, but the decaying corpse in the corner had helped to soften the impact.

It was Wiz who regained his focus first. The Centuria would have heard the crash in the lift shaft, they'd know that's where they were hiding. They had to exit fast.

'Dillon, get up, we need to run!'

Dillon tried to force himself up, but he was unsteady and shaken by the fall.

'We have to go now!' Wiz shouted at him. They were still in darkness, but he reactivated the WristCom to give them some light. There was blood on Dillon's forehead. Wiz hoped his pallor was just a consequence of the shock. He'd barely had time to register what had happened. He had thought he would be carrying Dillon's severed torso on his shoulders when he'd crashed to the ground.

Wiz had some fast thinking to do. The Centuria must have heard the elevator crashing to the ground but which floors did they have covered? He thought he and Dillon must be below ground. Most elevators had a pit beneath them. Were they in the pit? That should give them a head start. The Centuria would at least be at ground floor level.

Wiz used the WristCom light, frantically hunting for a floor hatch. Most elevator cars had one, but he couldn't locate it.

'Damn it!' he cursed. He could hear activity above them. The Centuria had heard the sounds in the lift shaft and were prising open the doors on the levels above them to figure out what was going on. It wouldn't take them long to work it out.

Wiz wondered if using the WristCom would be of any use, but he didn't think he'd have time to send a message. He got no further than activating the device before the sound of Centuria overhead forced him to take action. They had to get out of the lift shaft.

'Any ideas, Dillon? There should be a hatch in here somewhere.'

'Try underneath the dead body,' Dillon suggested. 'It might be there.'

Wiz retched at the thought of having to push his hands into the stinking, fetid corpse, but if he couldn't force himself to do it they'd both be joining whoever it was who'd already lost his life there.

Wiz pushed his hands through the fleshy waste, scratching to find the floor. There was activity in the shaft above them, and a shot fired. Wiz scrambled harder. His fingers found the vinyl of the floor covering underneath the body. He managed to get traction on the edges. He pulled at it as hard as he could. No movement. He tugged at it again. The weight of the corpse was too great for him to lift it.

'Dillon, help me, we need to move this body.'

Dillon was beginning to regain his wits, but wasn't keen to assist Wiz. It took another bullet ricocheting in the lift shaft above them to force him into action. Between them, they scraped the mess of flesh and bones away from the hatch in the floor. Dillon felt something solid and thought it was a rib at first. It turned out to be a small knife. It was sharp and deadly. He handed it to Wiz.

'Nice, we might need that later,' he said. There was a small hatch with a metal loop concealed within the floor. After some pulling, it lifted at last. It needed to be twisted as there was a locking device built in. It was stiff after so many years, but Wiz still managed to prise it open. He peered down into the darkness below. He could hear the sound of rats scuttling to get out of the way. They must have known what was coming next.

'We've got to jump down there, Dillon. I hope you don't hate rats as much as your brother.'

Fortunately, Dillon's fear was not rats, though he wasn't particularly happy about jumping into a shallow black pit filled with live vermin and sheared cables. Wiz went first, as he figured that being taller would help. He gently lowered himself out of the tiny floor hatch and dropped to the ground. He knew it was fairly close from the sound of the rats, but he couldn't judge how far in the darkness. As it turned out, it was far enough to twist his ankle. Wiz cursed his bad luck, the injury would slow them down.

Dillon passed down the bag of tech and a rat brushed Wiz's hand as he carefully placed it out of the way. Wiz decided that worse things had happened that day. He helped Dillon down from the elevator car, it was a much bigger drop for him. When Dillon was safely back on the ground, Wiz used the light from the WristCom to check out the area. There was a steel ladder leading up out of the far side of the pit and cautiously, quietly they climbed up it. Wiz's ankle gave a painful twinge as he placed it on the ground. That was going to be a problem.

As far as Wiz could tell, they were in a basement, below ground floor level. It wouldn't take the Centuria long to be swarming the area. He could hear the screens' audio at the front of the building, the trial must have reached an exciting stage because the commentary sounded frenetic.

'We need to find an exit out the back,' Wiz said. 'Let's head over this way.' Behind them they heard a door opening. It required some force, it sounded like something was blocking it. There was a commotion, it was the Centuria. They were coming for them.

'Keep moving,' Wiz whispered, struggling to take his full weight on his foot. They were in an underground storage area which was all but empty so they could move freely. The Centuria activity was increasing at the door, they were trying to sort out lighting. Even the Centuria weren't stupid enough to enter an enclosed pitch black room without checking what was in there first.

Wiz was running out of ideas on where to go. It had to be in the opposite direction to the Centuria, but there was no guarantee there would be a way out when they got there. He was beginning to panic. The first light went on at the far end of the storage area. They were out of range of the beam, but it wouldn't take long until they could be seen.

'We're going to get cornered if we're not careful,' Dillon whispered. Wiz knew that, but there was nowhere to go, they had to keep pushing forward. Wiz counted six lights, attached to weapons, following them through the darkness. The Centuria were cautious, perhaps expecting an ambush. All Wiz and Dillon had between them was a bag of tech and a small knife, they'd be unable to put up any resistance.

'We're in a corner,' whispered Wiz. 'Damn it, we're in a corner. Can you see any way out, a door or a window light?'

'I can't see anything,' Dillon's voice came out of the darkness. 'They're getting nearer, Wiz. They're going to find us.'

There was nowhere left to go and no place to hide. They were trapped. It was only a matter of time before they'd join Jena in the hands of Fortrillium.

Fury

Damien Hunter was furious and exhilarated at the same time. He'd had to intervene rapidly when he saw what was happening in The Grid, but the disappearance of Joe Parsons and Lucy Slater meant there was hope. Events were quickening now. He had a feel for drama – Hunter knew how to create it and how to read it.

Where had they gone? They'd disappeared into thin air. He'd contacted the Gridders – they hadn't a clue what had happened, it was not of their doing. Hunter had been so busy barking orders over his WristCom, he feared he was losing his grip at one point. He got the live screen feeds killed first of all, then demanded to know what was going on. He was monitoring events in The Grid via his own console, and he saw Delman's intervention. It was unprecedented that the President should get involved in a trial. Justice was in the remit of Fortrillium to deliver, and Damien Hunter was the man in charge.

He'd heard Delman's warning. What had forced his

hand to make him reach out directly to Joe and Lucy? Damien Hunter considered the stories about Delman. Supposedly, he was the only person ever to have got out of The Grid. How had he done it? Had Parsons and Slater discovered his secret? How had they passed through the exit when the other Justice Seeker had been killed instantly by the red beam? The thought of there being a way out of The City was intoxicating to Hunter. But there was danger there too – Miron Panko had been killed trying to exit The Grid.

Hunter was anxious not to miss his chance. He would have to declare against the President. If he did it too soon, Delman would kill him and his family. Too late and he'd miss his chance.

He could feel things coming to a head. He'd spent his early evening torturing Mitchell Cranshaw – how good that had felt. It had served as a release to Hunter; he drank in the sensations of power and control. Mitchell had put up a feeble resistance – he'd revealed everything Hunter needed to know. Hannah James was arrested immediately on hearing Mitchell's revelations and a team of Centuria dispatched to Talya Slater's house confirmed she was nowhere to be found. She had vanished into thin air.

Word had also reached him that evening of Max Penner's arrest. That one had taken some digging, but a fingernail removed from Mitchell's left hand had made him squeal enough to help Hunter make the connection. Mitchell didn't have Max's name, but when Mitchell revealed that Talya's source was somebody she'd met on her tour of Fortrillium's prison facilities, it was easy enough for him to piece together.

Mitchell had also handed him Jena Parsons, her son, Dillon, and Shen Li, the one they called Wiz. He'd been frustrated to hear that two of them had escaped in The

Climbs, but Joe Parsons' mother was the perfect addition to The Grid.

He'd ordered that they all be prepared for immediate inclusion in the trial. They'd been rushed through Psych-Eval and readied for their debut on the screens. Hunter had also thrown in the Centuria traitor, Julia Levett, for good measure. The viewing audiences loved to see a Centuria perish in The Grid. It made the fools believe there really was some sort of justice in The City.

There was no doubt about it, the trial was shaping up to be the best ever. He'd be relying on that, and when his moment came he'd need to be agile. There would only be one opportunity to take out Delman, but Damien Hunter would be ready. If the residents of The City were glued to the screens, nobody would be watching when he made his move. He was waiting for Delman to step out of the darkness, it had to come soon.

He'd monitored the conversations between the President and the person on the other side of the wall, and he was more convinced than ever that this was Catharsis. He believed it would be connected with some pivotal event for the residents of The City ... but what?

Hunter was running blind and he knew it. The pages of The Pact referring to Catharsis had been torn out. Delman had gained an early advantage. But he didn't know that Hunter was monitoring him, he had no idea there was someone breathing down his neck.

With Teanna Schaelles on his side, he would make a formidable adversary. She had a burning hate for Delman too, but she was without a history. He was unable to find the usual information on her in the Fortrillium database. She had no Gen-ID, the same as the President. It was probably because Teanna was part of his inner circle, but she intrigued him nevertheless.

Damien Hunter had lined up his soldiers ready for the final battle. He didn't yet know when and where the fight would take place, but he'd drawn up his war plan.

His enemies were in The Grid, they'd be sacrificed one by one. The Gridders were under new instructions to make the gameplay as powerful and compelling as possible. He wanted the watching crowds to be aghast at what they were seeing. As each traitor died, so would any chance of rebellion or resistance when he seized control of The City from Delman.

Teanna would monitor Delman's movements. Their plan was for her to copy the pages relating to Catharsis from The Pact. It was out on Delman's desk all the time now, it should be easy for her to capture an image on her Wrist-Com. Delman trusted her, he would never think her capable of such deception.

Unknown to the President, Damien Hunter was now monitoring all communications with the mystery person on the other side of the wall. No conversation would go unheard. Delman had lost his anonymity.

Hunter was ready, there were just a few loose threads for him to tie up. Where Parsons and Slater had gone was troubling him greatly, and not even the Gridders could throw any light on that one. It was an unknown area, a function at The Core that nobody had any knowledge of. Max Penner had been of no use, he'd just confirmed what everybody at Fortrillium knew already. The bots performed maintenance tasks which were pre-programmed, nobody got to see what they were up to in The Grid. It appeared that this bot had malfunctioned and performed a maintenance check when it should have made its way back to Fortrillium.

None of that rang true to Hunter, but he couldn't find any evidence to show otherwise. Had Delman been controlling the bot? He thought it unlikely. But who would have known about the exit at The Core of The Grid? The answer was directly under his nose, but he failed to see it. He didn't believe Max Penner could possibly have orchestrated such a scheme. He also didn't know about the WristCom that had been smuggled inside The Grid.

There was another thing troubling him too. He'd thought he had Talya Slater exactly where he needed her. She'd been destined to join her daughter in The Grid after her short tribunal the following morning. Not only had she broken the laws of The City, Hunter now had sufficient evidence to prove she'd been colluding with the Fortrillium operative, Max Penner.

Hannah James had also been working with Talya. He'd need to be a bit more careful about how that particular traitorous activity was presented on the screens, but from a Law Lord point of view he'd caught her. Only he hadn't quite succeeded, she'd slipped through his fingers and disappeared.

Still, he had that one under control too. The Centuria, Julia Levett, had been only too happy to strike a deal when he'd threatened her family members. No torture had been necessary. She'd been willing to give what information she had about her conspirator friends, Leo Bachus and Jody Carn, though it was only of limited use to him. They'd vanished into thin air, like Talya Slater, rats scuttling away into dark alleys.

It was the information she'd feed to him from inside The

Grid that would be invaluable. All of the protagonists were there and she'd win their trust. She'd also be within reach of the exit at The Core. If Delman made a run for it, Levett would stop him. Levett was armed and equipped with a WristCom. He'd promised to spare her life and the lives of her family if she worked with him. What choice did she have? Damien Hunter was adept at making offers nobody could refuse.

Part of him felt smug at having set everything up so carefully. There was nowhere Delman could turn without word getting back to him. But there was still the uncertainty over Joe Parsons and Talya Slater and her daughter; they were proving troublesome and difficult to kill. Perhaps he should have worked with Talya. Would it have been better to team up rather than fight each other?

It was too late to change that now. Hunter was committed to his chosen course of action. He'd learn everything he needed to know about Catharsis, quash any hope of rebellion within The City, set up Delman for an almighty fall and then take The City as his own and reclaim his family. He'd let Delman bargain for his life to win back his family, but then he'd just kill him anyway.

Damien Hunter could see the final battle coming, the storm clouds were gathering. There were one or two annoyances still to resolve, but he could almost taste the power. Soon The City would be his to rule, he'd be reunited with his family and there would be nothing that could stop him.

Rampage

President Josh Delman had wondered if things were beginning to slip away from him when he saw Joe Parsons and Lucy Slater leave The Grid. He'd been the only person in The City ever to enter and exit via that gateway, with the exception of Teanna Schaelles and a few others who'd made the journey with him under heavy sedation.

He'd been watching on his live video stream, but was grateful Damien Hunter had had the presence of mind to cut the feed to the public screens. There would be riots if the residents of The City had seen their escape. But it meant that Hunter had seen exactly what he had seen. Would he know what had happened? It was unlikely, but he couldn't rely on that. Hunter was a danger to him, he'd caught a glimpse of a secret that only Delman knew.

The President had tried to prevent the exit. He knew straight away that he would have to step out of the shadows to try to stop Joe and Lucy leaving The Grid. It was the desperate effort of a man who was fighting to preserve the one advantage he still had. He'd had to appear via a holographic image – that was not normally his way of communicating, but he was President and if he wanted to do it he would. He'd made a last appeal to Parsons and Slater not to exit The Grid. They'd ignored him. In doing so, they'd forced his hand. They'd exposed him to Damien Hunter, and he was vulnerable now. Delman could kill Hunter's family at the press of a button. He'd taken the precaution of activating the switch-off sequence in the Umbilica. It would just take the press of the remote activator in his pocket to shut down their life-support systems. If there was a confrontation coming, that would help to focus Hunter's mind.

There had been one last chance that Parsons and Slater might not make it out of The Grid. He'd prayed that the BioSweep would take their lives. But Joe and Lucy were the children of Matt Parsons and Tom Slater, so of course they passed through unscathed. They were clear to exit The Grid just as Delman was, the same as Teanna. They were special. There weren't many of them, but they were all linked by something unique.

When the Justice Seeker Miron Panko had fled to the exit, he'd been caught by the scan. Delman knew Damien Hunter would have seen that on his private feed, it would unnerve him. It was the one good thing about those recent events – at least Hunter understood that it wasn't just as simple as walking out of that place.

Parsons and Slater were a threat to him now they'd discovered there was something outside. He'd have to kill them when he too left The City, he couldn't allow them to survive. He'd lined it all up when he'd exited The Grid with Teanna all those years ago.

Delman would hold all the power when Catharsis came. It was a plan he'd put in motion many years previously. They had to work with him because he had the power to destroy them all.

Delman didn't usually dwell on the past, but a memory came back to him at that moment, one which he'd not thought about for some time. It was probably because it was related to the Parsons family. They'd been a curse to him for several years.

It had begun with Matt Parsons and Tom Slater. They'd very nearly revealed The City's darkest secret to Damien Hunter, but Delman had managed to head it off just in time, in the same way that he'd attempted to do by sending the holographic message to Joe and Lucy in The Grid. He'd managed to retrieve Tom's WristCom and conceal it in the body of the man known as Jay who had perished in The Grid. The secrets contained on the WristCom device had died with him.

Delman wondered what had made him recall that episode again. He'd tidied up the threat posed by Matt

Parsons and Tom Slater a long time ago. Damien Hunter had even helped him to do it. The irony of it, Hunter had helped to destroy the two men who could have answered his prayers. Sometimes Delman wished he'd got somebody to share these things with, he kept a lot in his own mind.

He'd get his chance to live again soon, it was why he'd taken Teanna Schaelles, she was his guarantee. When Catharsis came, he'd return to The Core and claim his new life. In the process, he'd save humanity from extinction.

CHAPTER THREE

Strategy

Talya didn't know whether to laugh or cry. The stress of the past few days was catching up with her. She felt as if she'd been staggering at the edge of a precipice, and she craved rest and release. There would be no break for her until she'd found out what had happened to Lucy. She didn't know what to make of this latest information. Leo played back the video loop on his console.

The feed had faded to black right at the end, just as it had when Matt Parsons had been in The Grid. She'd seen it before. But something had very definitely happened in those final moments. The promos were trying to tell her that Lucy was dead. It looked as if Joe had been slaughtered by the creature. But there was no proof of death. There were no bodies, just as it had been with Matt. Death was assumed, but where was the evidence? They usually liked to show the bodies on the screens. Still, silent and finally at peace, it was often a relief to see that the torture was over when a Justice Seeker died. But there were no bodies for Joe and Lucy. If there were no bodies, there was still hope.

'Take it away, Leo. I don't need to see it again.'

'I don't think it's conclusive, Talya. We have to assume she's still alive.'

Talya nodded. She wanted to scream and fly into a rage, she felt so powerless in this fight. If it wasn't for her daughter, she could throw herself into the final assault. But all the time she had to be mindful of Lucy and Joe. Her actions could get them killed, if they weren't dead already.

'What do we do next, Leo? What's the plan?'

Talya decided to focus on the things she could control rather than dwelling on what might be.

'We have to strike fast,' Leo began. 'Hunter will know all about us now – if he's got to Julia, he'll know. She has family, he'll have threatened them, and Julia will have had no other choice than to tell him everything she knows.'

'And what does she know?'

Talya wasn't entirely sure she wanted to hear the answer.

'She knows about the resistance, but she's never been here. We kept her out of it. With family to protect, it would have exposed her too much.'

'Why did you involve her in the first place, if she was such a risk?'

'My hand was forced when we all got caught up in one of Damien Hunter's killing sprees. I'm no murderer, Talya. I do what I can to save lives. We had to bring her in on it, but she didn't really have a choice. We're all doing what we have to do to stay alive.'

Talya knew about that. It was difficult to apportion blame in The City, everybody had to make the best decisions they could to keep breathing. It was those at the top who were responsible, Delman and Hunter. There was no need for The City to operate in that climate of fear.

'Are we safe here, Leo? Is there any chance Hunter can flush us out? You know he won't stop until he finds me, don't you?'

Leo knew there was no way Hunter would rest until he'd located Talya, Leo and Jody. He wasn't stupid, he'd be piecing it all together just like they were. Hands were being forced, they were all being pressured into making the first move.

'We're as safe as we can be here, Talya. This place has been used by the resistance for many years now, and it's secure and well protected. It helps that we're in The Climbs, there's much less scrutiny out here.'

Talya wasn't so sure about that, she knew what Damien Hunter was like. He'd already taken her husband's life. It was quite possible that he'd killed her daughter, and he was coming for her next.

'How can I help?'

Leo looked uncomfortable and Talya sensed that she wouldn't like what he was about to say. She fought her battles with words and alliances, she was not a warrior. Although there was a lot of weaponry in that headquarters, she was certain that what was coming next would be a very different battle.

'We need you to make an address on the screens in The Climbs. They're connected by a cable loop which we've been able to access for some time – we can hack into them, although we can't get to those on Silk Road. We need someone like you, Talya. It has to be someone who people trust.'

Talya could see the sense of that. She would be hard-pressed to find anyone more suitable than herself.

Someone like Leo couldn't do it, he was unknown and the Centuria were despised. Law Lord Sivil couldn't do it, it was a close thing who was hated more, the Centuria or the Law Lords. She saw that it had to be her, she was the right person for this job. She was respected and well-liked on Silk Road and in The Climbs. It was probably the only reason why Damien Hunter hadn't disposed of her outright. Talya understood her power. It hadn't been much use to her so far but in this battle she could be a leader. She would call on every last drop of trust and credibility she'd earned in The Climbs to inspire the residents to action.

'So what do I say when I'm on the screens? What are we going to ask them to do?'

'We're not going to ask them to do anything, Talya. We're just going to show them the truth. We've gathered quite a show reel of atrocities that have taken place in The Climbs. All you have to do is to tell them it's the truth. You just have to plant the seed. The rest should take care of itself.'

Gameplay

Linwood was scared now. Hannah had been escorted out of the Fortrillium premises and the room was filled with armed Centuria. Would they figure out that they'd been working together? He rapidly worked through Hannah's code, but there was nothing in there to suggest they weren't testing out some new ideas in a rendered environment.

They'd created their cityscape model in a part of The Grid that was clear of Justice Seekers. It was normal practice. They'd had to do it to fight whoever was working against them. Linwood wondered if he should raise the matter with the Head Gridder. Was she in on it? Did anybody else know that there was outside interference?

A drop of sweat splashed onto Linwood's hand as he worked at his console. He'd have to take care not to show how rattled he was, he didn't want to give the game away.

His mind was racing about what might have happened to Hannah, but he had a feeling that he knew already. When five new Justice Seekers had been thrown into The Grid, Linwood knew what had happened. It had to be Hannah. There were two women in there of her age, but he couldn't tell which was which. He'd need to work it out – would she think to give him some clues? Hannah would know that Linwood could only see her as a pixelated image, there would be no names and no ID for him. He'd watch carefully, hoping she would know he needed a sign from her to confirm her identity. Just as Hannah had been oblivious to Joe and Lucy's presence earlier, so he would have to ascertain which of the figures on the screen represented her. He wasn't even sure she was in there, her removal from the team of Gridders had not been accompanied by any explanation.

Things were extremely tense among the Gridders. It had all happened very quickly. Hannah and Linwood had lost control of the gameplay once they'd created the new cityscape to give the Justice Seekers a way out. Whoever was controlling events in The Grid was intent on killing everybody, it seemed.

Something had happened with the bot. They'd agreed with Fortrillium to keep it contained in an area out of the way of the Justice Seekers until it could be safely returned, but it had suddenly started moving and making its way to an area right at the centre of The Grid.

At that point their screens had gone down. Only

Damien Hunter could do that, not even the Head Gridder could deactivate the live feed. The trial had gone dark for a couple of minutes, and there had been panic and confusion. Nobody knew what was happening – it had never occurred before.

A few minutes later, the screens were back. There was a top-level order from President Josh Delman demanding that the centre of The Grid be heavily defended. As far as Linwood could see, it was just a water butt. They were defending a water butt. And the bot was still there.

Another command came in from Damien Hunter. He wanted a full report on what was going on. But none of them knew what had happened.

Linwood worked with the other Gridders to deploy snipers. They were created so quickly that they were only partially rendered 3D models, but the Justice Seekers wouldn't get to see them. The snipers were just needed to keep them away from the centre. You didn't get an order from the President and ignore it.

Once the feeds were restored, Linwood was astonished to see another five Justice Seekers had been thrown into the arena, and it was only then that he noticed Joe and Lucy were missing. Two Justice Seekers had completely disappeared. How had that happened? It was impossible.

Shortly afterwards, Linwood saw one of the Justice Seekers run to his death, but that had been nothing to do with the Gridders. He'd been annihilated immediately by a threat unknown to him. It was a good job the public feed hadn't been restored at that stage. What was going on? He'd never seen anything like it. And there had been something going on with the water butt too, the pixels were changing, as if somebody was fighting to restore it. Every now and then a doorway to an elevator would emerge.

Orders were being issued all around them – it was like being in the heart of a battle. The Head Gridder wanted the entire labyrinth environment re-rendered as a cityscape. When the public feed was switched back on it would have to look as if the disruption had been caused by a Mode change. But who was it who was working to conceal whatever lay hidden by the water butt? What was there? Why had the Justice Seeker run at that area, only to be killed by something that was not of the Gridders' creation?

It occurred to Linwood that backs were being covered. Delman had his agenda, Hunter seemed to be doing something completely separate and the Head Gridder was just doing her best to keep them all out of trouble. Something very serious had happened, and a lot of senior people had become seriously rattled.

It took some time for things to settle down among the Gridders. It wasn't until The Grid had been re-rendered as an entire cityscape, the bot destroyed and the existing Justice Seekers regrouped behind a concrete barricade that they began to relax a little.

Linwood had figured out that Hannah *must* be one of the new Justice Seekers, and he reasoned that the panic that had taken place was probably related to whatever it was she and her friends had been plotting. He was scared for her life and terrified he might be caught up in these events after his association with her. But a part of Linwood didn't care. After his brother had disappeared, he'd felt helpless and useless. Now he felt empowered. At last he could make an impact.

Of course, he was petrified they'd be escorting him from the room next, but so far he seemed safe. He'd keep his head down. Only now it was Hannah he was trying to keep alive in there, not Joe and Lucy. Where had they gone? There was something in The Grid that none of them knew about. He hoped that Hannah would be able to stay alive long enough to find some answers.

They'd received instructions to give the Justice Seekers a short reprieve. There was some serious covering up going on. The promo teams were working overtime to account for the timeline of events the citizens had seen broadcast on the screens. None of the Gridders saw these promos, they had to be kept away from the real identities of the people they were slaughtering. The video feeds were re-cut to make it look as if Joe had been killed in his final battle with the creature. It wasn't difficult, they just used a shot showing the beast charging at him. It seemed he couldn't possibly survive. There was no moment of death, just the strong inference that he'd died.

Lucy's final fight with Schälen was similarly re-edited. A few edits here and there, the use of some close-ups from their first fight, it wasn't difficult to achieve. Again, there was no moment of death, but it was clear to those watching on the screens that Parsons and Slater were no longer part of the trial. To them, they were dead, two more casualties of The City's justice system.

Linwood carried on working into the night, oblivious as to how events in The Grid had been portrayed to the residents of The City. He could see there were a number of badly wounded people in there, and he decided to give them a break. He was the only Gridder at his console, while the others were chatting and exchanging ideas at the other end of the office. Linwood placed some food, water and medical supplies at strategic points in the cityscape. He could see that two search parties had split off from the main group. He was not doing anything unusual in The Grid. It was accepted that recovery time for the participants was good, it made the engagement scores better if the Justice Seekers were capable of fighting back. They'd have to make what followed strong and compelling though.

He'd done what he could. It was late at night and the crisis had been contained. Besides, Linwood had another project in mind. Whoever was interfering with the game-play was snooping around again. It wasn't obvious at first, but Linwood had noticed there was some patch-up work going on at The Core. Whatever was concealed there, the mysterious Gridder wanted it hidden away.

Linwood was onto him. If he was going to get Hannah out of there alive, he would need to be able to fight this invisible opponent. He'd nearly beaten him once before, but next time Linwood was going to be ready. He began to create a search program to figure out how the hidden assailant could be blocked.

Sport

Wiz and Dillon shrank as far as they could into the furthest corner of the basement. The torchlights probed the dark-ness, and it could only be a matter of time before one of those lights found them.

'Turn your back to the wall, stay as still and as quiet as possible. If they spot us, you stay still, I'll stand up. They might not notice you if I draw them away.'

'What will I do if they capture you, Wiz?'

Wiz sighed. They were running out of options.

'Take the tech bag and try to contact Talya. Don't speak to Mitchell, he's not to be trusted anymore. And take the WristCom. You'll need to find a Centuria called Leo Bachus. I think you can trust him.'

Dillon nodded and ducked as a beam of light swept over

their heads. Wiz handed over the WristCom. It was still activated, and he turned it off in case its dim light drew unwelcome attention.

'Get down!' Wiz whispered. He was seriously considering giving himself up to save Dillon. Would Dillon be strong enough to help the others stay alive? He wasn't sure, but how could he sacrifice Dillon to preserve his own life? He was probably Joe and Lucy's best chance of survival, but he couldn't send Dillon to his grave to save them.

The Centuria were sweeping the further edges of the basement now. It was only a matter of minutes until they were discovered.

'Remember, if they spot one of us, stay still. Let me draw them away from the area, okay?'

The searching beams of light swept over their heads, then began a scan at floor level. Wiz felt the light pass over him. For a moment, he hoped he'd been missed. But the light came back and settled on him. There was a shout, followed by several other lights.

'Stand up and turn around slowly!' came the order. The Centuria didn't mess around, all weapons were now primed and aimed directly at them. Wiz turned around, hoping Dillon would stay still, as he'd instructed.

Wiz was dazzled. They'd been in darkness for so long his eyes needed to adjust. There seemed to be a swarm of Centuria, there were far more bodies than there had been lights in the darkness. He could hear the electronic charge of their weapons. He emerged from the corner with his hands held high so the Centuria could see them. He jumped as there was a single shot in Dillon's direction.

'And the other one. Come out slowly so we can see your hands!'

Damn. They'd spotted Dillon. Wiz turned to him and

nodded to give him reassurance. There was little point trying to make any smart moves, there was nowhere for them to go.

'Kick the bag over here!'

Dillon kicked it towards the Centuria who'd issued the instruction. It was heavy with tech and didn't travel very far.

'I want both of you to turn around slowly, kneel on the ground, hands behind your heads. Any sudden moves and we shoot.'

Dillon and Wiz had seen enough of the Centuria to know this was no joke. There were no sudden plays to be made, no smart moves. If they didn't follow orders, they'd be shot. If they did follow every instruction, they still might be shot.

One of the Centuria walked towards the bag and scanned it with an electronic device.

'Safe!' he called, and the bag was retrieved and searched. Two more Centuria came forward. They patted down both captives, removed the knife Wiz had taken from the dead body in the elevator, and secured Wiz and Dillon with electro-cuffs before kicking both of them to the ground.

Wiz wondered if they were going to finish them there and then in the basement. Surely they'd make a spectacle of them and throw them in The Grid? It was a waste of body count if their demise didn't get to play out on the screens. It looked as if they were going to be roughed up first. Maybe the Centuria were going to opt for the best of both worlds, physical violence then death in The Grid.

Wiz felt remarkably clear-headed, bearing in mind his life might end in the next few minutes. He was angry they'd come so far and got caught anyway. He was frustrated that any hope for Joe and Lucy's survival was diminishing. He'd really hoped they might make a difference. He also felt frustrated that they'd got so close to finding out The City's secrets, yet the tentacles of Fortrillium had spread around them until their efforts were extinguished. They'd done well, they'd come as far as they could. He still had fight left in him, he'd do what he could until they stole his last breath.

It seemed that was not too far away now. One of the Centuria had opened a direct Comms line to Damien Hunter, they could clearly hear his voice over the WristComs.

'Suspects apprehended, sir. How do you wish us to process them?'

'You can kill them, but I want it all recorded on film from multiple angles for the screens. Make it slow and make it dramatic. Make it look like they're running away. I want the bodies too, don't leave the bodies there!'

The Centuria shut down the WristCom and gave a signal to the others.

'Remove the electro-cuffs and activate recording devices.'

Each Centuria touched a button at the side of their helmet. Red lights cut through the darkness indicating that the helmet cameras were in record mode.

'I want the exit blocked. We'll give them ten seconds to run, then we hunt them down. Make it look like they're on the run. Wound first. We only kill on my command. Make sure you record everything.'

'This is it,' Wiz turned to Dillon. 'I'm sorry, Dillon, I thought I could get you out of here.'

Dillon was putting on as brave a face as he could, but he hadn't yet grown accustomed to the more barbaric aspects of life in The Climbs. He began to sob. Wiz wondered how he could make it easier and quicker for

Dillon. What was about to take place was being done for sport. Damien Hunter wanted a good manhunt to broadcast on the screens. It would need to take some time, so they'd go for wounding shots first. No point in making a quick kill when you're trying to entertain the crowds. They'd torment them and injure them, finally going for a bloody and horrible death. Wiz was ready for it in his own mind, but he wanted to protect Dillon from the ordeal. What could he do? Perhaps grab one of the weapons from the Centuria and kill Dillon himself? Fast and with mercy. Hunter would get his dramatic video shots still, but Dillon would make his exit cleanly. They'd make it worse for Wiz as a result, but he felt a sense of responsibility to Joe's brother. He was so young, too young to suffer what the Centuria had planned for him.

Two Centuria stepped up behind them to release the electro-cuffs. Wiz was close enough to grab the knife that had been confiscated earlier. It had been clumsily placed in the utility belt which formed part of the Centuria's uniform.

Wiz made his decision. What had he got to lose? He'd take the knife and try to finish Dillon quickly himself. What choice did he have? Either he could do it now, without fear or pain, or it would be hung out for sport and entertainment. As the cuffs were released, Wiz made directly for the knife. It caught the Centuria off-guard, and he immediately reached for his weapon. Wiz moved the knife across the Centuria's neck. He hadn't any idea how to cut a throat. Wiz thought he'd failed at first, but then a jet of blood sprayed out over his clothing as the Centuria collapsed on his knees. Wiz grabbed his weapon before it hit the ground and pointed it at Dillon's head. All around him he could feel the other Centuria levelling their weapons at him. He'd have very little time to execute Dillon before they started to fire. He had only a momentary advantage, they'd be on him in no time.

'I'm so sorry,' Wiz said, as he began to squeeze the trigger.

The Deal

President Josh Delman was the last person Clay would have expected to call him on the WristCom. For starters, it seemed impossible that Delman could have known which portal to connect to. He was astonished that anybody should be trying to get in contact via the device.

However, the President knew this particular WristCom well, and its portal details were already established in his own device. It had, after all, been he who had taken the device from Tom Slater six years previously. It had been Delman who'd ensured it was hidden inside Jay's body before he perished inside The Grid. And it was Delman who'd worked out whose WristCom was in The Grid. He'd recognized it on the video feed as soon as Lucy threw it to Clay. There was only one way it could have got in there in the first place and that was contained in a BioPouch. It didn't take him long to work out what had happened. Now Joe and Lucy had discovered his little secret at The Core, it was time to make some deals.

Clay looked at the image of the President's face on the WristCom screen and was unsure whether he should respond to the call or not. He showed it to Julia who raised her eyebrows when she saw who it was. Clay accepted the incoming feeds and Delman appeared on the screen. He didn't speak, instead his image was accompanied by a text message.

Don't respond verbally to this message. Microphones

may pick up conversation. I need your help. I can get you out of The Grid if you assist me.

Clay made sure that Julia could read the message. He had no intention of doing any deals that didn't include the other Justice Seekers. He typed his reply.

We're receptive to any offers. What do you have in mind?

Clay wondered if anywhere was safe to talk, since it would make life a lot easier. He'd been aware of fixed cameras and camera drones as they'd been making their way through The Grid, but much of the time he'd been more preoccupied with survival than following their where-abouts. Although they were able to keep the Justice Seekers in view most of the time, Clay thought it unlikely there would be comprehensive microphone coverage. He decided to take a chance. He moved into the doorway of a ruined tower block and positioned himself so he could be seen on camera but where any microphones couldn't be placed close enough to pick up what was being said. He indicated to Julia that she should make herself look busy to distract the attention of those watching them. Clay turned in to the doorway so that his lip movements couldn't be seen and switched to a video and audio feed.

'What's the purpose of your call, President Delman? As you can see, we're busy here trying to stay alive.'

'Mr Hillman, are you certain it's safe for you to talk?'

'You're the President, aren't you? How dangerous can it be?'

'Believe me, Mr Hillman, we have never lived in more dangerous times. I need to know what you saw when Parsons and Slater exited The Grid.'

At least he was straight to the point. Clay guessed he was about to learn why the President had intervened with his warning message.

'We probably both saw the same thing. They found a doorway to an elevator which was concealed by a water butt. The bot did something, the water butt disappeared, and an elevator door was there. Joe and Lucy went through the doorway and now they've gone. Miron tried to do the same and got killed. Why was that, President Delman?'

'I'm sorry to tell you that an identical fate awaits anybody who tries to do the same thing, Mr Hillman. Your friends Joe and Lucy will also be dead, I'm afraid to say. There really is no exit from The Grid.'

Clay had heard the rumours about the President, and he sensed he was being played. There would never be a better time to ask the question.

'Yet you walked out of here alive, President Delman. I'm assuming you know all about that exit?'

Usually President Delman appeared calm, in control and authoritative, but for a moment he looked rattled. Clay pushed again, he had nothing to lose, they were all dead anyway unless Delman was lying about Joe and Lucy.

'I don't think you're telling the truth about Joe and Lucy. I believe you know exactly what's at the heart of The Grid and I think you're worried we might expose your secret.'

Clay was on a roll, he would never have dared to speak like this to any figure of authority, let alone the President, but he sensed that he was annoying Delman and that's exactly what he wanted.

'Mr Hillman, I need to remind you that I could end your life in an instant. You don't think for one minute that you're going to get any justice in there, do you? The Grid was created to dispose of people like you, the ones who don't know when to stop pushing. I advise you to adjust your tone. It only takes an order from me and you'll be crushed under a falling piece of masonry, or we'll create more snipers to finish you and your friends off. Do I make myself understood, Mr Hillman?'

The power suddenly returned to Delman. Clay should have understood that he had no ability to bargain in The Grid. Delman had them all where he wanted them. Clay nodded in acquiescence.

'Thank you, Mr Hillman. I have no desire to end your life just yet. You have the potential to be very useful to me. Now, are you ready to listen, or shall we continue to figure out who's in charge here?'

'I'm sorry, President Delman. I hope you'll understand that it can be very stressful in here.'

Clay resolved to play compliant, he'd get more information that way. He'd decide if he was going to work with the President after he'd listened to what Delman had to say.

'You're quite right, of course. I have been in The Grid before, but I have also walked out of The Grid alive, Mr Hillman. You should remember that if you want to do the same thing. I'm offering you a chance to live, but I need your help.'

'And what about the other Justice Seekers, President Delman. Do they get to live as well?'

'I can't guarantee anybody's life, but all you have to do is to stay alive for another eight hours. Those who can keep themselves alive will be able to walk out of there, you have my guarantee.'

Clay was unsure, but the President seemed to be offering them all a chance. The probability was that they would all die anyway – they still had to survive the third Mode. What could he lose from continuing to listen?

'Do you guarantee that all Justice Seekers who stay alive can walk out of here?'

'I guarantee that they will walk out of The Grid alive if you can keep them safe from whatever Hunter has planned for you. Can you do that, Mr Hillman?'

Clay wanted to know what the deal was. There was always a price to be paid.

'What do I have to do in return?'

'I think it likely that Damien Hunter will be making you a similar offer. It won't come for some time, but when it does it will be in desperation. You need to assure me that you will reject it when it comes. He cannot make any guarantees to you, he has nothing to offer.'

Clay was intrigued. If Hunter and Delman were in conflict, something very interesting was going on. Delman was the only person to have walked out of The Grid, and he was senior to Hunter. Clay felt the President was probably the better bet.

'I agree to those terms,' said Clay, although he knew he didn't really have much to bargain with. Certain death or the smallest possibility of making it out alive, he had to take whichever offer looked most likely to preserve lives. If he could get any of the other Justice Seekers out of The Grid alive, he'd take his chances.

'Excellent!' came Delman's reply. He looked at ease now. The power had returned to him, he was more accustomed to it that way.

'Shortly I will be entering The Grid myself. I will have help to protect me when I arrive, but I expect Damien Hunter to put up the fiercest resistance. I need to get to The Core, Mr Hillman, just like Parsons and Slater. I need you to get me there. You have shown yourself to be an excellent Justice Seeker. You will be the last man standing whatever happens. Your job is to guide me safely to The Core and to allow me to exit in the elevator.'

'Won't you be incinerated, like Miron … and Joe and Lucy?'

Clay added the last names in an attempt to convince Delman that he'd bought his story. He hadn't, of course. He was sure that Joe and Lucy were alive. And he knew they would be doing everything they could to rescue the Justice Seekers.

'There's a reason why I can leave The Grid, Mr Hillman, and you cannot. I am the President after all. But I will require your services as an escort. It's likely to be a tough journey to the centre, although we will have some help. If you can do that, Mr Hillman, I can guarantee that shortly afterwards you will walk out of The Grid alive.'

What choice did Clay have? By the time Delman arrived, he might be dead anyway. He would agree and continue to assess his options. If Hunter was going to make a similar offer, things might take a sudden turn anyway. There were possibilities now, none of them very attractive, but at least it might not end in a bloodbath.

'I'll accept your offer, President Delman. May I inform the other Justice Seekers? We'll be able to keep you safer if there are more of us.'

'It's important that nobody knows about our conversation, Mr Hillman. I have the feed from The Grid on my console, and remember that I can watch any camera view. I'm not restricted to the edited highlights on the screens. If I get any inkling that you're trying to deceive me, Mr Hillman, I will use my rights as President to intervene with the trial. Is that understood?'

'I understand.'

'Excellent. I will enter The Grid very soon. We have no way of knowing what will be happening with the Modes at that time. I will do everything I can to keep you and your friends alive, but please understand that events inside The Grid can never be completely controlled. I cannot be held responsible for any deaths that occur in the meantime. Above all, *you* Mr Hillman must stay alive. You will guide me through The Grid to The Core. When I have safely made my exit, you will be able to walk out to your freedom.'

Clay nodded. It seemed like a chance, although one that would have to be worked for. There was still a fight to survive. Maybe he really could get some of the others out alive.

Delman closed down the feed. The call was over and he'd got what he'd come for.

Clay would have to keep this secret to himself. He'd have to give Julia a good story, maybe suggest that Delman had been warning him away from whatever killed Miron. It was in her best interests after all. He'd struck a deal that could keep them all alive. Delman would be monitoring their conversations, so if Clay confided in anybody he would be putting them all at risk. He'd made an agreement that could save lives. At last there was a chance that some of them would get to walk out of The Grid.

Delman had meant it when he promised that Clay would be able to walk out of The Grid alive. He would be as good as his word. Shortly after Delman made his exit via The Core, Catharsis would begin. Clay and his friends would certainly walk out of The Grid alive. But if Delman didn't achieve his objective in time, they'd all be destroyed by a process which would end the lives of everybody in The City.

CHAPTER FOUR

Stolen Identity

Joe had been fighting the wrong battle all along. They all had. He'd thought it was about discovering the truth after the death of their fathers, but that had never been the real fight. People in The City thought that the conflict was with Fortrillium and the only struggle was staying alive every day. But the true challenge was now, and it had been set a hundred years ago. There was a darker shadow cast over their city, only nobody had known about it. Their fates had been sealed, and much of it seemed to come back to Delman.

'Can anybody else stop Catharsis?' Joe asked his father. 'If you can start something, surely it can be stopped too?'

'The Sectors were created in a state of emergency when the plague came, Joe. The disease mutated into three strains, which meant they had to create two additional Sectors at great speed. It was far from perfect, but something had to be done to save the population. The pandemic was spreading at a frightening pace and it had to be stopped in its tracks. Our records show that the person we know as Delman was to blame for the original mutation of the disease. But it's also Delman who can save our city, he's our only hope now.'

'There has to be another way. Millions more people are going to die. Why can't they be left in their cities?'

'That would work until the resources dried up, Joe. You know what it's like in The City. The tower blocks are crumbling in The Climbs, so what will happen when the population is forced beyond the walls to seek food and shelter? It'll start with unrest and riots, and people will be forced beyond The City's boundaries. The pandemic will begin again as the three strains merge once more, wiping out whoever is left. We had to be contained while the rest of the world beyond the walls burned up with plague.'

'But if we could buy ten more years, surely we could figure it out? Does it have to end this way? The Sectors have survived alongside each other for now.'

'It was all determined that way before we were even born, Joe, and we can't control it. We gave ourselves a hundred years to cure the plague but we've failed to do it. The Sectors cannot continue to survive indefinitely without moving beyond their existing walls for new resources. If we do that and merge our populations, the plague deaths will begin again. Catharsis was to have destroyed the three cities but would have preserved Centrum. Delman's sabotage means that Centrum will be now destroyed too.'

'There has to be a better way to solve this. We're going to wipe out millions of people. What does Delman have to do with it all? How will he survive Catharsis?'

'There's no way to control it, Joe. I've been here for six years. Believe me, we've tried. At the heart of it all is Delman. He holds the key to Catharsis and we need him here at Centrum. He's cutting it fine if he intends to come back. He must have a plan to preserve his own life, but we don't know what it is.'

'If you're an Immune, why didn't you leave The TriPlex like Delman did? Couldn't you have just walked out and come to us? We thought you were dead for six years. We were thrown into The Climbs after you were taken.'

Joe was angry. It had happened slowly, creeping up on him. He'd thought he'd have been relieved to see his father, it was all he'd thought about since Matt had been taken from the house by the Centuria. Now he felt resentment that his father had abandoned them to live in this place of comfort. He'd been alright all the time so why didn't he come for them?

'I can't leave via The TriPlex, Joe. I had my implant removed when I exited. We didn't know what their purpose was at that time. The surgical team here thought it was a danger or it could be tracked. Turns out they were wrong and they should have left it alone.'

Joe didn't like the sound of what he was hearing.

'Implant?' he asked, not really wanting to hear the explanation.

'You went through Psych-Eval, yes? It's the most painful thing I ever experienced, and I'll bet it was for you too. That's because they placed an implant directly into your brain. It controls how you see and experience The Grid, it feeds into your senses. The Grid is an artificially generated setting which doesn't actually exist. The implants control your senses so you think you can see, hear, touch, taste and smell the environments. They're not real, they don't exist. I had mine removed as soon as I got out of The Grid. It was destroyed in case it created any security issues. If I enter The Grid without an implant in place, I'll be terminated immediately. It's like a one-way valve. Nobody is supposed to leave the Sectors, nobody is supposed to enter them. We've tried to send people without the implants. It's not nice what happens to them.'

'So how did Delman get out if the rumours are true?'

'There's a lot you need to know about Delman, Joe. This all comes to rest at his feet. He has no Gen-ID, nobody in Centrum has one. We all know him as Delman, but that's not his body. The reason he can come and go as he pleases is because he's hijacked the body of the most senior person in Centrum. He's using the body of our legally appointed President. All of our leaders have been placed in Cryo.'

Joe could barely believe what he was hearing. Less than an hour ago he'd been fighting for his life in the labyrinth, now he was being told some incredible story by the father he'd thought dead for the past six years. Much of it made sense, the implants especially. He'd seen what had happened when the water butt had pixelated and turned into the elevator. It made sense that The Grid environments were generated in some way, how else could they be able to control the Modes? But he'd seen people die, that was no illusion. When people perished in The Grid, it was for real. Or was that a deception too?

Joe could see that Matt wanted to move on. He seemed frustrated at having to explain so much, but Joe needed to understand.

'What's Cryo?'

'It's a state of suspended animation – bodies can be frozen and re-awoken at a later date. Delman should be well over one hundred years old by now, but he's been body-hopping. His original body is here in Centrum, but his consciousness is using another host body which is younger.

'It's a lot to take in, Joe, I know, but I need you to believe me. You have to trust me as we have very little time now. It's a different world down here, and it took me some time to adjust to it. We must get Lucy patched up and then there's something urgent we need you to do.'

Joe was beginning to see where this was leading, but he wanted to hear it from Matt first.

'How did Delman exchange bodies? Why did he do it?'

'It's the reason he can go anywhere he pleases, Joe. He's in the body of the President, a man called James Morgan. Morgan was the President before any of this happened, the power of leadership resides with him. He has access to all areas, including the Sectors; he has a unique implant which allows him to do this. For some reason, Delman stole Morgan's body and went into hiding in our Sector. We always knew him as our President in The City, but down here he's the most senior person in Centrum. We need you to bring him to us. He's our only chance of stopping Catharsis. We need to know why he did what he did.'

'Surely he'll perish too when Catharsis comes? What can we do to get to Delman?'

'You can go back into The Grid, Joe. You and Lucy. If we don't remove the implants, you're safe to go back in there. Nobody else can get in, only Delman has the ability to come and go. We don't know how he does that, but he's figured it out. Delman is the key to all of this so if we can get to him we may be able to postpone Catharsis and try to buy more time, find another solution.'

'What is it that you want us to do when we're in there?' asked Joe, terrified at the prospect of having to enter The Grid again.

'We need you to get to Josh Delman. Somehow we have to get some answers from this man. We need to know why he took Morgan's body and what can be done to avert Catharsis. Delman is the key to all of this.'

Extraction

Wiz's eyes were closed. He could barely force himself to watch. He couldn't believe what he was doing, this was his best friend's brother. The City drove everybody to do crazy things eventually, it was one twisted place. Most of the blame for that came to rest at Damien Hunter's feet.

As Wiz began to complete the squeeze on the trigger, Dillon's sobbing was replaced by the flash and boom of an explosion. It was suddenly mayhem in the basement area. A steel rod was lodged in the chest of one of the Centuria but he was still standing, as if he hadn't registered that he was supposed to be dead.

The other Centuria were covered in dust and everywhere there were small fragments of concrete. Dillon was face down in a cloud of dust, completely grey except for a rich, red circle of blood which was beginning to pool by his head. He'd been struck by a concrete fragment.

All Wiz could hear were the muffled shouts of Centuria. What had happened? There was a bright light in the room which made it difficult to see. The Centuria were falling, one by one, and there was gunfire, the spatter of blood and flesh as bullets found their target. The Centuria were all dead, and there was firing from the far end of the basement where the guards at the exit were being shot at. Who was shooting? Wiz wondered if he was still alive, had he been shot? Had he killed Dillon or had he been wounded in this battle?

Wiz stood there, dazed. He didn't know whether to run or fight back. This didn't seem to be about him. The dust began to clear and he turned to see who was responsible for the carnage. He didn't recognize anybody, they weren't Centuria, so who were they? He was surrounded by exploded concrete, iron bars and dead bodies. Dillon was being attended to – somebody was giving him medical attention.

'Is he alive? Did I kill him?' Wiz asked, dazed and shocked. His ears were still ringing. He couldn't hear properly, the voices sounded as if they were in another room even though the people speaking were right next to him. Then a face he recognized emerged from the dust. It was Jody, the Centuria he'd met on the rooftops earlier. It took him a moment to place her.

'What's going on?'

'You're safe, for now,' Jody began. 'You made it difficult for us when you switched off the WristCom, we couldn't track you. We had to take a chance in the end and blow out the wall. We had to hope you wouldn't be near the blast.'

Wiz got it. They'd picked up the signal when he'd activated the WristCom when they were in the elevators. They must have tracked them. And he'd turned the WristCom off, probably just when they needed the tracking signal most. Well, they'd intervened in the nick of time, a second later and he'd have executed Dillon. How could he have lived with himself if he'd pulled that trigger and survived himself?

'Is Dillon okay, will he be alright?'

Jody looked at the medic who was attending to Dillon's head wound.

'He's suffered some minor head trauma, he'll be okay when we get him back to base.'

'You're lucky, Wiz. We had to gamble when we blew the wall. We knew you were in here somewhere but we didn't know where. We need to evacuate the building fast. This block is a nest of Centuria, they're coming down from the upper levels.'

The dust had settled enough for Wiz to fill in the rest of the story. A hole had been blasted through the wall to his side – it must have taken some serious explosives to get through that. There were twisted steel supports and concrete rubble strewn all over the floor of the basement. Dillon had been lucky only to get a head wound. Wiz could barely believe his luck in escaping unharmed. There were armed men and women securing the area and engaged in a gunfight with the Centuria who were gathering around the doorway, alerted by the blast and the commotion.

'Okay, let's move out!' Jody shouted, indicating to Wiz that he should follow her.

'Blow the door!' she yelled to the fighters at the far end of the basement. There were three more explosions, smaller this time, and then the firing stopped. Wiz was aware of armed soldiers moving through the hole in the wall. It was quite a struggle for him to squeeze through and not the first time his height had caused problems for him during recent events.

They had to run up a bank to get away from the building. His ankle was still troubling him, but he was moving more easily than before. Jody urged him to take care, the Centuria had begun to gather outside the tower block now and were firing on them. There was a black vehicle waiting at the roadside. Wiz was bundled inside it along with Dillon who had been placed on a makeshift stretcher. He was still out cold. Jody jumped in behind them, pulled the doors shut and the van screeched off into the night.

'You okay?' Jody asked. Wiz nodded, his hearing was beginning to return, though there was still a high-pitched whine accompanying everything that was said. He could hear the gunfire outside fading into the distance. Whatever their destination, it seemed to involve a lot of twists and turns, hurling them from side to side as the van lurched one way and then another. The medic was holding Dillon's head as steadily as he could but it wasn't the best environment for a casualty.

'What will happen to the others? Will they get away?' Wiz asked.

'Now we're out safely, they'll just blend into The Climbs. The Centuria will never be able to track them.'

'What about their Gen-IDs, won't they be able to locate them that way?'

'We have a fix for that, Wiz. You'll need to get yours sorted as soon as we arrive at HQ. Dillon will need his fixing too. Place this over your tattoo for now.'

Jody handed him a metallic sheet which wrapped around his arm and adhered to his skin. The medic was doing the same to Dillon.

'What happened?' asked Wiz, still not sure what was going on. It had taken place so fast: one minute he was about to kill his best friend's brother, the next he was in the middle of a gun battle. He'd never seen such blood and carnage before.

Jody looked at him, unsure whether he was ready to grasp the enormity of the situation.

'We just started the revolution, Wiz. Fortrillium know we exist now. It's a fight to the end, and it just began in that basement.'

Rebels

Talya felt that events were moving to a critical point. So far she'd not had to declare her hand fully, but now she had to take sides. Once she'd made her appeal to the citizens on the screens of The Climbs, that would be it. There would be no more subterfuge, no more skulking in the shadows. President Delman and Damien Hunter would know exactly where she stood. She was making a direct challenge to their authority. She would become the enemy, not just a pawn or a thorn in their side, but the target of their hate.

She would commit Lucy to this course of action too. Wherever Lucy was, she would become an immediate target when Talya appeared on the screens. She'd stayed alive in The Grid. Talya had watched the replays over and over again looking for clues and she saw no evidence Lucy was dead. The highly edited film made it look that way, but there was not a single shot of Lucy's body. The same went for Joe. There were some horrific fighting scenes with the creatures, and he'd certainly been struck, wounded and knocked to the floor, but in the highly edited montage there was no view of his dead body, just the implication that he'd died. Talya was sure it was trickery.

Something had happened, just as when Matt was in The Grid. She struggled to remember the precise details, it had been a long time ago. A lot had happened since then. Matt had been in the final stages, and she'd been certain that death was not far off for him. He was tired, weak, bruised and weary. The threats were coming thick and fast, while all the other Justice Seekers in that trial had been finished off. She'd suppressed the memory, it had been hard to watch at the time. She'd seen it in his eyes, she actually saw the point at which Matt had given up. He'd resigned himself to certain death, he'd seen that he couldn't evade it anymore.

The cameras had been merciless, zooming in on his face, showing every last bead of sweat, splash of blood and agonized expression. The light faded in his eyes before he was dead, but then the screen went blank. It was black, as if the feed had failed. The commentators seemed confused, they had no idea what was happening. They'd filled in the time, recapping the action and speculating on what had happened to Matt. The screens must have gone dark for over ten minutes. It felt like an eternity to Talya who was waiting to find out what Matt's fate had been. Replays and montages were hastily played on the screens, rousing disquiet among the viewing audiences. They knew this was an execution, they understood what was playing out in front of them, but they wanted the man put out of his misery. He'd been hounded and tormented in The Grid, he'd put up an amazing resistance and encouraged his fellow Justice Seekers to fight and survive. He deserved a fast death with whatever honour was possible in such a terrible place.

Talya had never seen Matt's dead body on the screens. None of the replays showed a body. They displayed some horrific scenes, and Matt was certainly under great threat. But there was no evidence. And now exactly the same thing had happened with Lucy and Joe. Was there something she was missing? Had a deception taken place? Was there a way out of The Grid? Had a deal been struck? Whatever had happened, Lucy was either out of The Grid or she was dead. Talya needed to carry on, and she thought it unlikely her actions could place Lucy in any more harm. Lucy had already shown herself to be an awe-inspiring survivor. Talya thought she could probably learn a few lessons from her own daughter. Talya had been hasty and foolish. She'd placed Lucy in enormous jeopardy when she'd made her outburst to Damien Hunter. She had a highly trained legal mind, yet she'd displayed the same erratic behaviour that she'd feared would land Lucy in trouble. She'd let her emotions rule her actions – her maternal instincts had dominated her professional reactions. That's why she'd become so popular among the citizens of The Climbs and Silk Road. Her passionate outbursts and emotional appeals had cut through the bland official speak of Delman and Hunter. There was something in her passion that resonated. Perhaps it was just her ability to speak the truth, it was in short supply in The City.

Lucy had grown up, she was a woman now and a formidable one at that. Talya felt a pang of pride that, however this all turned out, her daughter was amazing. Tom would be proud of what she'd become. Talya had to leave Lucy to her own devices now, if she was still alive. She and Joe were more than capable of taking care of themselves.

Talya watched the replay of Lucy and Joe's final moments one more time. Leo and Jody were right – she was the best person for the next difficult task. If she'd known there was a resistance movement six years ago, after Tom's death, she'd have joined it straight away. Perhaps they could have changed things sooner if the rebels had made themselves known to her earlier. They seemed well equipped, and it was remarkable that Law Lord Brad Sivil was involved. There were so many deceptions in The City – people seemed to be one thing but were often another. She had thought Brad Sivil was the enemy, yet like so many others within The City's walls he was just biding his time, waiting for the moment to strike. Who would have thought it?

There were new and shocking developments in The

Grid to take on board too. The noose was beginning to draw tight, she felt as if she was beginning to choke. So many people who'd helped and colluded with her had suffered in terrible ways. Talya was beginning to think that she was the mark of death.

Hannah was in The Grid now so Delman must have worked out what she was up to. She looked as if she was in reasonable health. Had Talya been the one to expose her to Fortrillium? Mitchell was in a terrible state, his eyes had become resigned and lifeless, much as she recalled Matt's in his final moments. And Jena, how had they caught Jena? She'd been so fragile, but now Talya could see a new determination in her eyes. That light had been extinguished six years previously, and she was beginning to see the signs of her old friend returning.

Talya was saddened to see Max among the new Justice Seekers in The Grid. That was her doing, she had no doubt about that. The poor man, she'd tortured him and threatened him until he had no choice but to comply. And for his trouble? He'd been thrown into The Grid. She felt responsible for Max, he was just an ordinary citizen who'd got caught up in something that was none of his doing. She owed him one. Talya was in his debt.

There were others in there too. One of Leo and Jody's friends had been thrown in The Grid, and they were anxious to save her. There was the man from the Institute, Rampage they called him on the screens, and Clay and Ross, who'd both worked so hard to keep Joe and Lucy alive. Their lives were inextricably linked now, they were bound together by a common purpose. To survive and conquer.

What would happen if they succeeded in overthrowing Delman and Hunter? Was that the objective? Talya wondered what might replace their rule. If the rebels were not destroyed, there would be some monumental changes required in The City. Talya felt overwhelmed by the enormity of it all. On a minute-by-minute basis, survival was all she could think about, her survival and that of those who were in imminent danger. The rest would follow after that.

She had to do what they were asking of her, it would be her contribution. There was still hope for Max, Jena, Mitchell and Hannah if they could turn events in their favour. At least if they failed, they'd have died trying.

Talya was grateful for having had some time on her own. She'd reasoned there was little she could do to impact events until her address on the screens. She needed to eat, build her strength and prepare for what was coming. The rebels had created an impressive base below ground in what must have been a large storage area for vehicles in the pre-plague years. They'd accumulated weapons, medical supplies and Silk Road technology. The resistance was made up of ex-Centuria, Silk Road residents and those who lived in The Climbs. It was remarkable it could have existed for so long without detection. How had they evaded Fortrillium?

Talya shut down her console and left her small room in the Med-Centre. The control area was alive with activity, it was as if they'd been waiting for her to arrive. There didn't seem to be an appointed leader, it appeared to be more of a collaborative arrangement. Leo had authority, Sivil seemed to command respect too, but she'd seen no clear leader.

She walked around the control area, impressed at what they'd managed to achieve. There was a dedicated medical area – it seemed well supplied, it was clean, organized and as good as anything she'd encountered on Silk Road. If only she'd had access to this when Harry had her accident, might they have saved her?

There were a couple of meeting rooms and offices, some guarded weaponry areas and several military vehicles, including three that were armoured. Talya speculated about how they could have procured those vehicles without detection. Fortrillium must have known about the resistance movement since there was no way that level of deception could have remained concealed.

There were video feeds of the trial all over the control area. These were mixed with other views: of Fortrillium's main security gate, of the entrance to the President's quarters, and of the security gates positioned between Silk Road and The Climbs. They seemed to have everything sewn up. Talya could not believe that so much had been achieved by so few. She wished that Wiz had had access to this area. They could have made so much more headway without the constraints of operating from Harry's cramped apartment.

Her attention was caught by activity in one of the far offices. There was a camera being set up and lights and screens were being arranged. They were preparing for Talya's address, it would happen soon. This would be her moment. Everything would change forever once the citizens of The Climbs knew there was something else besides the horror of Fortrillium rule. There had been no hope for so many years, but at last a small flame was beginning to glow in the darkness. They would have to move fast and confidently to keep it burning. The minute Damien Hunter saw what she'd done, he'd do everything in his power to snuff out that tiny flame.

CHAPTER FIVE

Edward Schaelles was grateful for the solitude of the Cryo-Lab, it was a relief after twenty-seven years of custodianship to have finally reached this day. The man in the Cryo chamber held the whole of humanity in his hands, his awakening would set the world on a new course. If there was one person who could stop it all going up in flames it was JD2022. The level of destruction in the other Sectors had finally been confirmed, it was time to reawaken their only hope.

JD2022 looked calm in his frozen sleep. But once awoken in his new body, he would walk into a firestorm. As a CryoBiologist, Edward hadn't had much cause to get involved in politics. Most of his work after the plague had been in Centrum, and it had been a long time since he'd bothered to wonder what was outside, it hadn't mattered for years. There was nowhere to go anyway. But when he'd discovered what Morgan was up to, he'd had to take action for the sake of his son, if for no other reason, and now for his granddaughter.

Edward had vague memories of the world before the plague. He'd been a young man then, twenty-three years of age, just at the beginning of a promising career in Cryogenic preservation. What had once been a way for the rich and famous to try to live forever had quickly become a means of self-preservation for the key leaders of the human race. The ruling elite who'd invested their money in Cryogenic chambers were swiftly thrown out and replaced with more important contents. Their frozen bodies were left on the surface, naked and exposed, never to awaken from their deep sleep. Most would have preferred it that way, Edward believed. The world they would have inherited after the plague was not one they would have chosen.

They'd made considerable progress since he first entered Centrum. JD2022 was lucky to be in there, sleeping soundly and securely, safe from the perils of this new world.

JD2022 was prepared for awakening. The nanotech readings had confirmed all was well physically. The subject was thirty-one years old. In fact it was his thirty-first birthday that very day. There was some poetry in that. This man had requested a rebirth on his birthday. He was actually eighty-one years old, but his physical and mental deterioration had been stalled by the freezing process. He'd need a young man's constitution to handle what was coming next.

Edward Schaelles was tiring of life. So many years away from the blue skies and beautiful landscapes of his youth had taken their toll. He'd not had much to celebrate since the plague years, and after the death of his wife there was only his work and his son to live for. His life's work was almost over, it was time to pass the responsibility to his son.

Once Philip had a daughter, he'd understand why Edward had had to take such drastic unilateral action.

Taking JD2022 out of his Cryogenic state was his final task. His son would continue his work after that had been completed. Edward was ready to sleep, he envied the slumber that these people had been allowed to enjoy. He'd hang on a little longer because he was desperate to see Philip's child born. It would be like finding a flower growing in the desert – beauty and wonder at last in a place of desolation.

JD2022's body began to jump. It was always the same as the brain was reactivated. It was literally a rebirth, a flood of memories finding sudden motion after a break of almost fifty years. As consciousness was confirmed on the console in front of him, the confidential details about the man would be unlocked. His files had been top-level security, and only when his brain patterns returned to normal would the data be unlocked.

Edward had never seen anything like this. Most of the Cryos were politicians or scientists with specialist expertise, put on ice to guarantee the passage of knowledge through the years. Nobody had yet been under as long as this man, he was special.

Edward monitored the screen and waited for the lock to be opened. Although tired of life, he was still fascinated to see how this process worked. He'd been taking care of JD2022 for twenty-seven years, ever since the initial transfer took place in complete secrecy. It felt as if he'd been waiting for this day forever.

He could see that the console was polling the man's brain, extracting data and matching it with things that only he could know. It was a padlock, and the combination set with uniquely personal information. He couldn't see the questions or the answers, it was an electronic process, but he was able to watch it taking place on his screen.

There were ten pieces of data, ten bars on his screen. As each challenge was made to JD2022's brain, the correct answer was received and the bars changed in colour from blue to green.

This was top-level security, it went over everybody's head. There was no higher level of authority, it superseded everything that had gone before. When Edward had taken on the task of managing this awakening, it had been in the strictest confidence. If he'd ever shared what he'd found out it would have been punishable by death, even more so if their leaders ever discovered how he'd deceived them.

It was for their own sake. He had to take action to save them all. If he hadn't done it covertly, Morgan's team would have killed him. He hadn't even told his wife before she died. He regretted that. No man should live with secrets, he'd understood that only after she'd left him.

The console changed again and a password request box appeared on the screen. He'd remembered this information for many years, it would be ill-advised to record it anywhere. He entered the data carefully. The panel unlocked and JD2022's file was presented on the screen.

There was a security code which would confirm to anybody in authority that what was about to happen over-ruled everything else. JD2022 would have control of the entire infrastructure from this point on. The agreement between them was clear. Edward would complete this essential process, and then it would be over as far as he was concerned. It would be another fifty years until the final action was taken. He would be long dead by then, but it would save his son and his granddaughter.

JD2022's eyes opened and Edward looked into them for

the first time, searching for clues as to who this man was. He had a name now, and he would need to welcome him back to their terrible world.

Edward pressed a button at the side of the Cryo chamber and the lid slid open. He could see that JD2022 was struggling to make sense of it all so he took the initiative.

'Welcome back to Centrum. My name is Edward Schaelles. If you recall, I'm the CryoBiologist charged with your awakening. You'll be unsteady on your feet at first, just take a moment to come round, it can be very disorienting at first …'

JD2022 stepped out of the chamber and walked over to Edward's screen. There was his file and Morgan's, just as he'd left them before his long sleep began. Schaelles had been as good as his word, he'd delivered on everything he'd promised. He could feel Morgan's consciousness, but it was weak and subjugated like a distant echo, it wouldn't trouble him. He'd got access to everything he needed from Morgan. They'd taken care of that fifty years ago.

Everything he required was there, but he'd have to move fast to cover his tracks. He needed to get to a place where they'd never come for him. When he was ready, he'd come to them. It would be another fifty years until that moment.

He read the data on the screen and committed it to memory. He was still struggling to orientate himself after the awakening, but there was no way he could trust that data to any electronic device. It had to stay in his head. These codes would eventually save humanity.

Once the information had been safely stored, JD2022 began the deletion process. The data begin to erase just as he'd always intended, starting at the bottom and working to the top of the screen. There had to be no history of these events. For him to make his final move, he had to remain undetected and unchallenged.

He and Edward Schaelles had plotted this forty-nine years previously. He'd been a prisoner then, scarred and tortured by the man whose careless and callous actions had created a second pandemic. Schaelles had saved him. He was supposed to have been stored as a replacement host body for President Morgan but instead it was he who was stealing James Morgan's body, and he would inhabit it for another fifty years until the time came. Morgan had supped with the devil and JD2022 would use his body to put things right, unopposed by Morgan's political cronies. Schaelles had seen JD2022 as their salvation. He'd been blamed for the second wave of outbreaks of the plague but now he'd be able to make restitution. Schaelles believed him to be an honourable man. He was trusting him with their survival.

Edward was not a brave man, but he'd known that Morgan had to be stopped. JD2022 was their only hope as far as he could tell – he'd learned what Morgan's plans were and they were not in the interests of Centrum or humanity.

Edward watched JD2022 work through the deletion process. There could be no trace left here – the transition to Morgan's body would need to be secret. Unknown to Delman, Edward would pass that secret to his son. It was on a timed secure message ready to send after the baby was born. He didn't want to trouble Philip until the baby had arrived, it would prove a heavy burden for him, just as it had been for Edward. He'd understand when he had a child of his own.

He looked at JD2022 as he stood in front of the computer terminal trying to peer into his soul. Had he done the right thing? They were all going to perish anyway if Morgan had got his way. Edward was taken by surprise as he saw the man staring at him. Before he knew it, a hand was gripped around his throat and he couldn't breathe. The more he struggled and panicked, the faster the life drained from him. He wondered how this man was so strong. He'd just come out of the CryoPod and it usually took some time to regain full strength.

As Edward struggled to take his final breath, his thoughts turned to more important matters. He'd never see his granddaughter. A tear ran from his right eye, but it was too late to cry, he was as good as dead. As the life drained from him, he placed his finger on the keypad next to the console. This would send an archive of the data to his son's file area so he'd be able to piece together what had happened. His body slumped to the floor and the grip was finally loosened from around his neck. At seventy-three years of age, Edward had been unable to offer any resistance to his assailant, a man he'd believed to be his ally.

JD2022 waited until he saw the last two words disappear on the screen – his real name – which had been right at the top of the file. He turned, ready to begin the next phase of his life, with his consciousness now controlling the body of the President. He would have to leave Centrum to stay safe, and return when it was time to do what had to be done.

The last text faded from the screen: his name, Josh Delman. The man in whose hands the future of the entire human race now resided.

Allies

'How did you get caught up in all of this?' Jena asked as she and Max moved off in the opposite direction to Clay and Julia.

She was nervous about what they might encounter,

she'd barely drawn breath since her fight on the stairwell. They'd shot her with an electronic device which had knocked her out on the spot. She recalled waking in a medical area where the lights were extremely bright. Jena was accustomed to The Climbs where, other than sunshine, there was virtually no light. The brightness was ferocious and she was experiencing incredible pain. She woke up as needles were being inserted through her nose – it felt as if they were going directly into her brain. She'd cried out, thinking that they were subjecting her to some form of torture, but it had ended soon enough and she was placed in a holding cell where she'd been joined by Julia shortly afterwards.

'I work – I *worked* for Fortrillium,' Max replied to Jena's question. 'I'm here because I got involved with Talya Slater.'

'Joe Parsons is my son,' Jena responded. 'If you helped Talya to keep him alive in there – in *here* – thank you, I appreciate it.'

'Doesn't seem to have done me much good, but no problem. To be honest, I feel terrified, but it feels like the one good thing I ever did in my life. I've been a coward, this feels like the right thing to do.'

Jena felt ashamed. She was embarrassed by her reaction to Matt's death. She saw now that she'd been useless to Joe and Dillon. She understood what Max was saying. Her gunfight on the stairwell had been the first honest thing she'd done in six years. She'd just retreated after Matt's death, horrified at the enormity of what had happened. When she started to fight back, she finally understood that's what she should have been doing all along. It was much better to be fighting. She felt a rage that she had suppressed after Matt's death, it came flooding through her veins and it felt good. With every shot she fired, it seemed that the balance was being redressed for her years of silence and fear.

'I understand exactly what you mean,' Jena replied. 'I kept quiet too long. My son has been in The Grid setting an example to everybody and all I could do was cower. Well, enough of that. I'm scared still, I'm terrified of what's happening here, but they're not going to steal my life one day at a time. If I die here at least I'll be fighting back. I'll keep pushing forward until I take my last breath. I owe that much to my sons.'

Max understood. He had a vague recollection of her husband's trial, but it didn't take long for one death in The Grid to merge into another. He'd lost count of the times he'd dispatched the bots to clean out The Grid after a trial. He seldom had to make direct contact with the bloody remains, but the regular squelches as the bots expelled the crushed bodies through their pipework served as a reminder that human beings were losing their lives. He'd kept his eyes averted but his silent acquiescence had stolen his soul, one piece at a time.

Like Jena, he had realized that fighting back and helping others was the right thing to do. He knew that the minute he'd decided to help Talya Slater rather than hinder her. It had come as a relief to him once she'd finally forced out the truth about the hidden WristCom. He'd gone through all that pain and resistance – and a mangled hand – to work out that he was ready to change sides.

The moment he'd programmed the bot to perform its maintenance checks at The Core of The Grid, he'd known what the right course of action was. He was petrified yet exhilarated, fearful but alive. He knew the dangers. Of course he didn't want to die, but resisting Fortrillium, in any small way that he could, made him feel useful. That was it. He was useful again. People needed him. He'd been like a ghost for many years, existing alongside everybody else, but not being a part of anything. That had changed and he was ready for the new journey, whatever it brought.

Already Max was among good people, he was part of a team, they had a common goal. He understood the chances of success weren't high, but it felt empowering to be part of something so important.

'I agree with you. When Talya Slater did this to my hand I learned that you can bear pain and survive it. It didn't kill me, it forced me to confront who I am. I'm grateful to Talya for doing this to me. It hurts like hell, but it took this to make me see sense at last. If I die in here, I'm going out fighting.'

Max and Jena were walking cautiously through the ruined city. The newly rendered landscape in The Grid was fully established, and it seemed this was where the next Mode would take place. They were nervous about snipers. It had been a sudden and violent start to their time as Justice Seekers, but Clay had kept them safe, directing to them to cover.

As they walked past the ruined tower blocks, several rats crossed in front of them and ran into a building. Max jumped. He'd got used to a life on Silk Road without the creatures. Jena didn't flinch, she'd grown accustomed to vermin since moving to The Climbs. They were every-where and there was nothing you could do to stop them. You had to accept them as a way of life.

Seeing the rats made Max and Jena turn and take more notice of the building they'd run into. There was a faded and heavily rusted sign above the shattered windows. It had once been a Med-Centre but had probably been stripped clean many years ago. It was wrecked, decaying and unwelcoming, but Jena and Max decided to step inside, it seemed a good place to start. Mitchell and Ross were in a bad way and even discarded bandages or dressings would help.

Their hunch was well rewarded. Unknown to them, Linwood had placed fresh supplies in the area. He'd had to take care not to show too much generosity, but they were more plentiful than Jena had ever seen in her six years living in The Climbs. When she thought how they'd had to scratch around to find dressings to help Harry, her anger began to burn once again, and her resolve to fight back was renewed.

There were two bags in the Med-Centre, both placed there by Linwood. It was he who'd triggered the rats to cover his tracks and make it look like a natural part of the gameplay. Inside the bags were water, bread and a collection of dressings. There was even disinfectant, Jena had not seen that in many years. Hygiene was something you had to let slip in The Climbs, even on Silk Road disinfectant had been hard to come by.

'This is good,' said Max. 'This must have been placed here for us to find.'

'We can get Mitchell and Ross patched up with this. I'm not sure how mobile they'll be when the next Mode begins, but at least we can clean the wounds and stop their bleeding.'

It was something positive at least. They could eat and recuperate, and they would be able to make the wounded more comfortable. Jena and Max returned to the main group, walking in silence. Jena was preoccupied with thoughts of Joe and Dillon, Max was wondering what Talya Slater was up to. She was a strong woman, she would be plotting something. If they hadn't caught her yet, she'd be trying to protect them. That much he'd learned from their brief encounter.

There was an immediate lifting of spirits when they rejoined the other Justice Seekers. Hannah was particularly pleased to see what Jena and Max had found on their journey. She didn't want to say anything in case it was picked up by the microphones, but as a former Gridder she knew it was no coincidence that the supplies had been found. In the same way she and Linwood had left food and water in the labyrinth, Linwood was sending her a signal to tell her he was watching out for them. His hands would be tied, just as hers had been, but at least she knew that he was doing what he could.

Jena set about dressing wounds straight away. She attended to Mitchell first – he was barely moving, whatever had happened to him had left him weak and vulnerable. Chris was calm and had responded well to Hannah's company. He worked with her to bandage and clean Ross's wounds. Ross was tough, he'd sustained several injuries but none so bad he wouldn't be able to fight back when the next Mode began.

It wasn't long until Mitchell and Ross were patched up. There were sufficient supplies to re-dress Max's hand wound as well as allowing Chris and Jena to clean up the minor cuts and lacerations they'd sustained in their own battles.

'Hold some back for Clay and Julia,' Max suggested. 'Clay was in a bad way, I didn't notice if the Centuria had been hurt at all.'

The food was divided up and eaten, the water shared and information exchanged between the Justice Seekers about their experiences and reasons for being in The Grid.

It seemed as if things were going well. The two casualties were comfortable, even if Mitchell had barely uttered a word since his arrival. It was easy to forget this was a controlled environment which was created by other human beings. Nothing was real, their surroundings were artificially constructed on consoles by Gridders who'd been specially selected for their gaming abilities. In The Grid appearances were always deceptive.

The Gridders had just put another plan in action for the Justice Seekers. It was a small diversion, a minor digression to keep the group on their toes before the final Mode was activated. But before the hour was over, it would leave two of them dead.

Punishment

The Gridders were in a state of high alert. Damien Hunter was paying an unannounced late night visit and the rumour was that he was taking scalps. They'd relaxed too soon, they thought they'd be off the hook once they'd covered up whatever had gone wrong in The Grid. They should have known better. Hunter had been more attentive than usual on this trial, he wasn't going to let it slip. The Head Gridder gave the team a five-minute warning of the visit. She warned them to be on their toes.

Hunter had stormed into the room, throwing it into immediate silence. The Gridders stood up when he entered – there was something about the way he burst through the doors that demanded it.

Linwood had taken care to cover his tracks. He knew he was vulnerable because of his collusion with Hannah, but so far they'd left him alone.

There were already extra Centuria in the area, placed

there after Hannah's arrest. They seemed particularly alert once Hunter was in the building.

Hunter walked along the rows of desks, saying nothing, just looking at the Gridders. He approached Linwood, he could feel himself sweating. A drop trickled from his temple, down his cheek and onto the floor. Did Hunter see it? He seemed to miss nothing.

Damien Hunter walked up to Linwood, staring him directly in the face. Linwood averted his eyes, not wanting to appear confrontational. He could hear Hunter's breathing, the room was in complete silence.

Without warning, Hunter drew a weapon and placed it to the head of the Gridder who was standing to the side of Linwood. He pulled the trigger. There was a loud bang and the Gridder dropped to the floor. A splat of brain passed Hunter and landed on Linwood's cheek.

A ripple of shock ran around the room, but nobody said anything. They continued to stand in silence, terrified of what he was about to do next.

Hunter barely flinched. His shirt was speckled with the blood of the man he'd just killed. The body was twitching on the floor, it was the only movement in the room. At last he spoke. It was a relief when the silence was finally broken.

'I'm a little bit annoyed about what happened in The Grid earlier. You need to make sure that I don't become extremely annoyed. We will now be monitoring all of your consoles continuously for unusual activity. I want these Justice Seekers tormented, but I need to keep a few of them alive, potentially up to twenty-four hours longer.'

Another bead of sweat trickled down Linwood's face. Was everybody else in the room sweating like he was? He daren't turn to look. He thought it must have been obvious to Hunter, but so far no bullet through the head.

'If any of you were working with Janexx2, please step forward now.'

Linwood hadn't been expecting that one. His face reddened, he felt himself burning up. Should he step forward? Would Hunter kill another colleague if he didn't?

'No volunteers? Very well, if you step forward now, your death will be swift. If we find you out later, I can promise it will be very slow and extremely painful. Now, does anybody have something that they want to tell me?'

Linwood hesitated. To step forward would mean instant death. He was no use to Hannah if that happened. Hunter couldn't have known if anybody had been working with Hannah, they'd have been escorted out of the building alongside her if he had. Linwood thought he was safe from detection. Hunter would kill Gridders at random if he wanted to, but there was nothing he could do to prevent that.

Hunter was walking up and down the rows of desks again, looking into the eyes of the Gridders one by one. The tension was electric, Linwood just wanted it to end. He had decided to gamble. Hunter couldn't have known he had been working with Hannah, they'd been careful to cover their tracks. He'd opened up a secure socket before Hunter's announcement so his attempts to track the outside source of interference should avoid the scrutiny of Fortrillium. He'd have to take great care over what help he gave to the Justice Seekers. He was relieved to have placed the MedPacks earlier, before Hunter's visit, he wouldn't have dared do it after the warning was issued.

Linwood chose to stay alive. He was going to help his friend Hannah and the other Justice Seekers. And he was determined to track down whoever was interfering with the trials. He had to find out what was going on. If he was discovered, he'd take his chances. It didn't seem to matter to Hunter if people were guilty or not, everybody's life was balanced on a knife edge anyway.

Hunter stood at the front of the room. There was complete silence again. The body of the dead Gridder had stopped twitching, but there was a large pool of blood around the blasted skull. Hunter spoke again, moving to the side of the Head Gridder who looked as terrified as everybody else in the room.

'I have one more announcement before I leave. We're making an internal re-organization. We're removing a tier of management.'

Linwood looked at the Head Gridder's face. She had guessed what Hunter was referring to. On Damien's final word, she began to run along the aisle between the desks, jumping over the dead body obstructing her exit. The Centuria raised their weapons and pointed them directly at her, fingers poised on triggers and ready to end her life.

'Stop!' shouted Hunter, holding up his free hand.

He levelled his weapon as if he had all the time in the world. The Head Gridder was almost at the office door, surely they weren't going to let her run? She placed her hand on the ID panel and it turned red.

'Access Denied' came the electronic voice.

Frantically, the Head Gridder placed her hand on the panel again.

'Access Denied.'

She turned to look at Damien Hunter. She knew she was on borrowed time and couldn't believe she was still alive.

Hunter waited until the Head Gridder looked him directly in the eyes, then shot, right in the centre of her forehead. She dropped to the ground. There was an audible gasp this time. The Gridders couldn't contain the tension any longer.

Damien Hunter handed his weapon to a nearby Centuria and began to head for the door, ignoring the shocked faces of the Gridders.

'Consider your department reorganized,' he said, as he stepped over the body of the woman whose life he had just ended.

'Make sure this trial is good, or next time I visit I'll be looking for some new people to fire.'

The last thing he did as he left the room was to turn and point directly at Linwood.

'You're in charge,' he said. 'You have two hours to do better than the dead woman over there.'

CHAPTER SIX

Opportunity

'I want you to be ready to leave immediately, Teanna.'

Delman had made the announcement out of the blue. He'd summoned her after hours, she'd barely had time to change her clothes after the interrogation session with Damien Hunter in the back of the van. Hunter was a madman, she'd ended up with Mitchell's blood on her suit. She'd had to burn the clothing.

Teanna had been disturbed by the level of Hunter's violence. Mitchell was only young, he'd have confessed anything at the sight of those torture instruments. In fact he'd told Hunter everything they needed to know within minutes. Hannah, Jena, Joe, Lucy, Dillon and Wiz, he gave them all up in no time at all. The rest was purely for Hunter's own entertainment.

Teanna wondered if she was doing the right thing by colluding with Hunter. She felt forced into it. She knew Delman wasn't being straight with her – he wouldn't tell her the truth, she knew he was lying. If they could just put the lies behind them she would work with Delman.

Hunter had been making overtures to her for several years. She'd resisted all of them, but in a moment of frustration when Delman had blocked her questions one time too many she'd relented. She made her deal with the devil. It was her insurance. She would still work with the President – if she wanted to see her father again she'd have to. But Hunter was another iron in the fire. If things turned bad, she wanted him ready and primed.

It had also saved a lot of messing around with Mitchell. The kid was a weasel. She didn't approve of Hunter's techniques, but at least she knew everything at last. They were getting dangerously close to the truth.

She'd never seen Delman so agitated. Something was up – he was usually cool, calm and in control. He couldn't stop reading that document on his desk. He'd been thumbing through it every time she'd been in his office for the past few weeks.

'Are we returning soon?' Teanna asked. 'Will I see my father again?'

'I'll keep my end of the bargain so long as your father does, Teanna. If he plays ball this will all be over soon.'

Teanna wanted to ask her question again, to find out why her father had been so angry with Delman. She thought better of it, it wasn't the right time.

The President picked up his papers and walked over to his safe. He placed the papers on the shelf, shut the heavy door and keyed in his code. Talya watched closely, she'd never caught the final digits, his hand always covered them.

This time, though, he was more careless about entering the code. It must have been because his mind was on other things, he was usually so cautious. Teanna was certain that she'd caught it. She already had the first eight digits memorized, but she'd never caught the last two. He'd left the outer cover open. That part required the President's DNA, but he'd just pushed it closed, it hadn't clicked shut. The DNA part was always going to be the challenge, but he'd left it wide open. He trusted her anyway, why would she think to betray him if he held the key to seeing her father again?

'I'll be back in five minutes, Teanna. I want to discuss Damien Hunter with you when I return. Stay here please.'

Delman left the room. Teanna had five minutes, maybe more, maybe less. The moment the door slammed shut, she made for the safe.

She pulled open the outer door, incredulous that Delman hadn't activated the DNA lock. She tapped $VX9+1ByP$ into the keypad. She'd known that part of the code for some time. She added To onto the end and hesitated. She was doubting herself. Was that a letter or a numeral at the end? If she got it wrong, the alarm would sound. In her mind she replayed the President's finger movements. She'd seen the button he pressed, but she had to recall its position to figure out if it was a zero or not.

Delman had been out of the room for about a minute already, she either had to take a chance or wait for another opportunity. She wasn't sure she'd get one. Teanna opted for the zero, confirmed the code and held her breath. She heard an internal whirring from the safe as it considered the code. She expected the alarm to sound at any moment. Instead, the door opened.

There was nothing inside the safe except for Delman's copy of The Pact and some torn pages. At the top of those pages was the word 'Catharsis'. Teanna took her WristCom and swiftly scanned the torn pages. She didn't have long, but she could see that the sheets had been ripped out of another copy of The Pact. She guessed that was what was taking up most of the President's time. It would probably be the only opportunity she would get to access the safe – she hoped the risk would count for something.

Teanna rearranged the papers in roughly the same order they'd been in when she disturbed them. She closed the safe door and pushed the outer door so it half closed. The door to the office began to open, she moved silently over to where she'd been standing when the President went out. He picked up his conversation as if he'd never been gone.

'I'm moving things forward slightly, events are getting out of hand in The Grid. I want the trial to be over, but Hunter has just placed five new Justice Seekers in there. The man is an annoyance, I can't wait to be rid of him.'

Teanna nodded in agreement. It was a good job there were no cameras in the President's office. It was the one place in the entire building that wasn't covered in them. The President had to hold top-level and secret meetings. In the running of The City there had to be one place where those private conversations could take place.

'You'll need to dress practically, Teanna. I think we're going to have a tough time getting back to your father. You'll need to come armed too.'

Teanna knew nothing about this process. Delman had refused to tell her. It was another secret he'd kept from her. All she remembered from their last crossing into The City was the warning from her father, then her departure. She'd been sedated, that was part of the deal with her father. Delman had implanted one of the devices in her brain using some terrible medical tool he'd brought with him. She vaguely remembered an elevator but her recollections after that were non-existent. She didn't know what had happened after they exited the elevator. She regained consciousness in a medical facility. Delman continued as if nothing had happened. She stayed in the medical facility for a few days and was released to Silk Road where a house and new identity was awaiting her.

She trained with the Centuria, but never became one. Delman moved her to his side where she'd been ever since. She had no memories of their journey through The Grid and no idea what their return would entail. She knew it would be the only chance she'd get to see her father again. But his final warning to her was sounding loud in her ears. It was a nagging doubt which was building to a crescendo inside her.

She'd been warned not to trust Delman, but he seemed to be on her side. There was no suggestion that he was not going to reunite her with her father. Would he turn at the last moment? She was covering herself, just in case. Hunter was in position. She hadn't told him anything, he was still clueless, but like an unfed dog he continued to follow her on the off chance she might throw him some scraps to eat. If Delman tried to betray her, Hunter would be only too happy to move in and challenge the President. She also had the documents. She'd study them later, but they should reveal what was going on.

Teanna could feel that events were moving to a conclusion, though she was unsure exactly where they were heading. The storm clouds were gathering, but the rain had not yet begun. It would come soon enough and she would be ready. When the time came, she would need to decide quickly whose side she was on, who she could trust.

President Delman was working up to something. She could always tell when he was about to make a special request.

'Teanna, before we leave, I need you to take care of something for me. It's an extremely sensitive job and you'll need the utmost discretion.'

This wasn't unusual. Teanna was an expert at discretion, she'd performed many covert operations on behalf of Josh Delman.

'It concerns Damien Hunter's family. They're in the Umbilica, as you know, but we're going to need to set up some insurance for our passage through The Grid. I want you to do some reprogramming for me. If Hunter catches wind of what we're doing, it may be necessary to remind him of the small print in his contract. Any nonsense from him, and we're terminating his family.'

Haven

Wiz was relieved to be in the rebel HQ. He couldn't quite believe he'd managed to escape from Harry's tower block. There had been several times when he'd expected not to make it out alive. He was relieved too that Dillon was still breathing. Wiz had crossed a very dark threshold when he'd begun to squeeze that trigger.

They were in an underground medical area, still somewhere in The Climbs. It was lit, they had power. Wiz wasn't used to that level of lighting, it was daylight or darkness if you lived in The Climbs, artificial light was a rare experience. They'd sorted out his sore ankle, and he was feeling much better.

He'd never seen such plentiful medical supplies. Wiz was accustomed to trading on the black market in The Climbs, but most medical supplies were smuggled in from Silk Road; they were difficult to source, whatever you were trading.

He was pleased to see somebody attending to Dillon – his wounds were being taken care of and he was showing signs of regaining consciousness. Wiz was covered in small cuts, scrapes and bruises. He hadn't noticed them as they'd been fleeing for their lives, but now they were being cleaned he could feel each one as the disinfectant entered the broken skin.

Jody had handed them over to the medical staff. She was keen to update Leo on her progress. All Wiz wanted to do was to sleep, but he knew he'd have to keep moving. He allowed himself a few minutes to get cleaned up and sorted out. He figured it would help him to carry on in the hours ahead. He'd seen all the tech as he'd walked through the Control Room area. He still had the remnants of what Mitchell had brought over from Silk Road – they'd managed to retrieve the bag that was taken by the Centuria. Before he'd even entered the doors of the medical area, Wiz's mind had been racing.

The aerials on the tower blocks were still in place. The Centuria had been onto them in the apartment, but it was unlikely they'd figure out that he was hopping signals across The Climbs. All he had to do was to get wired up in the Control Room and he'd be away. He would be able to monitor the external feed from beyond The City's walls and interrogate Matt's data card. He'd have no power issues either, there appeared to be everything he'd need in the rebel HQ.

Wiz wasn't sure of their location. The van had careered from side to side and he'd lost track of the turns. He was well away from his own neighbourhood, that was for sure, so they might need to hop the signals over a few more tower blocks. With what Wiz had seen on his way through the rebel HQ, they weren't short of resources. He'd be able to make himself immediately useful.

The medical staff were doing their final checks on Wiz when the door opened. It was Jody and Leo. They were followed by Talya.

'Talya? How the hell did you get here?'

'Good to see you, Wiz.'

Talya walked over to Wiz and hugged him. She looked towards Dillon whose eyes were just beginning to open.

'Is he okay?' she asked.

'Just a bit shaken, he'll be fine,' replied the doctor who was attending to him.

'You did well, Wiz, thank you. Thank you for keeping Dillon alive.'

'They'll have smashed up the tech, Talya, but I think the masts will be safe. We should try to use those.'

'What happened to Jena? Did you know that she's been thrown into The Grid?'

'I haven't been able to see what's going on, Talya. Are Joe and Lucy still okay?'

There were many questions to ask and be answered, it took some time to work through everything that had been going on. Wiz took a few moments to let it all sink in. Everything had flipped while he and Dillon had been trying to escape from the Centuria. The stakes had been raised even higher. It sounded as if Mitchell was getting what he deserved though.

Wiz thought about Mitchell a while longer. He wasn't sure what to make of his friend. His former friend. Had he really betrayed them? Mitchell had sent a warning message and without that Wiz and Dillon would have been captured, maybe even killed. But had he caused all of the problems in the first place? Wiz hadn't a clue what to think about Mitchell. He decided he'd have to postpone judgement on that.

Leo and Jody were concerned about their own friend too. Wiz had been uncertain about Julia. He was pleased she was the one in The Grid, rather than Leo or Jody. He felt that he knew where he was with them, Julia had been a little harder to read.

So many lives were exposed, the hurdles seemed overwhelming to Wiz. Yet here he was in a rebel base surrounded by friendly faces. Perhaps things weren't so bad after all. He would never have thought a resistance movement to be possible.

'Leo, I want Wiz to be able to continue the work he was doing. Can you facilitate that?'

Talya was already beginning to assert her authority, Leo didn't challenge it.

'We'll get onto that straight away, Talya. I can also deploy some tech people to assist with any additional masts. Wiz, we need to know what's going on beyond the walls.'

'Talya, I have to tell you about Matt,' Wiz began. 'I think he's still alive, he recorded a message for Joe. When I get the tech area set up, I can show you, but he wanted Joe to come and find him.'

For a second Talya's heart jumped. Matt alive? Surely that was impossible? But she hadn't seen him die, just as she hadn't seen Joe and Lucy's final moments. She'd never seen Tom's body either, the Centuria had denied her that. Was it possible they were both alive? She dared not even think about it.

'I need to see that message as soon as you can restore it, Wiz. Could we use it in the address?'

Leo considered it for a moment, then nodded.

'That would be an amazing thing to show,' Jody picked

up. 'If we could prove that Matt didn't die in The Grid, it would convince people that they've been deceived all along.'

Leo could see how this might play out, it was the best opportunity they'd get to ignite a rebellion.

'This might be just what we need. Wiz, make that your priority. We need to know who's sending those messages to Delman from outside The City too, let's get those masts set up as soon as we can.'

'I think we should delay my address on the screens until Wiz can replay Matt's message,' Talya suggested. 'It's so powerful, I really think this could force people into action.'

'How long will it take, Wiz?' asked Leo. They needed to make the broadcast as soon as possible. Fortrillium knew they existed now, they wouldn't let that rest. They'd try to flush them out and finish them, there would be no delay. Damien Hunter would find the nest and exterminate the infestation.

'Give me a power source and my bag of tech, I can have it done in no time—'

Wiz didn't get to finish his sentence. Sivil had just walked into the room. His face was grey.

'You need to see what's happening on the screens. We've just lost another Justice Seeker.'

The mood changed in an instant, another life lost, another casualty. When would it stop?

'What happened?' asked Talya.

Like everybody else in the room, she knew there was a good chance it would be somebody she cared about.

'I don't know what happened, I thought he was dead,' Sivil continued. 'But he's back, somehow he's returned from the dead. Schälen's back!'

Recovery

It was not the family reunion Joe had been expecting. He'd dreamed about his father being alive, that it might have all been some mistake. He was no different from anybody else who'd lost a loved one. The fantasy that it might be possible to wake up and find that it had never happened was a strong one. Certainly Joe had succumbed to it on many occasions. The dream had come true, but it was far from what he thought it would be. This was not how he'd imagined it.

He'd got his reunion, but all around him there was the threat of death and destruction. Neither Matt nor Joe could savour the moment, there was simply too much to do, too many lives at risk. Much as Joe yearned to spend more time with Matt to talk about what had happened and how he'd survived, he understood that it would have to wait. Dillon was still out there somewhere, as was Jena, and there was Lucy to take care of too.

If he thought about everything that was going on, it felt too overwhelming. Wiz, Mitchell, Chris, Clay, Ross, Miron – they all depended on him now.

'Dad, can we check in on Lucy?' Joe was resolved to focus on the mission ahead. 'The sooner she's patched up, the faster we can get back into The Grid. Do you have any way of monitoring what's going on in there?'

'No, we're blind to everything in all three Sectors. We see nothing, we can't enter without implants. If someone exits any of the Sectors, the alarms go off here so we know they're coming. We didn't know it was you and Lucy coming down in the elevator, your implants set off the alarms. I'm almost ashamed to admit that we'd hoped it would be Delman.'

'How often does it happen? Does anyone ever exit the Sectors?'

'It's never supposed to happen, Joe, but it has, of course. I'm here, just like you. I came down in the elevator the same way that you did. As for Delman, he seems to be able to come and go almost as he pleases. He's the real mystery, he doesn't trigger the alarms. He exited Centrum without raising any alerts.'

Matt still seemed to be holding back, his mind appeared to be processing what it was safe to say and what had to remain hidden. He was cautious as he spoke. Joe thought there was another question that needed to be answered.

'How did you get down?'

Matt was about to give his reply when he was paged via the intercom.

'We're all clear in the Med-Centre now, the patient is conscious and mobile.'

'That's Lucy,' said Matt. 'It sounds like good news, follow me.'

Joe hadn't got his answer. He was intrigued though. He and Lucy had been shown the exit by someone or something. How had Matt made his escape from The Grid?

'How did you get out, Dad?'

Joe pushed the issue, he wanted an answer. If he and Lucy were going back into The Grid, it might be the only chance he got to ask.

'The truth is, Joe, I don't know. I thought it was over for me, I really thought I was dead. We'd stayed alive for so long in The Grid, but towards the end it felt as if somebody new had taken over the trial. Everything changed, I couldn't fight back anymore. I thought it was over – then something changed in front of me. One moment I was looking at a concrete wall, the next it disappeared, it pixelated, and all I could see was the door to the elevator.'

Joe looked at his father. They'd had very similar experiences but he felt that the truth was on the tip of Matt's tongue, and that something was holding him back from sharing it with his son.

'Did President Delman intervene to give you a warning? He tried to stop us leaving The Grid.'

'No, it was as if someone had suddenly opened a door and given me a way out. Tom and I had known all along that there was an outside force at play. I left a lot of the information encrypted on that data card I handed you. I'm assuming you figured it all out if you're here?'

'Only some of it, but we found the outside source. So it's not coming from here?'

'You're thinking the same way as I did, Joe. When I came down to Centrum, I assumed this was some kind of control area. It isn't. Wherever that data stream was coming from, it's not Centrum. It may be one of the other Sectors, I just don't know.'

Delman and the data source were linked, they had to be, but what was going on? Joe felt as if he'd taken a huge step forward, only to be sent hurtling backwards once again.

'Tom and I believed there was something at the heart of The Grid too. It's hard to figure out when you're in there, everything is so disorienting. But we'd seen that from watching the trials. Whenever a Justice Seeker got close to the end, there was always an intervention, it was as if somebody wasn't letting them cross a certain point. I confirmed that when I was in The Grid. They were trying to finish me, then the doorway opened up. I still don't know why I got out. I'm an Immune, just like you, so it let me through.'

'None of this seems to make a lot of sense, Dad. Can Delman be behind all of this? How is he doing it?'

'I think we're going to find out soon, Joe. This whole situation is one big stalemate. We can't leave Centrum without the implants. Nobody can come down the elevators unless they're Immunes and have the implants fitted. That's if they can even access the doors like we did. If the three populations in the Sectors come together, the plague will fire up again and finish us all off. The few Immunes that are still alive may well perish alongside everybody else, we just don't know.'

Matt seemed to hesitate on these last words. He didn't seem entirely convinced as he said them. Again Joe felt he was holding back.

'We're immune to the second strain,' Matt continued, 'but I don't know if you or I would survive if exposed to the strains in the other Sectors. It's all locked in, Joe, there's no way to move. Delman is the key to it all. We have to get to him and put him in a position where he has to speak with us. Unless we can achieve that, we'll have no control over Catharsis.'

Joe allowed Matt's words to sink in. Only he and Lucy could re-enter The Grid. They were both Immunes and they had the implants fitted. It *had* to be them. How would they get to Delman? They still had to exit The Grid. He'd have to wait for that information. They'd arrived at the Med-Centre. What was it that Matt wasn't telling him?

Joe had been taking in Centrum as he and Matt walked through. The technology was extremely advanced, like nothing he'd seen on Silk Road. It appeared to come from another time and place. The environment was clean, fresh and modern. On every wall there were the digital screens. The countdown continued, purposefully and seemingly unstoppable, getting closer and closer to the eight-hour mark. Whatever information Matt was withholding, Joe had no doubt the deadline was for real.

They walked through the doors of the Med-Centre. Lucy was sitting on the side of a couch, ready to get going again. Her wounds had been cleaned and dressed, she'd been reclothed and looked like a new person to Joe. He'd not yet had time to get cleaned up. He was sweaty and bloody, his overalls ripped and smelly. Matt took the lead.

'You're looking better, Lucy. I'm pleased you've decided to work with us now.'

Lucy smiled sheepishly, embarrassed by her previous attempt at escape.

'You're very much like your mother, Lucy. Extremely capable and impressive, but that fiery temper can get the better of you at times.'

Matt smiled as he said that. The Parsons and the Slaters had been good friends once upon a time. It felt too long ago to Joe. They had seemed such carefree times. How had it all turned so sour?

'The doctor has been bringing me up to date with what's going on, Matt. If you escaped from The Grid, do you think there's any chance that ... is there any way ...'

Joe knew what she was trying to ask. Of course she needed to raise that question. They'd all thought that Matt was dead, could there be a way that Tom had survived? Matt was as gentle as he could be, but that flame had to be extinguished.

'I'm sorry, Lucy. Tom is not in Centrum, he didn't make it this far. What happened to him after I was arrested? I always thought they would finish us together in The Grid.'

Lucy explained how Tom had been killed in The Climbs. No body recovered and no evidence provided.

Matt was upset by the news. For six years he'd kept the hope alive that maybe Tom had been given a way out too.

Lucy recovered herself. Her eyes had begun to fill with tears when Matt revealed that Tom was not at Centrum. While she was in the Med-Centre she'd allowed herself to think of the possibility that her father might still be living.

'We never saw a body. If Matt is still alive, then I think my dad might have made it out too. I don't know how, but we never saw any real evidence, Joe. I still believe my dad might be out there too.'

Joe looked her in the eyes. He could see she really believed this, and he hoped she would get her wish as well. They'd spent too many hours talking about their fathers. It seemed cruel that Joe should be reunited with his dad and Lucy denied the same outcome. Joe had seen so many incredible things, he really believed that Tom might be alive. But where was he hiding if he was?

'Joe, we need to get you cleaned up and dress some of those cuts. You're in quite a bad way,' said Matt.

'They have good meds here, Joe,' Lucy smiled, breaking away from her thoughts. 'Whatever they gave me, I'm feeling pretty good again!'

'Okay, Joe, you get yourself clean and fixed up, then we'll get you both fed and fully briefed. We don't have a lot of time to play with. We need to get you back in action as soon as possible, within the hour if we can. If we can't get you to Delman in the little time we have left, we're not going to be able to stop Catharsis when it begins.'

CHAPTER SEVEN

Pressure

Nobody dared to breathe for several minutes. The Centuria were still stationed all around the room, but it looked as if Damien Hunter had finished. One of the Gridders gasped, another began to retch, two of them rushed over to the Head Gridder's body. It was futile, she was dead. Hunter didn't take prisoners.

Linwood began to breathe again. All he could manage were shallow, sharp bursts. His heart was pounding furiously in his chest, he was wet with sweat and his face red and burning.

He'd just been made Head Gridder. Did Hunter know? Was he just tormenting him prior to execution? There was no way Linwood could extricate himself from the situation and save his own life. He was ready to give himself up for dead.

The Centuria moved swiftly to remove the bodies. They were hauled onto barrows and wheeled out of the room. Cleaning staff moved in to remove the splatters of brain and blood from desks, screens and floors.

Except for the muted conversations in the room and the two empty workstations, it was as if the two dead Gridders had never been there. Linwood knew he would have to take control quickly, he could see that his colleagues were looking to him for leadership. He wanted to walk out of the building and never have to return, but The City was a place from which there was no escape. Life might have been easier on Silk Road, but its residents were no less trapped.

Linwood thought about his brother, Jacob. There was a big age gap between them – Linwood had only been twelve when his brother disappeared. Jacob had been a great gamer, it was his enthusiasm that had inspired Linwood to play.

Nobody had known what happened to Jacob at the time, only in retrospect. He'd taken part in the Gridder Games. Linwood had been there to watch his victory. Jacob had been amazing, he'd been so proud of his brother. Yet he'd changed so much after winning the games, starting from the day afterwards.

Jacob became moody and secretive. He finished his job in City Management Services and moved to a new department at Fortrillium. He would never discuss his work, and sometimes he'd disappear for days at a time. Often they wouldn't see him for weeks. If anybody asked him questions, he'd become moody and defensive. The brother that Linwood knew had changed the day after he won the Gridder Games.

Linwood knew exactly why, of course. After his brother's disappearance, he'd followed in Jacob's footsteps, taking part in the Gridder Games and, after several years of trying, eventually winning the contest.

He'd been approached by Damien Hunter, signed the appropriate contracts and then learned very quickly why his brother had become so secretive and defensive. His mother and father had watched it happen all over again, first their eldest son, then the only son that they had left.

Linwood had worked hard to win the Gridder Games because he was desperate to find out what had become of his brother. They'd never known what had happened to him when he disappeared, there was no body. That wasn't unusual in The City, people often disappeared without a trace. But they were usually in the public eye, people who'd been foolish enough to challenge the President or Damien Hunter. Jacob was invisible, why would anybody need to dispose of him?

It had been difficult growing up not knowing what had happened to Jacob. There was no official explanation, no evidence trail. He'd just gone missing. There were no messages either, Jacob had left the house one day and never returned.

Linwood had hoped to find some answers by winning the Gridder Games. He'd certainly discovered why Jacob was so secretive and bad-tempered all the time. That went with the job. But he'd moved no closer to the truth about his disappearance, and there he was, trapped in a role from which there was no escape. The Gridder Games were simply a way for Damien Hunter to find new killers.

Linwood had struggled with his conscience just as Jacob must have done. His family were at risk if he didn't comply with Hunter's requirements, and the deaths in The Grid would continue whether it was he who was creating the scenarios or somebody else. He had to sit tight, make his kills, then walk out of there still breathing. With his mum and dad still alive what choice was there?

If at any time he'd considered that Damien Hunter might be making idle threats, he'd now seen the truth. Hunter was deadly serious. If you crossed him, you died. The two Gridders who'd lost their lives didn't even get the chance of a Justice Trial. What he'd just seen was summary execution.

Hunter had placed Linwood in charge. As he stood there considering what to do next, he wondered if Jacob had just disappeared. Perhaps nobody had killed him, maybe he'd just run away and hidden. It was what Linwood wanted to do. If he could have just disappeared at that moment, if he'd thought it was an option, he would have done it.

Linwood was torn. What could he do? He desperately wanted to keep Hannah alive. He was sure she was in The Grid, but how could he carry out Hunter's demands and still protect his friend? If he didn't make the trial look good, Hunter would place a gun to his head. He'd used some of his best gameplay already, he'd need to come up with some new ideas. His team of Gridders looked as if they all wanted to run away, and he wasn't sure how much use they'd be. They were all in shock from what had just happened, there was no hiding behind pixelated images on console screens anymore.

He would have to make the gameplay good and rely on Hannah to survive. He'd give them weapons and supplies, he'd place clues where he could, but she would have to do her best to stay alive. Linwood needed more time to think, he couldn't see a way out of the situation which didn't involve death.

He decided to seek some help from his brother Jacob. He'd been an amazing gamer, and Linwood had looked on in awe as he'd watched his brother rise to victory in the

Gridder Games seven years previously. He was going to deploy a few techniques that Jacob had used to win his own contest.

Firstly, Linwood intended to bring back Schälen. He'd not seen that technique deployed in a long time, but it always played well with the watching crowds. Schälen was a great villain, but he was beatable. Lucy had fought him off, Chris had killed him. Hannah would be able to do the same if it came to that. He would clone three Schälens, recreate rendered versions of the madman – that would generate some immediate tension in The Grid.

Then, for the third and final Mode he'd use a brilliant idea his brother had come up with. He'd beaten all of his opponents in the Gridder Games using this technique, and it would give Hannah a fighting chance too. Rather than depending on strength and fighting skills, the final challenge would be psychological. He'd seen that Hannah was strong, but she'd have to fight her worst demons to survive. He was sure she could do it.

Linwood walked over to the Head Gridder's console at the end of the room and indicated the remaining Gridders should gather round for a briefing. He was going to play as a different Gridder now, in honour of his own brother's amazing talent. It was his brother's fate that had led him to that place, it would be his brother's skills that would now keep him – and his friend, Hannah – alive.

Instead of continuing the trial playing as 97TRaider, Linwood would now attempt to step back into the mind of his brother Jacob. He would have to live, breathe and act just like his brother's Gridder ID. Linwood would have to become his brother Jacob, known in the gaming community as Reevil96.

Tech

Wiz was impressed. They'd given him everything he'd asked for and more. If only he'd had access to this equipment when he'd been in Harry's apartment.

To his side he had the live stream of the Justice Trial on a console screen. He'd been shocked to see Schälen back in The Grid again, but it was being played for maximum drama. The Schälen clones hadn't yet located the two parties of Justice Seekers.

Wiz knew it was now a race to get ahead. Two teams of rebels had been sent out to attach aerials to three new tower blocks. Wiz had advised them to forget the aerial on Harry's block and to reroute the signal from the sewers to avoid detection. They were quite some distance from where Harry had been based, but there were three tall towers available to them.

Reports were coming back that The Climbs were alive with Centuria. The news of the rebel attacks had been suppressed on the screens, but word had got out among the residents of The Climbs. Nobody remembered ever seeing a battle where the Centuria hadn't come off best. There was a new buzz in The Climbs, and it wasn't just about the latest trial.

Wiz set up the tech he'd managed to salvage and cabled it up to the new equipment he'd been given. There were no issues with power supplies, no solar packs to nurse and no looking over his shoulder to make sure he was safe. He would be able to work fast and effectively, there were even tech people on hand to help him where normally he'd have called on Mitchell's skills.

Wiz was angry with Mitchell, but he had no desire to see him harmed. They all did things in The City which they'd have preferred not to have done. He'd been about to kill Dillon. He was going to blow out the brains of his best friend's brother. As an act of mercy! How screwed up was that? How could Wiz ever explain that to Jena, Joe or Dillon? Yet, in the moment, it would have been the kindest thing to do for Dillon, to spare him the agony and torture of being hunted like a beast by the Centuria.

In that moment, Wiz forgave Mitchell. Whatever he'd done, he was only human. None of them were perfect, they all had to make deals with their consciences every day. Mitchell was no better or worse than anybody else. He wasn't evil, he wasn't trying to get them killed. Whatever had happened to him, he was probably just trying to do the right thing. Of course, Wiz was annoyed and felt betrayed, but he resolved not to judge Mitchell. He'd got them this far, and if it wasn't for him they wouldn't have the masts set up on the tower blocks, Lucy would have been caught in The Climbs after Segregation, he never would have been able to find the message from Joe's dad.

Mitchell had made a bad mistake betraying the whereabouts of his friends, and now he was paying the price, stuck in The Grid, wounded, bloody and beaten. He was just trying to survive like the rest of them. If Wiz ever saw him again, he would forgive his friend. And he sure as hell was going to do his best to get him out of there, along with Hannah, Jena and all the rest of the Justice Seekers.

There was no point in dwelling on the things that had passed already, it was time to seize the future.

Exit

Teanna was relieved to get to the relative safety of her apartment within the presidential complex. She needed to catch her breath, events were moving fast. Alliances were being tested, she would soon have to make her final choice. Would she throw in her lot with President Delman or take a chance on Hunter? She knew that Hunter would make a formidable ally. He was ruthless and without mercy, he also had the motivation, but would he be able to reunite her with her father?

If she carried out the President's instructions and made a move on Hunter's family in the Umbilica, she'd have to declare her hand. She wasn't yet ready to make her choice. Delman might betray her at the last minute when they crossed through The Grid. There was no longer any reason to keep her alive once he'd safely returned to Centrum. Hunter did not hold Delman's power, he had no ability to get through The Grid. Still, if she needed a killer on that side of The Grid, he was her man. She'd seen the look in his eyes as he'd tortured Mitchell. She'd wanted to step forward and spare the boy from the ordeal, and in the end she prevented Hunter from slitting his throat. He was poised to do it, but Teanna had suggested that he should be thrown in The Grid as a traitor. Hunter had hesitated a moment. He'd actually been disappointed not to be able to cut Mitchell's throat, but he could see how placing Mitchell in The Grid would be a direct challenge to the President. He wasn't going to let a throat cutting get in the way of a spiteful strategy. Teanna had saved Mitchell's life, or, at least, prolonged it. He'd seen what she'd done before he passed out. He knew she'd stepped forward and manipulated Hunter.

Teanna drew out her WristCom and transferred the images to her console. Finally she would get to know the truth about Catharsis. It took a moment for the pictures to transfer. She'd taken them on the highest resolution, she wanted to be able to read them clearly.

It didn't take Teanna long to understand what the President had been hiding from her for so long. That's why they were leaving in such a hurry, Catharsis was about to begin.

She'd been shocked to read about the process of destruction that was coming. The time had to be approaching if Delman was leaving. But what was he up to? What was his plan? Her father was caught up in it all too, it's why he'd taken her in the first place. Had her father known about Catharsis and hidden the secret from her? Wherever Delman was heading, it would be safe from Catharsis, that much she knew.

Teanna's father was a CryoBiologist, they didn't even have those in this city, it was an unknown technology. The Umbilica was the only evidence that kind of knowledge had ever existed, but it was primitive and basic compared to her father's work. Her father had something Delman needed – it's why he was crossing back to see him. And Teanna was part of the deal, it wouldn't go ahead without her, she was her father's security. The men had made some sinister bargain many years ago, and it was almost time for them to collect.

Teanna couldn't make up her mind which way to jump. If she betrayed Delman, she would be putting her father at risk. What did he have riding on his arrangement with Delman? He'd warned her not to trust him, those were his parting words to her. Was that a hidden message, did he want her to stop Delman?

Then there was Hunter, crazy Damien Hunter. She was certain he was unstable, but he was also dangerous and powerful. He commanded the Centuria. If anybody could stop Delman it was Hunter. And he certainly wanted Delman dead. With his family caught in the Umbilica, Delman had Hunter exactly where he wanted him. Hunter had to toe the line. However much he wanted to kill the President, he would not put his family's lives at risk.

Yet the President had asked Teanna to give him direct control over their fate, he was going to put a knife to the throats of Hunter's family much as Hunter had done to Mitchell earlier that day. He'd asked Teanna to begin the process of termination. It would not be instant, she would selectively begin to shut down their bodies, leaving them in a state of half-life. They would be teetering on the edge of death, but not quite dead. The President wanted them that way so he could kill them at the click of a button. It would be instant. It would give Hunter no thinking time, nothing to gamble with. If he didn't comply with the President, he would lose his family. Delman would paralyse him with the threat if it came to that. Delman might have seemed to be the saner option, but they were living in a world surrounded by madness.

Teanna thought through her options. She needed to create some insurance of her own. She had no bargaining power with President Delman, she'd never had any power. If she wanted to see her father again, she had to be fully compliant. She had to make sure she had some kind of hold over the President just in case it was needed.

Teanna made her way to the Umbilica and partially followed through on Delman's commands. She began the process of termination, but she would not make it quite as perilous as the President had requested. She needed to buy Hunter some time. If Delman put him under pressure, if the President really killed his family, there was no telling what he'd do. Teanna thought Damien Hunter was a man best left with options. So she altered some of the settings in the Umbilica, but she had every intention of keeping Hunter's family alive.

Only Teanna and the President had control access to the Umbilica, and Delman was the one with final authority. But before Teanna left the area, she made a minor change in case it came in useful later. Hunter would do anything to keep his family alive, Teanna had seen that already. So she made sure he could access the Umbilica. Just as the President had done in error earlier the same evening, Talya left her account partially open. It was encrypted at password level, but the DNA recognition was left open. If she needed to, she could convey her access information to Hunter and he would be able to reverse the termination process. It might just buy her some time if things turned ugly with the President.

Unleashed

Mitchell was feeling wretched, but he was more capable than he'd led the others to believe. He was ashamed, humiliated and contrite. Not only had he betrayed his friends, he'd been a fool to fall for the President's flattery. Joe, Wiz, Hannah and Lucy had been good to him, they'd welcomed him into their circle of friendship. His response was to look down his nose at Joe and Wiz and to desert them in favour of the highest bidder as soon as the going got tough.

He wasn't ready to talk with the others yet, he needed some time to straighten things in his own mind. How could he recover from this? Hannah was an arm's length away from him, she was the one whose attention he'd been trying to attract all along. Look where it had ended up. They were both in The Grid and their plans to take on Fortrillium had come to nothing.

Mitchell blamed himself for everything. If he'd just helped Wiz a bit they could have sorted out the tech, saved

Joe and Lucy, and had a good stab at taking down Damien Hunter. If he'd kept his mouth shut and just fed Delman lies and mistruths, he might have kept his friends safe. Would Delman have fallen for it? He wasn't sure how much choice he'd really had in the matter.

Teanna Schaelles had been the biggest surprise for him. She was in league with Damien Hunter. The President didn't even know. If he could get that news out into the open it would create massive problems. However, Hunter had tied up all the loose ends. Mitchell was stuck in The Grid and there was no way any of that information would get out into the open. He'd missed his chance, he had misjudged events and got it completely wrong.

In the van, Hunter had been like an animal. Mitchell had told him everything before Damien even touched him with any of the deadly torture instruments in his bag. But Hunter had tortured him anyway. He'd sliced off pieces of skin, stuck scalpels underneath fingernails and impaled him with small skewers which kept him alive but created excruciating pain. Much of the pain had been psychological. It was the threat and the waiting which made it so bad, it had almost been a relief when he'd got on with it. Teanna had saved him in the end. He'd thought it was over, but she'd stepped in and saved his life. Had she really been offering Damien a better way to deal with Mitchell, or had she hesitated when she'd seen what was being done to him? He'd probably never know, but he was grateful to her all the same.

He was in great pain. Hunter hadn't incapacitated him, just found many ways to hurt him. The dressings had helped, but every part of his body hurt. Hunter had been thorough and expert in his work.

Mitchell kept his eyes closed and stayed still. He'd let

them think he was still partially conscious, it saved him having to engage though he listened intently to the conversations of the others.

He heard how Hannah had successfully infiltrated Fortrillium and managed to help Joe and Lucy survive. It was even possible that they'd escaped. Clay was the leader, he'd done some amazing things. Mitchell was pleased to have somebody strong like that within the group of Justice Seekers.

He'd been surprised to hear Jena talking. She was transformed since he'd last seen her in The Climbs. Harry's death and Joe's arrest had shaken her out of the trance she'd been in. Mitchell was in awe of her as she described her gun battle on the staircase with the Centuria. He wondered if he would be able to show the same resolve if he was placed in a similar situation. He doubted it. He felt so scared all the time, he thought he lacked the courage to make a stand.

They all had incredible stories to tell. Max Penner sounded as if he'd had a terrible time. Talya had told them she had a source of information on Silk Road, but Mitchell never thought she would have used torture. Yet Max had already forgiven her, it had shaken him out of his own inaction and forced him to stand up and be counted. Mitchell yearned to have the same mettle as the others, but he was a spineless, treacherous little rat. He despised himself, how could he justify his place among such an impressive group of people?

There was some unease about the presence of a Centuria. They had all spent a lifetime living in fear of Fortrillium's military force. The consensus was that Julia was the same as everybody else, they were just people trying to survive in an impossible environment. Nobody got left out in The Grid, they were all Justice Seekers, they fought together.

Mitchell wondered how he could move on from where he was. Did the others even know what he'd done? Wiz certainly did, but at least he'd managed to send Wiz a warning. He'd done something honourable at last, but it was probably too little, too late. He lay there, churning over all the terrible things he'd done, and wondering how he could ever retrieve the situation.

The answer came sooner than he could have anticipated. Clay and Julia were still out on their scouting trip while the remaining Justice Seekers had created a temporary base behind the concrete block which had served so well as cover under sniper fire. The attack came without warning, nobody had been expecting it.

From nowhere, three men wearing black overalls appeared at either end of the enclosed area that had provided shelter for the group. Black overalls meant a serial killer. Three serial killers, all dressed in the overalls of Justice Seekers. Were they part of The Grid trial? The men were exactly the same. There was confusion as the pieces were put together.

'Schälen!' shouted Chris, who'd recognized the deadly clones immediately.

'Hell, you're supposed to be dead!' came Ross's voice as he turned to grab his weapon.

'Who's Schälen?' asked Max.

'Haven't you heard of me?' came Schälen's reply. 'Well, no worries, you can get to know us a little better right now.'

Schälen had the advantage of surprise. Ross was still in a bad way and not capable of doing much fighting. Chris's reaction had been to panic, he couldn't understand how he'd killed the animal and yet he'd come back. There were three of him. How was that possible?

Jena, Max and Hannah had not yet encountered the monster, though Hannah knew what it was straight away. She recognized him well enough from the pixel view she'd been able to access while working at Fortrillium. The black overalls confirmed it.

'They've cloned him. This isn't the real Schälen, he's been created by the Gridders. He's real to us though, and he's probably even more dangerous. Be careful, there may be more of them!'

There were only two weapons available to the group, a broken spear and a scythe. The Schälen clones were heavily armed. Each carried a long knife with a deadly serrated edge, a long spear and, in a holster slung over his back, a scimitar.

The clones were approaching the group with knife and spear ready. One neared Mitchell. He leapt up and joined the main cluster who were standing in a defensive line in front of Ross.

'Mitchell?' Hannah said, surprised at his sudden recovery. She immediately understood what had been going on. He'd been playing wounded all that time. It had taken a threat to shake him out of it. She was disappointed, shocked, but there was no time to talk. She understood what the Gridders were doing, this was an entertaining interlude before the final Mode. The clones were strong and intent, their sole mission was to take lives.

They began to move in on the group. Hannah grabbed the spear, Max took the scythe. There seemed little they could do. They couldn't attack, each clone was armed with a spear that would pierce them before they got anywhere near.

Jena had seen an opportunity. She picked up a fragment of shattered concrete, throwing it directly at the clone who was closest to her. It hit his head, sending him staggering back.

'Well, at least they can be hurt like the real Schälen,' said Ross, attempting to stand up so he could join the fight. The others followed Jena's lead, picking up fragments of concrete from the floor. The clones had been forced into action by Jena's move. One ran directly at Max, his blade grazing his side as he violently thrust his spear. Max gave a cry but managed to use the scythe he'd been holding to knock the spear onto the ground. Mitchell retreated behind Ross. He held a piece of concrete in his hand but dared not throw it. He watched as the others bravely fought.

Only Jena, Max and Hannah were offering any real resistance. Chris was doing his best to throw pieces of rubble but seemed unsure what to do. He was overwhelmed by the situation, completely daunted by sight of three clones of the man he thought he'd killed.

The clones seemed to have been implanted with the real Schälen's memories because they were intent on getting to Chris. Max passed his scythe to Hannah and picked up Schälen's dropped spear while Jena fought with her broken weapon. Ross did his best to throw stones, but he was slow and sore.

The clone fighting Max had drawn his scimitar. He was looking Max directly in the eyes. Max thrust the spear every time the clone got closer. He continued to approach, cautiously and tentatively.

Jena did the same with her clone. He approached and she tried to fend him off. Hannah was embroiled in full combat. The clone was swiping at her with the serrated knife, grazing her cheek twice, she felt each tear of skin as it did so.

Without warning the clones, in unison, changed direction and ran at Chris. He threw the stone he'd been clutching and screamed. They were coming for revenge. It took Max, Jena and Hannah by surprise. One second they'd been engaged in direct combat, the next their opponent turned and rushed at a new target, one that was unarmed and exposed.

One of the clones raised his scimitar and brought it down on Chris's arm. He'd just picked up another stone, ready to throw. The weapon cut right through Chris's limb. It dropped to the ground, still holding the small fragment of concrete. He let out an agonized cry and fell to his knees, clutching the bloody stump where his arm had once been.

Jena jumped onto the clone's back, thrusting her spear end into the neck of the abomination. It threw her off onto the ground, she struck her head and was dazed by the violence of her fall. Another of the clones drew back his spear and thrust it into Chris's stomach. The third threw down his own spear, drew his scimitar from its sheath and drew back his arm. Max could see what he was intending to do, and he thrust his own spear into the back of the clone. The clone stopped momentarily then continued with its deadly objective. The sharp blade flew through the air, removing Chris's head effortlessly before he'd even had a chance to see it was coming. His body fell to the ground.

Two of the clones were wounded, but one was still unharmed. Jena could have sworn afterwards that time stood still for a moment after Chris's execution, but it couldn't possibly have been so. All of the Justice Seekers looked at Chris's corpse. Hannah called his name in disbelief. Max froze for an instant.

The mortally wounded clone dropped his bloodied scimitar and drew his knife. Holding it by its tip, he aimed it at Mitchell. Ross saw it was coming and pushed Mitchell out of the way. Before the clone had dropped to the floor, dead, it took one more life. The knife that had been aimed at Mitchell sank deep into Ross's eye, lodging in his brain. He died immediately, clutching Mitchell's arm.

Mitchell observed the precise point at which things changed for him, in spite of the pace of events. It was then and there, at the moment of Ross's death. He'd been terrified, shielding himself from the fighting, and cowering in the corner. When he saw what Ross had done for him, the fear left him. He became enraged. He realized this was exactly what had happened to Jena and Max. Every person had their limit. They would inhabit fear until it was forcibly ejected from its sphere. Mitchell had avoided engagement until the last possible moment. But when he had to look death directly in the eyes, he stepped forward. He chose to live.

Mitchell lowered Ross to the ground, as Max, Hannah and Jena attempted to repel the remaining two clones. Mitchell calmly extracted the knife from Ross's eye socket. He heard the squelch of brain tissue as the blade exited its victim. He'd never held a weapon before in his life, but he gripped the handle with the surety of a hunter who knew he was about to make a kill. Summoning all the anger he could muster, Mitchell ran at the wounded clone, pushing between Max and Jena, and plunged the knife straight into the beast's heart.

This Schälen dropped to the ground. Mitchell looked towards Hannah. The final clone had her cornered, raising his scimitar ready to smash it through the middle of her skull. Letting go of the knife, Mitchell turned to run at the clone. He saw that it was about to begin its final, deadly swipe. He was not going to let Hannah die. He'd secretly adored her from afar, but he'd been unworthy of her attention. He had betrayed her and let her down. He'd been despicable, but it ended there. He knew he'd never win Hannah's heart, but that no longer mattered to him.

As he ran towards her, he grabbed Max's scythe by the blade. Its sharp edge cut through his hand, but he'd experienced terrible agonies from Damien Hunter's torture and he knew the pain could be survived. He held his gaze on the scimitar all the time, watching as it began to make its journey to the centre of Hannah's skull. He leapt as high as he could, flipping the scythe in his hand and plunging it with every bit of strength he could muster into the wrist of the clone.

It cut right through. The hand dropped to the ground, and the scimitar fell at Hannah's side, missing its target. Mitchell delivered one more blow of his weapon, this time driving it into the head of the clone. The final assailant dropped to the ground. All was silent, except for the adrenalin-fuelled breathing of the survivors.

There were two dead, Ross and Chris, and all of the clones had been stopped. Hannah had been crouched on the ground waiting for death to come. Max and Jena had been astounded by Mitchell's speed, it had taken them by surprise. They'd survived, but there were terrible casualties. They'd lost two Justice Seekers, everywhere there was blood.

The clones began to pixelate, then disappeared, leaving no trace of weapons or blood. A holographic image of Damien Hunter appeared before them. They knew what it was. Surely not? They needed rest, they weren't ready.

As Damien Hunter began to speak, the three Justice

Seekers could only stand there and listen to his words. It was the beginning of the third and final Mode. There was to be no break and no rest. It was the early hours of the morning, yet they were going straight into battle again. There was to be no delay. For some, it would be the final battle.

CHAPTER EIGHT

Vanished

Tom Slater had felt uneasy all through that day. Something was going on that he didn't know about, and he couldn't put his finger on it. When the moment came, in the short time he had to reflect, he was grateful for the way he'd parted from his family that morning.

Lucy had been up and awake, as had Talya, and he'd enjoyed a pleasant breakfast with both of them. His Fortrillium shift began early, as did all work in The City, so it was not unusual for him to be out of the house at 06:00. Talya was due in The Climbs that day on some pro bono work for somebody who'd got himself into a skirmish by stealing power from one of the Centuria devices that were situated throughout the ruined tower blocks. She was doing her best to keep him a free man. It was only because he'd been a former Silk Roader that he hadn't been incarcerated already. Tom thought it unlikely she'd succeed. He felt that Talya was being humoured by the authorities, but he supported her efforts nonetheless. Lucy was her normal happy self and had asked Tom to drop something off for Joe Parsons on his way to work – Tom and Matt always walked in together. The families were close, so he was happy to do that for his daughter.

The walk to work was nothing unusual. He called for Matt, exchanged pleasantries with Jena, Joe and Dillon, and set off towards Fortrillium with his friend. What had begun as a routine walk to the workplace had become valuable time in which the two men could discuss their activities without fear of being overheard. It seemed they were drawing closer to the conclusion, they'd have all the evidence they needed very soon.

'Are you sure the data is safe, Tom?' Matt had demanded. 'If we put our families at risk in any way, I'll never forgive myself – or you.'

'There's no trail back to Talya or Jena. If we get caught, they're completely out of it, it's you and me in for an encounter with Damien Hunter. Our WristComs can place any evidence directly onto a secure area on your Fortrillium storage area. Everything we've got is stored there. It's DNA encrypted so – even if they found it – it's invisible to them. Only you can get to it, or your immediate family members, of course, but they'd have to get into your Fortrillium account to do that. It's safe, Matt, honestly. I don't know how to make it any safer.'

'Okay, I'm transferring all of my images, notes and video evidence today. That's everything we have on Hunter. It's damning stuff. Surely he couldn't survive that if it was leaked to the screens?'

'Who knows with that man? Nothing ever seems to stick, I'm beginning to think he's untouchable.'

'Where are we up to with the data stream? Any further on?' Matt continued.

'It's tricky. I'm certain it's not Fortrillium technology and I also don't believe Hunter is involved – or aware. I'm beginning to wonder if Delman is up to something too. It has to come from outside The City, I just don't know where.'

'It's frustrating. I wish we could make some progress on that. Can you forward me the information? I'll place it in the files. I want this information stored somewhere secure. It's been risky concealing it in the open, we need it somewhere safe now. I've got everything on a personal data card ready for transfer. It's no use to anyone without DNA decryption or Fortrillium network access. If it gets lost, it would just look like a family photo album.'

The conversation changed as the men neared Fortrillium's offices. They would never risk discussing their plans in the building. They were playing with fire as it was, but they had to keep going.

It had all started with a simple cover-up. They noticed a discrepancy in the number of dead in an incident in The Climbs. Although she never knew it, Talya had helped them to put the pieces together. She'd mentioned that The Climbs was alive with rumours about a massacre during the night. It had been suggested Damien Hunter was involved, but that rumour never made it over to Silk Road. Something had made Matt dig a little deeper. He'd investigated the recordings from the Centuria cameras to help to verify the numbers, but they'd been tampered with. Initially Matt had involved Tom in a professional capacity – he'd been genuinely concerned to make sure their data was correct.

However, after only cursory investigation, it became clear this was not the only case of evidence tampering. Using Tom's skills with technology, they were able to restore the missing video time codes from the server and piece together what had really happened. Damien Hunter was a lunatic, he was freely slaughtering the citizens of The Climbs. The evidence was there on the servers, but it was being covered up.

The men had argued about what they'd found and had heated discussions on what action to take. There had been many hushed conversations in their homes, much to the interest of their wives. They kept the information to themselves, not knowing what to do with it. In the end, they'd decided that Hunter should not be allowed to stay hidden. They had no capacity to expose the truth, they'd probably be killed if they did, but they were going to make sure the evidence was safely stored. If ever there was a time when the information could be leaked in a safe way, or even used in judicial proceedings if it ever came to that, they would be ready. Until then, they'd watch and wait, gathering up the evidence against Damien Hunter and biding their time.

One thing had led to another. In watching Damien Hunter's activities more closely, they'd noticed that he, in turn, was watching President Josh Delman. Like everybody in The Grid, Tom and Matt knew all the rumours about Delman. A little bit of digging revealed there was no love lost between Hunter and Delman, and that's what started the checks on the conversations between them. They weren't ever able to listen in, but they were both privy to basic communications logs. It became apparent that Delman was making calls elsewhere, not within Fortrillium. The data trail showed a call initiation and a call duration, but there was no identifiable destination.

Tom put it down as a technical issue at first, but the President was making a lot of these calls. Who was he talking to? There was no way of telling since they were unable to listen in or intercept, but they thought the calls must be being routed somewhere else, outside The City. With Delman's mysterious past, that seemed to make sense.

Tom had been right to have an uneasy feeling on that day. He knew something was amiss, but he couldn't work out what it was. Matt had succeeded in transferring the data securely and undetected by Fortrillium. Tom was certainly relieved that had been accomplished. He was also keen for Matt to get the files erased from his personal data card, but he'd have to do that at home. It was to be that delay which allowed Matt to hand the card to Joe before he was detained later that evening.

Just as Tom and Matt had been monitoring his actions, Hunter too had seen that something was awry. He'd noticed that deleted data was being accessed and it didn't take him long to figure out which of Fortrillium's employees was doing it. He made his plans to apprehend both men later that day. He wanted them taken in front of their families. It always created more of a stir on Silk Road when homes were raided. It would serve as a warning to all of the other residents.

Matt Parsons was arrested and detained as Hunter had planned. However, he never completed the arrest of Tom Slater because he met with a mysterious accident that very evening in The Climbs.

Unknown to Damien Hunter, Tom Slater had been approached by President Josh Delman earlier that day. Not even Matt knew about the meeting. Tom decided to keep it to himself until he knew what it was about. He didn't want Matt involved if it might help to steer him clear of any trouble.

Delman wanted a meeting in The Climbs that evening before Tom returned home. Tom wasn't accustomed to entering The Climbs. He admired his wife for her pro bono work, but he'd always thought the place to be dangerous and full of hazards. There was nothing he could say to Talya to prevent her from going there, but he chose to avoid it. However, when President Josh Delman gave a summons it was best not to disappoint.

Tom crossed over at 19:00. It was precariously close to Segregation. He hoped the President knew what he was asking. Delman had instructed Tom to meet him at a location deep into The Climbs and Tom grew more and more concerned that he would miss Segregation. Would the President's request protect him? He wasn't so sure about that.

Tom entered a quiet and dark square. He waited underneath the screen there. Nothing was being broadcast, so there were no crowds and very little light to enable him to see what was going on. If the request for a meeting had come any other way, he'd have ignored it and gone home. But it had been sent via confidential internal memo from the President's office. It was authenticated, this was definitely the President who was making the request.

Tom waited and waited, glancing at his WristCom to monitor the time. He peeled it off his arm, playing with the device nervously. He ran his fingers over the initials TS. It was a touch of vanity having initials marked on a Wrist-Com, but one which Lucy had wanted to indulge on his last birthday. Birthdays were still celebrated on Silk Road, they'd long since become superfluous in The Climbs.

Half an hour until Segregation, twenty minutes to walk back to the gates, Delman was cutting it fine.

Then the black car drew up. A well-built man stepped out. He wore a smart black suit and he was armed. He didn't acknowledge Tom, just moved over to the far door and let President Delman out.

'Thank you for coming, Tom. I appreciate it.'

'That's no problem, sir, but can I ask, you are aware how close we are to Segregation? We're quite some way from the nearest security gate here, I will need to set off shortly.'

'It's no problem, Tom, don't worry. I can assure you that Segregation will not be a problem for you tonight. Troy, get the equipment please.'

Without a word, Troy took a case from the front of the car. In silence he took out some medical equipment.

'Hold out your arm please,' Delman instructed. 'We need to take a small sample of blood.'

Tom was about to protest but did as he was told. It was the President after all, how could he protest?

A sample of blood was taken, Troy ran it through a console and then nodded at Delman.

'You're sure, Troy? It's complete compatibility? We get this wrong and it's all messed up.'

Troy nodded again, this time speaking. He was a man of few words. 'It's a complete match, sir.'

'Excellent. Tom, it's probably best that you're not conscious for the next bit ...'

Before Tom could move, Troy had injected him in the neck. It was the same serum that would be used on his wife six years into the future. Just like his wife, the serum was used to temporarily kill him. This would be required to allow him to pass through the security gates undetected. He'd have an implant embedded in his brain too, to give him safe passage into The Grid alongside Delman.

Tom's WristCom fell to the ground. Delman picked it up and placed it in a shielding container. The last recorded data from that device would indicate that Tom Slater disappeared somewhere in The Climbs. His WristCom was assumed stolen, no body was recovered.

In the few seconds that passed between Delman's last

words to him and Troy injecting him from behind, Tom thought back to his family, Lucy and Talya. He considered what a lovely morning they'd had and how pleased he was to have spent some time with them before setting off for work. That would be his last memory of them for six years.

The Return

Joe wasn't sure if the presence of the countdown clocks was a good idea. Every digit that changed, it felt as if time was burning up in front of their eyes. They'd got less than seven hours to re-enter The Grid and get to Delman, and then what? Ask him nicely not to destroy The City?

He'd just returned from his first shower for six years. He'd forgotten how good it felt and for a moment, as the hot, clean water had cascaded over his sore, cut and bruised body, he'd just wanted to walk away from the problems and leave them to somebody else. As he stepped into that shower and felt the delicious warmth of the water, it had taken him back to his simpler life on Silk Road. Before the death of his father.

It was his father's disappearance that had torn that life away from him. His father was alive, it was unbelievable. But his mother and brother were in a city destined to be destroyed by Catharsis. Now his father was asking him to return to that city and seize its President. This was terrorist activity, but apparently it was the only thing that would bring Delman to the negotiating table.

Joe longed for the comfort and peace of the shower again. Something so simple, yet it represented so much to him. He'd had his wounds patched up, he'd got new clothing and he was sitting in the Med-Centre with Lucy, awaiting final checks.

'We're just going to run a BioScan on both of you,' the medic had explained. 'We need to be certain of a couple of things before you re-enter. It's for your own safety.'

It seemed crazy to Joe that so much care was being taken over their wellbeing when they were about to be thrown back into The Grid.

'Stand here please,' the medic indicated to Joe. Joe stood at the centre of a black circle on the floor. A blue light formed around its perimeter and scanned him up and down. A 3D rendering of his body appeared on a large console screen in front of him. The medic pressed a few buttons and two specific areas became highlighted on the screen.

'You'll see that your implant is currently inactive in your brain, but when you re-enter The Grid it will activate immediately. You need to understand that Fortrillium can track you online the minute you go back. They'll know you're there. You can't get in or out of The Grid without that implant.'

Joe finally saw what had caused so much pain during Psyche-Eval. It was a tiny unit placed in his brain via his nostrils.

'What can they do with that? Do I need to know anything else?'

'It's a key in and out of The Grid. No living being can enter that area unless they have one of these fitted. It has to be removed surgically or with a special device, it's why your father can't come with you, his was taken away.'

'Well, at least we know they can be extracted,' said Joe, but it didn't seem to be reassuring Lucy.

'What's that showing up in Joe's arm?' she asked.

'That's what powers your Gen-ID. We all have them in the Sectors, they're implanted at birth. It links to the markings on your skin. It contains a small chip – that's how Fortrillium keeps an eye on you.'

'You're very calm for a man who may well be dead within the next eight hours,' Joe commented.

'We just have to keep working and moving ahead. We've known about Catharsis for many years. It all hinged on Delman coming back. Your arrival here has given us the single best chance we've had. We had no chance before you two arrived. As far as I'm concerned, my life expectancy has just improved dramatically.'

Joe understood what the medic was saying, but it meant that everything was now riding on his shoulders. He wasn't sure he was up to it, though he was going to try his hardest to do as he'd been asked. They were all going to die anyway, so what did he have to lose? And if there was a chance to dish out some justice to Damien Hunter, that would be a revenge he would savour.

Lucy stepped into the black circle and a scan was run on her body.

'As you see, you're exactly the same, Lucy. You're an Immune, like Joe. We knew that – you wouldn't have got down here if you weren't. You have the implant too and the full Gen-ID insertion. I'm afraid to say that you're both good to go, you're the only ones who can help now.'

Matt entered the room. He was waiting for Joe and Lucy to be dismissed so he could take them onto their next stop.

'They're both cleared to go,' said the medic. 'Be aware, Joe, that your heart has taken quite a shock somewhere along the line. I'm not sure what you can do about it, but you've sustained a big hit physically. If you can, take care.'

'That will be in the cells, Joe, when you were calling out

to get help for Chris. That electronic device knocked you right back,' said Lucy.

Joe nodded.

'It hurt a lot whatever it was that they used on me. I'm not sure what I can do about it, but thanks for letting me know.'

Matt escorted them out of the room and rushed them over to a new area. Neither of them had seen this section so they were interested to discover what Matt had planned for them next.

'This is our arms area,' he announced, sensing their inquisitiveness. 'When you go back into The Grid, you won't be empty-handed.'

He hadn't exaggerated. They were given new overalls with lightweight protective armouring on the legs and arms, offering much better protection than the ones they'd been handed by Fortrillium. Utility belts were placed around their waists.

'You've got med supplies, ammunition, a knife, and food and water in there. You'll also need to take these.'

Matt gave each of them a hand weapon. Neither Lucy or Joe had used one before. Matt gave them a quick lesson.

'Point, aim and press the trigger. That's it. And try to hit whoever is attacking you, okay?'

Joe wasn't reassured, but it felt better to be entering The Grid with at least some defensive capability. He'd learned to use the primitive weaponry given to the Justice Seekers in The Grid. He'd been surprised at how fast you could learn when somebody was trying to kill you.

Disappearance

Jacob Carley gave a non-committal grunt as he left the house that morning. There was another Justice Trial and he was finding the secrecy involved to be overwhelming. His family knew something had changed, but he was unable to discuss it with them. He'd signed the contract, sworn the oath, and he would be putting all of their lives in danger if he disobeyed.

Like most keen gamers, Jacob had aspired to a win in the Gridder Games, Silk Road's most prestigious gaming event. They all knew the games were based on real-life trials that had taken place in The Grid, but the event was about gameplay, strategy and skill. The games had little to do with death or slaughter.

There was some suspicion that the best gamers ended up working for Fortrillium and devising the new challenges for the real trials, but there was no proof or to support the theory. The reality was that once the contracts were signed there was no talking about life as a Gridder.

When Jacob had won the Gridder Games – not at the first time of trying, like so many players before him – he was immediately contacted by Fortrillium's head, Damien Hunter. A short conversation and a lot of veiled threats later, and Jacob had signed the contract, like those before him and the many who would follow in the years ahead.

Things became tricky at home. His younger brother Linwood idolized his champion brother and wouldn't stop talking about gaming. His parents wondered why he'd quit his job at City Management Services and continued to ask probing questions about his involvement with Fortrillium.

What was he supposed to say? 'I can't tell you anything

because if I do you'll be arrested by Fortrillium and never seen again?'

That wasn't an option. Much as it had hurt him to behave in this way, he'd been evasive and dismissive of his family to protect them. When he disappeared for days on end, his family must have suspected that he was connected with the trials in some way. He'd leave the house on the day The Justice Trials started and get back home the day after. Questions would be asked, but in the end it became too difficult for everybody. The questions stopped and Jacob said nothing. It was better that way, it would keep his parents and brother alive.

Day by day, Jacob's soul was dying. His only release from this prison would be to make his hundred kills. He wasn't sure his conscience could take that burden. It wore him down, he wasn't fooled or distracted by the pixelated images that were supposed to make the killing more palatable, he wanted out. There was no escape. His family would pay the penalty if he tried to walk away. He was stuck.

Promoted to Head Gridder, Jacob quickly began to learn more of The Grid's secrets. He was particularly interested in what was based at its centre. Whenever a new environment was rendered in the arena, it would first be created at the heart of The Grid. If there was a problem, the centre would always be protected first. To begin with, Jacob figured that it made sense. The technical process had to begin somewhere – it was logical that it started at the centre then spread outwards. But there was more to it than that.

When he got access to higher level information as Head Gridder, it became clear to him that one of his primary responsibilities was to keep Justice Seekers away from The Core. No reason was given as to why, but it was to be given a protected perimeter within any trial scenario. This fascinated Jacob. What was it that made the centre so special?

There was no way that he could see The Grid on camera without an environment being rendered, it was technically impossible. He knew that bots entered the zone remotely, but no human had ever seen what went on in there away from the trials. Somebody must have built it, of course. There must at one time have been someone who knew all of The Grid's secrets. But that was pre-plague. A hundred years later, that information had vanished or was being kept well-hidden.

He'd been working as a Gridder for just over a year when he was approached by President Josh Delman. It came out of the blue – he'd always dealt with Damien Hunter on issues relating to The Grid. He had a particular distaste for Hunter. It seemed the man was unable to have a conversation without making some sort of threat. So when Delman got in contact, it was a surprise and it offered the prospect of change.

Like everything at Fortrillium, Delman's approach was shrouded in mystery. Jacob had become aware of being followed by a car on his way home one night. It had unnerved him at first. The vehicle drew up alongside him in a quiet spot where there was nobody to observe. A man beckoned him to enter the car. He approached cautiously, peering into the vehicle beforehand. The President was in the back seat and he indicated that Jacob should join him. The driver and the President's minder were instructed to make themselves scarce.

Jacob thought it highly unusual that he should be left alone with the President, but the reason for his secrecy soon became clear.

'I've followed your progress at Fortrillium with some

interest. You're a highly competent player. I'm going to ask you to work with me. There will be no contract to sign, but you need to understand that if you do not keep our conversations confidential or if you attempt to betray me, I will have you killed.'

That had shocked Jacob. There were none of Hunter's threats and veiled menace, the President just came straight out with it: 'Mess with me and you're dead.' At least there was no small print to worry about.

'You need to decide now, Mr Carley. You can work with me and survive, or within six years your family and everything around you will be gone.'

That got Jacob's attention.

'Why is that, sir? Are you able to tell me more?'

'Everything I say to you in this car, including everything I have said already, is confidential. If you ever breathe a word of it, I will first kill your brother. Linwood, isn't it?'

That made Jacob shiver. The President of The City knew his brother's name. That wasn't good. He nodded in reply, trying to conceal his feelings of terror.

'After that your mother will die. Once you've had sufficient time to endure that pain, your father will follow. I will kill your family first, I will let you live with that pain, then I will kill you. Do you understand?'

Jacob got it, he didn't need any more detail. His only choice seemed to be to walk away and keep his mouth shut or work with the President and keep his mouth shut. Was the President even giving him a choice? He thought not, but he had to be careful with his decision, he needed to think of his family.

The President had suggested a time in the future that they might be at risk. This intrigued Jacob, and he decided to push his luck in spite of his fear.

'You suggested that something is happening in the next six years, sir. Am I permitted to know what that is?'

'You're not!' came the angry reply. 'You just need to understand, Mr Carley, that if you don't work with me, your family will perish anyway. I will not be telling you the reason for that at any time. You will simply do as I ask, and there will be no questions from you or explanations. Is that clear enough for you?'

Jacob didn't know what to say next. Six years was a long time, a lot could change. Was it worth the risk? If he rejected the President's offer, would his family suffer anyway?

Like so many people before him, Jacob didn't really have any choice in the matter. When faced with the death of loved ones, what could anybody do? You had to take whichever gamble kept them alive longer, even if that was going to be just a day. You had to keep taking your chances, avoid getting involved until the last possible moment, then follow the course of action which kept the most people alive for the longest time.

You tended not to make many of your own choices in The City, events chose you. In his ignorance, Jacob had practised to take part in – and win – the Gridder Games. That had been his mistake. He had done so because he enjoyed gaming and he sought the approval of his friends. He had never expected it to have the terrible consequences that it did. That simple action had resulted in him becoming a sanctioned murderer and having a private conversation in the President's car which could place the lives of his family in immediate peril.

'Do you guarantee that my family will be safe if I work with you? Safe from Damien Hunter?'

'I guarantee you nothing, Mr Carley, only that your

family will die anyway if you don't work with me. I'm offering you a chance, it will be the only chance you get.'

Jacob hesitated. He thought of Linwood, how he wanted him to grow up safe and healthy on Silk Road. He considered his mum and dad who'd striven so hard to give their sons the best life they could in The City. He wanted to protect them. He knew he'd have to accept the President's deal.

'I accept your offer, sir. I will agree to work with you if it will help to protect my family.'

'Very well, Mr Carley, or should I refer to you as Reevil96? You will not be able to see your family again until this is over. You're going to disappear from The City tonight. Your new mission begins immediately. We will need to begin by placing an implant into your brain ...'

The Third Mode

Damien Hunter's sneering face looked directly at them. If he hadn't been a hologram, all of the remaining Justice Seekers would have set about him there and then.

Clay and Julia came running up, out of breath. They'd seen that the next Mode was about to begin and knew the importance of being together as a group when it started. They immediately took in what had happened, though they couldn't see the cause of the bloody scene that awaited them.

'What the hell happened here?' Clay gasped, shocked at Chris and Ross's hacked bodies.

'An eye for an eye, a tooth for a tooth, a life for a life. So it is in our city that any person who breaks the law shall find justice in The Grid. It has been our way since the plague years. It has kept our city safe and fair for almost one hundred years.'

'Stick it, Hunter!' Clay shouted. 'What happened here?'

Hannah was the only Justice Seeker who had any knowledge of Schälen, and she only knew him as a swaggering pixelated image. Max, Jena and Mitchell had seen him on the screens, though they had paid very little attention to him. It was Ross and Chris, the two dead men, who'd known him from the beginning of the trial.'

'It was Schälen,' Hannah began, still choked by what had happened. 'They sent three more of him to attack us. Mitchell finished them off. He saved me.'

'Six Justice Seekers remain in The Grid today. If any find justice there, they will walk away with their freedom. This is how our society preserves truth and honesty.'

'I said to stick it, Hunter!' Clay shouted again.

'Look, whatever happened here, you all need to focus, okay? I know you're tired, I know you just want to sleep. But it's starting again, this is the beginning of the next Mode. Grab a weapon and stand in a circle, back-to-back.'

Once more, Clay gave the directions which had already helped to preserve lives. The group had at least gained some new weapons. Those who were holding the new blades brought in by Schälen were able to keep them. Those that were being carried by the three clones had disappeared. They were reasonably well-armed, but who knew what would be coming at them next?

The Law Lords came into view. There were only five of them this time. Clay noticed that Talya was no longer there, or the one called Sivil who'd drawn the Modes at the beginning of the trial.

Leianna Richwald stepped forward once again. Clay

was growing accustomed to her grim face getting the blood-shed underway.

'You six stand charged with crimes against The City. If you find justice in The Grid, you shall walk free.'

Hunter finished off the speech. Clay knew what was coming this time.

'Justice Seekers, find your justice!'

'Get ready!' Clay shouted.

The group braced themselves for whatever Fortrillium was about to throw at them next. They weren't ready to fight, Clay was aware of that. They'd had no time to recover from losing Chris and Ross – their deaths had struck every-body hard. There was just silence and darkness.

Had the environment changed? Clay listened, trying to stay sharp and be ready for what came next. Then a light came on in the darkness. It was from a flashlight. A voice followed.

'Clay?'

It was Joe.

'Joe, is that you?'

Clay held up his weapon, he was ready for a trick. They'd recreated Schälen already, he wondered if they were now going to have to have to fight Joe and perhaps Lucy.

'Hannah? Is that you?'

It was Lucy's voice.

'Lucy?'

The lighting around them was gradually restored, this time to give the appearance of dusk. Everything was the same as it had been before. The group was still based at the large concrete block where they'd first become separated.

Clay guessed that this was the real Joe and Lucy. When everybody had enough light to see, Joe rushed at Jena and

Lucy rushed towards Hannah. They all embraced, overwhelmed to be reunited. Joe moved from Jena to Mitchell to Hannah. There were tears of joy, a rare thing in The Grid.

Clay remained wary throughout, suspecting a trap or a deception. Joe explained to Jena that Matt was still alive, he'd just left him, but that they had work to do before they could be reunited.

'I knew there had to be something,' Max said, 'but I never imagined it would go to a whole new place.'

'It's amazing down there,' Joe continued. 'But we're in serious trouble, we've been sent here on a mission. We need to locate President Del—'

Joe almost finished his sentence before the drones came. There were six of them hovering silently overhead, emitting an almost inaudible buzz. Max saw them first, but it was too late for him. One of the drones fired a needle into his neck and he stood completely motionless. He simply stopped where he was.

'Max? Max? Are you okay?'

Joe shook his arm, there was no response. Without warning, the entire cityscape changed. It spun around them, then reconfigured. It was The Climbs, exactly as Joe knew it. A drone shot out a needle and this time it lodged directly into Mitchell's neck.

'Run!' shouted Clay. 'Spread out, there's one for each of us. Take cover, try to destroy them before they get you!'

Joe began to run with Jena.

'Go alone!' Clay yelled at him. 'They're hunting us, we need to separate!'

'Meet back here, Mum!' Joe shouted. 'Take this!'

He handed Jena a weapon. Lucy had done the same for Hannah. Mitchell and Max were paralysed, standing completely still where they'd been caught.

Joe ran down the street, he knew this place well. The drones were aiming for their necks – whatever they were doing, they had a specific target. As the four Justice Seekers began to run, so the drones split off, each one tracking a different target.

Joe needed to find some cover. The drone was right on his tail, he had to find a place where he could turn and shoot. He drew a hand weapon, ready to make his move. He turned down a long street, running as fast as he could. All the time the drone was on him waiting for its moment.

When he thought he'd drawn far enough ahead, Joe turned to shoot. The drone flew over his head and circled, targeting his neck. It shot its needle, but Joe was ready for it. He rolled on the ground, the needle missed him and lodged in the earth. Did they have more than one needle to shoot?

He got his answer straight away. The drone circled him again and shot. Another miss, the thing was persistent, that was for sure.

Joe moved to the right, bluffing the device, then darted off to the left. It gained him vital seconds to take cover under a concrete canopy which ran along the nearest tower block. He turned his back to the wall, neck protected, held out his weapon and fired.

The drone exploded and the debris fell to the floor. Joe sheathed his gun and began to walk over to it. As he did so, a new device materialized behind him and immediately released its needle. It flew directly into Joe's neck, instantly stopping him dead in his tracks. Mode 3 had begun.

CHAPTER NINE

Preparations

Philip Schaelles longed to see his daughter again. It would be time soon. He cursed the day the plague had struck the planet. His own father had told him stories about how life had once been. He'd never shared those with Teanna – it seemed unfair to give her a glimpse of a world she would never know. It was a world he'd never known too, he'd been born at Centrum.

As a boy, he'd loved it when Edward had reminisced about his life before the pandemic broke out. He'd describe things Philip could only imagine. His father was a man of science, but to hear tales of aeroplanes, ships, thriving cities and a life of free choice, it was the stuff of dreams. But as he'd grown up, he'd come to understand that the old life was over. He could dream all he wanted about the world that had been inhabited by his father, but it was gone, they had to accept that.

Before Edward died, Philip had asked him not to share

these stories with Teanna. He felt it would do more harm than good. The men had argued about that and the atmosphere had been tense for some time, but in the end Edward had agreed. As it turned out, he never got to see his granddaughter anyway. He was found dead in the Cryo-Labs before she was born. Philip was pleased they'd made their peace before his father's death, agreeing to put aside their differences and work together, dwelling not on the past but trying instead to create a new future. That future would come soon enough, along with the return of his beloved daughter. When Delman returned, the final pieces would finally be put in place.

They were both men of science. Edward had passed on his unique skills to his son and they'd accomplished great things between them in spite of the wrecked world they'd been forced to inhabit. Edward had bequeathed a heavy burden from beyond the grave. It had come when Teanna was only three months old, and the information in that message had changed Philip's world in an instant. His father had placed responsibility for the future of humanity in his son's hands.

Philip looked at the dials on his console, analysing the data and looking for problems. It looked good – the host body was in excellent condition, the brain had been kept alive and was ready for the transfer. If only there had been a world out there to admire what they'd achieved between them. He didn't like what he was doing, but he trusted his father and he had to believe in him now. It seemed unethical to meet Delman's demands, but if Edward's story were even partially true, there was nothing else he could do. Delman had to survive, he had to get what he needed.

Edward Schaelles had been a highly respected scientist

before the plague. He'd been celebrated all over the world at a time when countries were connected by a global network which permitted instant communication. That world had been gone for a hundred years. Nobody knew what was out there now or if the rest of the planet had even survived. Philip had loved hearing the stories of the old world. As a child, anything had seemed possible and he couldn't understand how science couldn't come up with a solution to the problem.

Humans had cured all sorts of diseases. Why not this one? Why had this particular pandemic beaten all of the best minds? He and his father had made remarkable breakthroughs in Cryo technology. Why could they still not find a cure for the disease?

He knew he had a tendency to take flights of fancy, it was something that happened to him increasingly as he got older. He missed his own father and he missed Teanna desperately.

Philip looked at the body in the glass container. He hoped it would all be worth it in the end. He'd learned from his father that sometimes sacrifices have to be made for the sake of scientific progress. But taking one man's life to save another? That was a hard concept to reconcile, but he'd done so, many years ago now.

Josh Delman would be one of the lives saved. He had appeared from nowhere six years previously, arriving undetected in the quietness of the night and making terrible demands. Philip knew who he was, of course. His father had warned him. And he knew there was no resisting his requests. Humanity depended on Delman countering Morgan's treacherous actions. But the price he paid was high, Delman had demanded his own daughter as security.

And he'd forced him at gunpoint to place that terrible device in her head to ensure her safe exit.

He wondered who the man was in the Cryo-Tank. He knew his name, but he knew nothing of his life. Did he have a family? Was he loved? Philip didn't know. He didn't get to know his lab rats individually, he had to focus on the science. Delman could save them all. The loss of one life would help them all to survive, there was nothing more important than that.

He wondered if the man in the tank was aware of what was going on. Did he dream of escape? His brain patterns were certainly active, they had to be for the transference to take place. Delman had been colluding on this for many years, ever since he'd made his first deal with Edward. Philip and his father had sorted out the science and it was up to Delman to deliver on his part of the deal. When he finally crossed over, the body that Delman was inhabiting would be old. It had already survived Cryo-Freezing once before, and chronologically it was over 130 years old, physically over eighty. Morgan's body would be discarded after the transference and Delman would take over the form of the younger man, using his brain as a host for his own thoughts, feelings and memories. Delman would live on in anonymity, free from the curses of his past. It was just collateral damage that the man's consciousness would have to die to protect Delman's new identity.

It would be less than a day. Whatever this man's thoughts and memories were, he had very few hours to enjoy them. Once Delman arrived, the transfer would need to take place quickly. It was the only way he'd get Teanna back alive. That was his part of the deal, the conclusion of his father's and his own work. Humanity depended on it.

As Philip Schaelles adjusted the dials, checked the configurations and monitored the results, he took a moment to look back at his files and remind himself of the name of the test subject. He'd become so accustomed to thinking of him only in terms of the science that he had to remind himself sometimes of the most basic details.

He scrolled up to the top of the file and read through the personal data section. Now he remembered. He was getting forgetful, he should have known that. He was a forty-seven-year-old male, an Immune, and in excellent physical condition. And his name was Tom Slater.

The First Visit

For Josh Delman, it was to be the third time he'd been in The Grid. It never scared him any the less. It was a terrifying place to be and he dreaded it. The first time he'd entered the deadly arena, he was running for his life in the unfamiliar body of President James Morgan and he had no choice but to walk through the valley of death. Once they found Edward Schaelles' corpse, they'd come after him. It would be a murder hunt, there was no refuge for him in Centrum.

He was a younger man then with a fit and athletic physique. He was strong, like so many of the Justice Seekers who survived until the end. He hadn't known what he would be walking into. He'd made his escape through The TriPlex and taken the elevator as the only possible way out. He knew they would never follow him there. It was forbidden, impossible. Had he been in his original body it would have been impossible for him too, but he was borrowing the body of another person. It gave him all the access that he needed: Morgan had had a special implant fitted right at the beginning of the project to build the Sectors and he could go wherever he wanted. He was an Immune too. He could access everything; he was the only one who could.

When Josh Delman walked into The TriPlex, he was faced with three exits, each one marked as a different Sector. Three Sectors, three strains of disease, it made sense to him. He made for the second exit. Sector 2 was the only area which had been spared from the testing of any cures. It had to be there, according to what Schaelles had overheard.

As the elevator began to ascend, Josh Delman caught his breath. He hadn't a clue what would greet him when the doors opened. He was armed, alert and prepared. The elevator came to its resting position and the door opened. He looked out into the final moments of a massacre. There were bloody bodies scattered all around, the last person had just been shot through the neck with an arrow. Delman hesitated in the doorway, but as he did the rural landscape in front of him began to pixelate, then disappeared, leaving a crisscross grid and a vast hangar. He stepped out of the elevator, which appeared to be right at the centre of the huge area. All he could see were bodies, some in front of him and others in various states of decomposition all around the arena.

He wondered if he'd have been better taking his chances at Centrum. As Delman stepped into the blue lattice markings that formed The Grid, he triggered a voice message.

'You sought and found justice in The Grid. You are free to take The Justice Walk. Please step onto the transporter to activate the release process.'

A circular platform appeared in front of Delman and he

stepped onto it. He was immediately scanned. The voice came again. It was automated, it sounded as if it was coming from a console.

'Welcome to Sector Two, President Morgan. You may now leave The Grid. Your full access rights have been reinstated. Please activate transportation.'

Delman recognized an opportunity when he saw it. He activated the control panel and it transported him away from the hangar. He materialized in a secure holding area where he was met by armed guards and a suited official. The man in the suit looked confused and in a state of panic.

Delman waited to see who would make the first move. The strategy worked well, and the official stepped forward, nervous and shaken.

'I'm delighted to meet you. My name is President – Acting President – Michael Noakes. Welcome to The City, Mr President.'

Delman seized on the confusion and played it to his advantage. He could work out enough of what had happened to piece things together. He'd taken over the body of President James Morgan in Centrum. As the most senior member of the ruling Government, Morgan appeared to have free access to this Sector and complete and unchallenged superiority in terms of rank. Josh Delman superseded the existing President, he had rights of office too. Not only had Delman just escaped with his life, he had walked straight into the most senior position in the Sector.

'Pleased to make your acquaintance, Mr Noakes. Thank you for your service. You are now relieved of your position.'

'May I ask, sir, what just happened? How did you get out of there?'

The man was completely confused. Delman didn't

know much more himself. He would behave as if he had every right to be there, then have the former President eliminated at the earliest opportunity. He would need to secure his position. The confusion was to his advantage, they couldn't argue with the computer systems which had clearly identified him as having seniority.

'I'm here to take charge of this Sector – 'The City' as you call it. You'll see from my authorization that I have full seniority here. You are not to refer to me as President James Morgan. For security purposes, I will be known as President Josh Delman and that is how you will address me from now on. Now, take me to my quarters.'

Delman was bluffing, but they seemed to accept his authority. They didn't like it, they didn't understand it, but all of their IT systems informed them that this man was who he was supposed to be – President James Morgan – and that he had full jurisdiction over everybody in the room. He didn't even have a Gen-ID, although everybody in The City was supposed to have one.

'We should introduce you to Luke Dreyfuss, the Head of Fortrillium. He'll probably be on his way down here already.'

It didn't take Delman long to piece together what he needed to know. He'd entered Sector 2. It was a walled city – he'd never been inside, but he knew the basic concept from when they'd been created during the peak of the plague years. He'd never made it to a Sector as he'd been moved over to Centrum before his ultimate detention by Morgan. Noakes was in charge in this Sector and it sounded as if Dreyfuss also had some seniority. Fortrillium had to be a form of government or law enforcement, it would be one or the other. He was President, he would have overall control over everything. Edward Schaelles had done well to give him Morgan's body. He'd be able to hide in The City for as long as he needed. They'd never be able to come for him, he was safe until the Centurial arrived. As long as his body survived, of course. Morgan's body had to last another fifty years, but he was fit and strong. He'd be over eighty when he left again, if he managed to survive that long. He had to live, for all their sakes.

'Tell Dreyfuss I'll meet with him later, I'm not ready to see him yet.'

Delman had learned that trick a long time ago in civilian life, before the plague days. Act as if you're in charge and nobody will question it. It worked – they agreed to everything he said.

Delman was escorted out of the holding area and taken to a vehicle. He quickly worked out he was in a Fortrillium facility, the logo was everywhere and the uniforms gave it away. He was driven to a gated complex not too far away from the Fortrillium buildings. Looking out of the vehicle window, he thought that life here seemed very similar to what he remembered from his former life, before the plague. There were houses, roads, trees, plants, just a few vehicles, and it looked clean and well ordered. After the artificiality of Centrum, it was good to see such familiar surroundings. It was good to breathe fresh air once again. The sealed environment of Centrum might have been secure against the ingress of infection, but it was sterile and claustrophobic for those who had known life before the pandemic.

Every time Delman stepped through a security gate or was required to place his hand on an ID panel, it activated without a problem. Delman could go anywhere and do anything without challenge. His demeanour was confident and authoritative. Every time he encountered any security he expected to be exposed as the impostor that he was. It didn't happen. He walked straight through as he was escorted to his office.

Delman dismissed the guards but asked Noakes to stay with him in the office. President Josh Delman received his briefing from the confused and astonished former president. In that one hour meeting, Delman gained access to The Pact and found out everything he needed to know about Catharsis. He saw that Edward Schaelles had been right all along about Morgan. His amoral alliances had sentenced humanity to oblivion. He also ascertained the nature of his presidential responsibilities, what his relationship was to Fortrillium, and the precise purpose of the place they called 'The Grid', from which his exit had created such a sensation.

Michael Noakes was dismissed from the President's office and Luke Dreyfuss summoned immediately afterwards. He was kept waiting for some considerable time by the President, even though Delman had been ready all the time. It was a technique Delman would use in future years for one of Dreyfuss's successors, Damien Hunter.

Dreyfuss had activated a complete rundown on the new incumbent by the time of his meeting. He looked for anything he could find to eject the man who'd so unexpectedly interrupted the comfortable arrangement he'd set up with Michael Noakes. It was an arrangement which had served them both very nicely since assuming their positions after the final closing up of the walls. The Grid had been of their making and between them they were assured a lifetime of luxury and leadership. Both men had expected to live out their lives in Silk Road luxury without any external interference. Yet here was President James Morgan – Dreyfuss knew it was him, except that he looked the same age as he did at the time of the plague. It was remarkable and unlikely, but the evidence was standing in front of him. However, it didn't seem to be quite Morgan, his attitude and demeanour had changed, but whatever checks and tests Dreyfuss had run there was nothing to suggest this wasn't Morgan, even though he insisted on being called something completely different. The BioScan data was correct, the access levels were built into the entire Fortrillium network – this new President was allowed to do what he was doing and there was no legal basis on which to challenge it.

He'd been seen to walk out of The Grid too. Dreyfuss had almost been caught out with that, it had tested to the extreme his ability to take decisions under pressure. The final Justice Seeker had been terminated and he'd thought it was all over. But just as the cameras zoomed in on the victim's final moments, Delman had clearly been seen to emerge from the pixelated scene in the background. He'd ordered the live feed to be taken down, but it was too late, it had been seen. In future re-edits, Delman would be removed, but the word was out in The City and on Silk Road that somebody had walked out of The Grid alive.

The President's meeting with Dreyfuss lasted a little longer than two hours. Delman adeptly ascertained the nature of the status quo and understood within five minutes that he'd rudely interrupted a very cosy working relationship between Luke Dreyfuss and Michael Noakes.

He discussed his appearance in The Grid and decided it would play nicely to his advantage. As the only person ever to exit The Grid, he had created a sensation within The City walls. He would quickly capitalize on that, making an address on the screens and seizing control.

Delman probed the relationship between the Centuria, the presidential security teams and the local constabularies and determined where his own power base would lie. He would need to incentivize and motivate a small team within the presidential guard to carry out some small housekeeping tasks for him.

The meeting with Dreyfuss was very useful and Delman had gleaned everything about The City he would need to know. He dismissed him and called in the senior member of the presidential guard.

Three hours previously, Delman had been a fugitive from Centrum, running for his life, hoping to put right his errors and save humanity from its fate. He had ended it as the man in charge of the second Sector, a place known to its citizens as The City.

Before the day had ended, The City's former president had met with an unfortunate accident while walking to his new, more modest, accommodation. He'd been struck and hit by a government vehicle – it had killed him instantly. It was a terrible tragedy.

Meanwhile the Head of Fortrillium had been found murdered in The Climbs. His death had been brutal and merciless. There had been no witnesses. It was another catastrophe in a night filled with incredible events. Delman had quickly learned that for him – and humanity – to survive, he would have to turn into a man who was more like James Morgan than the compassionate doctor he'd once been.

At the same time as those tragic incidents were playing out, The City's new president was making an address on the screens. Although the timing of the deaths had been uncanny, Delman had been broadcasting live at the time so his hands had to be clean.

The President had not bothered to explain how he had been in The Grid or why he had been seen to exit it. He was the only person ever to have walked out of there, and his arrival had already been seen as a victory for the people, in spite of nobody remembering him entering The Grid in the first place.

The new president immediately exposed the corrupt regime of the former incumbents – Noakes and Dreyfuss – and announced new arrangements to alleviate suffering in The Climbs. Although the residents wouldn't be aware of it, nothing would actually change, but it created enough enthusiasm to embed Delman into his new role and enable him to take control of Fortrillium and his own office.

The City had a new president and his name was Josh Delman. Some older citizens thought he looked uncannily like the president who had presided over the plague, but it was impossible, he hadn't aged a bit in fifty years. He had started the day as a fugitive and ended it as the man in charge of a city packed with several million citizens. Nobody was able to challenge his authority, there was no legal basis for an objection. The tragic deaths of Noakes and Dreyfuss made everybody step in line, and Delman's swift appointment of a new Head of Fortrillium ensured that all contenders immediately began work on impressing their new president. A new appointment was made, Delman's position was secure.

He continued to dwell in The City unchallenged and in complete control for more than forty years afterwards. He was safe for several decades until he was forced to take drastic action once again and re-enter The Grid. As he'd aged in The City, he'd begun to grow nervous that his existing body might not survive until the Centurial and became greedy for more life. He knew he could seize it too once he'd returned for Catharsis. But he would need a new body to inhabit. He would not return to his original body, he would take the form of a younger man. A new opportunity had arisen unexpectedly. It would involve risk, but it was worth it for the intoxicating chance of an extended life. There was no point saving humanity if you could not live to enjoy it. And to make sure he got what he wanted when he returned, he'd already taken the precaution of extracting someone very special from Centrum as his security.

Truth

Damien Hunter watched in horror as Joe Parsons and Lucy Slater returned to The Grid. The two Justice Seekers had walked back into the arena as if they'd been there all the time, emerging from a pixelated area which had appeared without warning. Whatever they'd done, wherever they'd been, Damien Hunter needed to access that knowledge.

They were dressed differently too. They were armed and had received medical attention. There had to be something – and someone – beyond the walls of The Grid. Hunter was prepared to bet on his family's life that this was where Delman was heading. The explanation for Catharsis had to reside at the centre of The Grid.

It had caused a stir when seen on the screens. There was no way they could conceal the reappearance of two Justice Seekers they'd claimed to be dead. Hunter had seen the show reels himself, he'd approved them, and they clearly implied that Joe Parsons and Lucy Slater were dead. Yet here they were, alive and well.

He would need to address the problem fast. This would cause a stir in The Climbs and might lead to unrest. Hunter contacted the Chief Centuria and ordered the deployment of more teams on the other side of the gates. He wanted to be certain he could contain the situation. People still talked about Delman's arrival in The Grid as if it was some sort of folklore. A generation had passed, yet still they talked about Delman being the only person to survive in The Grid. Now there were two more who'd stepped out alive. Back from the dead. He'd need a plausible explanation.

He thought through how best to play the situation. They could blank the screens, buy some time, and annihilate Parsons and Slater. Would they buy it in The Climbs? However much Hunter's instincts were to kill, he wanted Parsons and Slater alive. They were a source of valuable information now. Torture would be a more appropriate course of action, but he needed them alive to do that. Their friend Mitchell had caved immediately, they'd be just as easy to break, he was certain.

He reconsidered. He could use them to find out what Delman was hiding, they had to know the truth now. Why were they back? They'd come for something. Who would re-enter The Grid if they didn't have to?

Hunter connected his WristCom and demanded to speak to the show reel team.

'I want you to repackage the death scenes. Let the video sequences run on a little longer so we can see they were both clearly alive. Package it as a twist, a surprise, just like using the serial killer clones. I want you to make more of Parsons and Slater, accentuate a more positive story. Show how they helped the other Justice Seekers. Focus on Slater with that man from the Institute, show Parsons covering up the first Justice Seekers with dirt to protect them from the fire. Do it quickly, I want those show reels ready for approval in twenty minutes!'

He shut down his WristCom. He wasn't going to be discussing anything further with the team. They had their instructions. Hunter needed to move the story on so it would be possible to allow Slater and Parsons out of there alive. Perhaps he'd been too hasty to dismiss Talya Slater. He wondered if the diplomatic approach might have been more appropriate.

Damien Hunter replayed the video extract of Joe and Lucy's reappearance in The Grid. He zoomed in and played it back, frame by frame. All he could see was a water butt, some pixelation in the surrounding areas, and then the forms of Joe and Lucy stepping forward. He contacted the Head Gridder, 97TRaider, and asked if they were clones. The reply was in the negative. That gave Hunter the solution he was looking for.

'As far as the other Gridders are concerned, Slater and Parsons are clones, created on my orders. You are not to tell the rest of the Gridders otherwise. Understood? You remember what happened to your colleague earlier so do not think to disobey me on this. Do it now!'

He terminated the WristCom connection and reconnected with the show reel team. They'd just completed assembling his last set of requests.

'Delete the lot!' Hunter snapped. 'Parsons and Slater are clones, the same as with the serial killer. We've brought them back to disorient the other Justice Seekers. Make sure you show Parsons and Slater as dead. We've patched them up and given them new clothing and weaponry, just like we did the Schälen clones. They're not real – make sure that's made clear on the screens. Do it fast. I want it broadcast in ten minutes.'

Hunter had his play. By claiming Joe and Lucy were clones, it would make the problem of their reappearance go away. It would also enable him to broker a deal if one became necessary. He needed them to stay alive. He needed to speak to the Head Gridder again. He connected to 97TRaider.

'What have you got planned next for the Justice Seekers?'

'We're going into a Psyche-Trial, sir. We're going inside their heads to create scenarios based upon their worst fears and we'll screen those nightmares as if they are really happening.'

'How do you get inside their heads? What will happen?'

'You're aware, sir, what happens during Psyche-Eval before the trials begin? We place the implants in their brains so they can get in and out of The Grid, but also so we can access their vital signs and core memories.'

'Okay, okay, I know all that. How much information can we get out of their brains? Can we tell what they're thinking?'

'No, sir, it only accesses key data, the sort of memories which are stored long term in the prefrontal cortex. Historically, Gridders have tried to access short-term memories, but it puts the devices under too much strain. They have a tendency to explode in the head, creating an embolism. It's been deemed to waste Justice Seeker deaths and the most dramatic memories and fears are located in the long-term memory. It's been protocol for a long time not to use that technique.'

'But we could if we wanted to?'

'Yes, sir, it's possible. I could patch a feed through to you if you wanted.'

'That would be good. Do it for Slater and Parsons. Make sure none of the other Gridders know about this. I may be calling on you later, don't go off shift.'

Things were working out well for Damien Hunter. He'd

covered up Lucy and Joe's reappearance – it was fortunate that the Gridders had used the Schälen clones, the story looked plausible and convincing. Centuria were reporting more lively audiences in front of the screens, but the presence of armed officers on the streets was keeping things in check. Once the show reels began to play, it would calm down. If not, some random outbursts of fire into the crowds would soon sort it out.

He would try to access the memories of Slater and Parsons remotely. He might get all of the information he needed. He'd have to take care not to kill them, certainly not at first, that would be a huge inconvenience. However, if he could find the clues he was seeking in their short-term memory it might prevent him having to forge new alliances. Parsons and Slater could be killed or saved at a moment's notice, depending on whether he needed them or not. If he could get to Delman without making any deals, so much the better.

Hunter felt as if he'd got the situation under control, so he moved onto the latest updates regarding the day's explosions in The Climbs. They were troubling him, there hadn't been any incidents like it for many years. He'd clamped down on everything when he became Head of Fortrillium, he'd left no room whatsoever for even peaceful protest.

The use of explosives was worrying. It suggested some form of organization, not just a group of people getting angry about something or other. This was much more than that, but he didn't know what it was yet.

Things were coming to a head: Delman's secret conversations, trouble in The Climbs, the reappearance of Slater and Parsons, and the plot to hack into Fortrillium's servers via the sewers. Hunter's instincts told him these events were linked in some way, but he couldn't see the shape of it, it had yet to emerge. He was certain of one thing though, this was his chance to seize the initiative from Delman and be reunited with his family. Even if it meant striking a deal with the President, agreeing to suppress some key information, it could win him his wife and children back. If it was enough to take the President down, all the better.

Hunter checked in with the Centuria teams. The protesters had vanished into the ruins of The Climbs without trace. The explosives used had been stolen from Fortrillium – inventory checks were being run, and they'd know how they had been procured soon enough. The fugitives had escaped – alive – their whereabouts unknown.

The Head Centuria believed the unrest was connected to the three traitors, Bachus, Levett and Carn – Leo, Julia and Jody. That seemed highly likely to Hunter, it would explain where the explosives had come from. If they'd been on some misguided mission to rescue Shen Li – Wiz – and the younger Parsons boy, it would make a lot of sense. It was troubling that these fugitives were still at large, but they had no public profile. They were a non-story, insignificant residents of The Climbs. Easy come, easy go, they'd be caught soon enough.

Julia Levett was in The Grid, and Bachus and Carn would show themselves soon enough, they'd feel morally obliged to try to save their colleague. It was so predictable to Hunter, they'd all be apprehended and terminated soon enough. The situation was under control.

His attention was diverted to his console where the newly edited show reels had just begun to be screened. The editing was good, the voice-over work strong. He almost convinced himself that he was really looking at clones of Slater and Parsons. It was a good story, he was pleased he'd thought of it.

Two encrypted channel requests appeared on his

console. It was 97TRaider sending through the Psyche feeds. He'd have direct access to the minds of Slater and Parsons, and he had the rest of the night to figure out what was going on. For the first time in a while, Damien Hunter felt things were beginning to go his way. He could almost hear his wife's voice again and the laughter of his children. It wouldn't be long now.

Hunter had a thought. His best ideas always came like that, out of the blue. He connected his WristCom to 97TRaider who was sounding jittery. It was fair enough, Hunter thought, he'd shaken them all up a bit with his earlier visit. He'd need to change his shirt, there was still blood on it.

'I want the Centuria woman dead by the end of the night. I don't care if it's outside peak screen times, she has to be dead by 06:00. Slater and Parsons stay alive for now. Anybody else is fair game, do as you please with them.'

There was no more conversation. The WristCom connection was terminated. He'd given his instructions, there was nothing more discuss. Killing the Centuria, Julia Levett, would flush out the other two fugitives. That would lead him to Wiz and Dillon Parsons, as her death would inspire the predictable revenge attack. He'd get it nipped in the bud as soon as possible.

Damien Hunter was feeling smug, he'd got it all worked out. He'd spend the night working through the Psyche information feeds and by morning he'd know exactly what to do with Lucy Slater and Joe Parsons. He'd also have a good idea what Delman was up to. He'd be ready to make his move, Delman wouldn't see him coming.

Then his eye was caught by something on his screen. The feed from The Grid had been interrupted. It went to black then there was just interference. It was coming back, it seemed to have been a temporary technical fault. He was wrong. His screen was no longer filled with the feed from The Grid. Instead, he was looking at Talya Slater's face. And behind her, on a screen, a photograph of him holding a gun to a woman's head while she was still clutching her crying baby.

CHAPTER TEN

Sector 1

Matt felt completely useless. He'd felt useless for six years. After the sheer exhilaration of escaping from The Grid and saving his life, the implications had become slowly clearer.

When he'd first descended in that elevator six years previously, he hadn't had a clue what he would find. He didn't know if he'd survived The Grid and if it was The Justice Walk he was experiencing. Neither could he tell if something extraordinary had happened, something that was not supposed to have taken place. When the elevator doors opened on The TriPlex, he didn't know what, if anything, would be there to meet him. As he later discovered, there was no way he could have even got into the elevator if he wasn't an Immune. He'd have been terminated immediately. No warning, no alerts, just an instant violent death. When the Sectors had been created, it had been deemed essential for the survival of humanity that no plague carrier could ever enter The TriPlex. If the plague or a mutated version of the disease got in, the pandemic could begin all over again. If Centrum fell, the population was on its own.

It was equally impossible for those in The TriPlex to enter the Sectors. They were to remain sealed off zones, nobody was to enter or leave. The population in Centrum had been carefully balanced. It was made up of Immunes, of course. That was an extra level of protection in case any strains of the virus should get through, but also there was a balanced ecology of society in there: scientists, engineers, horticulturists, doctors, mechanics, teachers and political leaders were carefully blended to ensure Centrum would continue to thrive for the hundred years needed for humanity to increase its chances of survival. They did not know what their role was, only to maintain the systems of Centrum to ensure the system continued to operate correctly and to safeguard the disease-free integrity of the establishment at all costs.

Matt Parsons was the second person to make the crossing from the Sector to Centrum. As the elevator had worked its way below ground to its destination, he'd braced himself for a violent reception. He was familiar with working elevators, having lived and worked on Silk Road all of his life, so he understood there would be a momentary delay before the door opened.

He'd stood there, tired, wounded and weary, not sure if he had much fight left in him. He'd almost given himself up for dead in The Grid, then from nowhere the exit had appeared.

The doors slid open. A young man was there, unarmed.

'Come with me,' he'd instructed. 'This way!'

Matt followed his lead. Alarms were going off in the vast glass-domed area, and this man seemed to offer the chance of help.

They ran across to another elevator marked 'Sector 1'. The young man activated the door and they stepped inside. Matt saw guards appearing on a circular transportation area in the centre of the atrium as the elevator door closed.

'Where are we heading?' he asked, alert to the fact he might be about to step back out into The Grid.

'Don't worry, it's safe up here. It's very different to what you came from.'

The elevator door opened. They were standing in a vast hangar crisscrossed with blue lines. They were at its centre, they'd walked out into an empty arena.

'This is The Grid in Sector 1,' the man began. 'It's deactivated now, it's safe to come though. They're all dead here anyway.'

'What?' asked Matt, 'Who are dead?'

'The entire Sector,' the man replied. 'They've all been dead for years, looking at the decomposition levels. I never go out there, I can see it on the cameras though. Not sure if it's safe. It's much nicer out there than in Sector 2, but the bodies tend to spoil the view.'

Matt was stunned.

'There's another city? How can there be?'

'There are three cities actually, but two of them are dead.'

'But we were told we were the only survivors. It's not possible.'

'You're in Sector 1 right now. This is the first city. We're not in Fortrillium, they called it Sympozia: it was the same tech, same sort of set-up, but a different social structure and another group of people making the rules. I don't actually know that, I've just figured it out from what's left here.'

'Who the hell are you anyway?' Matt asked. He felt he was asking the right questions but in the wrong order.

'Jacob Carley,' he said, reaching to shake Matt's hand. Silk Road, Matt thought immediately.

'Matt Parsons.'

'What's happening, Jacob? None of this makes any sense to me.'

'I'm only slightly ahead of you, Matt, so don't worry. I was brought here by President Delman. As far as I can tell, I'm the only one alive in this Sector. He hasn't told me much, but as far as I know there are three Sectors. Two of them are dead, only Sector 2 has survived. I don't know what killed them, plague I assume, but who knows? Delman has me up here to stop anyone else coming down into The TriPlex.'

Jacob clocked Matt's expression. He saw that more explanation was needed.

'The TriPlex is where you just came from. Nobody is supposed to be there. It's the last point at which the plague can be stopped. Nobody enters The TriPlex and nobody leaves Centrum. Only it hasn't worked out that way. I'm here and you're here. And President Delman seems to have his own key.'

'This is incredible, Jacob. How can it have happened?'

'I don't know. I'm piecing a lot of this together myself. I think they created three cities when the plague came. They call them Sectors. We're in Sector 1, you've come from Sector 2. I haven't been to Sector 3, Delman told me not to even think about it. You never know what you're walking out into. I'm a Gridder, Matt. He moved me over here. I didn't have a choice really. He stuck one of those things in my head. Damn, that hurts – have you got one?'

Matt nodded, and yes, it hurt.

'Those implants are what got us through The Grid in the first place. Without them, we'd have died on entry.

They're dangerous things. He took mine out, he needed to use it on somebody else, I think. I'm an Immune apparently. I didn't know, but Delman seems to understand it. You must be an Immune too or you never would have made it into that elevator. You'd have been terminated. It's Immunes only here. The plague has to be kept out of The TriPlex. We've been specially chosen.'

Matt was struggling to take it all in. He was being presented with a lot of information – what Jacob was telling him challenged his entire world view.

'I need to get you out of here quickly, we don't have long. I'm not supposed to be talking with you and you're definitely not supposed to know I'm here. I got you out of The Grid, it was me who opened the door for you. You must never talk about me when they take you into Centrum. You can't visit me and you won't be able to contact me. Forget that Sector 1 is even here and do not tell Centrum that this city is dead.'

'Why did you contact me then? What are you doing here?'

'Look, I got caught up in this by Delman, I don't really have a choice. Same as you, I'm just protecting my family. But I think Delman is trying to save us, I don't think he's the bad guy here. Sector 1 is dead, our Sector is still alive, Sector 3 is gone. I've decided to trust him, I don't have much choice anyway – he'll kill my family if I betray him. You're my insurance, Matt. I need someone to know I'm here in case I'm wrong. We're going to wait for The TriPlex to clear, then you're going down there again and you're going to come out of the second elevator. Just like it should have happened all along. You're going to tell them you went back up and thought better of it. Then you're stepping out and you need to keep your mouth shut. Just remember I'm here and remember what I told you about Delman. I think he's here to help us, but I may be wrong. If it all falls to pieces, remember me in Sector 1. The Grid here is activated at all times, don't think of coming up unannounced. It's for my own protection.'

'What are they like in Centrum? Will I be a prisoner there?'

'Unknown. They're going to be pretty scared of you at first, but once they make sure you're plague-free, they'll relax. They'll want to know what it's like in The City, I'm sure.'

Matt nodded. He could see the sense of what Jacob was saying. Given that everything seemed completely mad, there did seem to be a grain of sanity in his proposal. He wasn't at all sure about what would greet him in The TriPlex, it couldn't be worse than what was in The Grid.

'Remember, Matt, you can't tell anybody about me, don't even think about it. We're allies, right? We're pretty well the only people who know we're still alive! We're each other's security if it all goes to hell.'

'Won't my family know I got out?'

'No way. Fortrillium blacked it out. They won't know what happened, but they can't come in after you anyway. If they do, unless they're Immunes, they'll die when they enter the elevator. And that's if the Gridders even let them get that far. Their instructions are to keep everyone away from the centre of The Grid. I'd always wondered what was there, now I know. The Grid is there to keep us all out of The TriPlex. It's all a big plan. Delman knows what's going on, I don't. You can send a message to your family if you want, if you do it quickly.'

'Can you get it to them?'

'Well no, not exactly. I can access Fortrillium's systems via the Sympozia network, it's how Delman and I are talking. He figured it out, if he wasn't so damn scary, we'd be admiring him as a genius. All the Sectors are linked by a central matrix. I never knew about it when I was working for Fortrillium, I don't know anybody who knows about it in Sector 2. But it's there. You worked for Fortrillium. Do you have a secure area I can drop the message into?'

'I was hiding data in an encrypted folder. I gave it to my son, Joe, before the Centuria hauled me away. It shouldn't take him long to figure it out, but we can leave it in there. Only Joe will find it.'

'Okay, I'm recording now. Just speak, I'll get it.'

Matt delivered the message which would be seen by Wiz six years later. It would lie hidden for too long to give Joe and his family any comfort, but it would prove essential to giving Talya Slater the confidence to press ahead with the rebellion.

'Okay, got it. I cut you off a bit sharp at the end. Can you leave me your codes? It'll take me some time to work out how to get that into your folders without leaving a trace. Hope you're confident your son will be able to access it, he'll have to be pretty good to get onto the Fortrillium servers.'

'Don't worry. I trust him, he'll get there eventually. I left him enough clues, and he's a resourceful kid.'

'Okay, Matt. Much as I love having your company, you've got to go. I'm on my own up here, just the occasional message from Delman and an instruction not to let anybody out of The Grid. You're lucky, Matt. You played well, you made it to the centre so I could get you out without a fuss. It won't happen again. You're my ally now, okay?'

Matt nodded.

'I'm still confused about what's going on here, but I'm grateful for you saving my life. There was no way I was getting out of there alive, I owe you that. I'm not sure about President Delman. I don't share your view of him but I hear what you say, and I'll reserve judgement for now. I'll keep quiet about you being in Sector 1, but if things change and I find out that something else is going on, I can't guarantee I'll stick to our agreement. For now, though, thank you. I appreciate that I'm still alive.'

It was the best Jacob could hope for. He was alone in Sector 1. He'd got plentiful supplies since he was the only one left alive. Power seemed to come from a central system. He was secure there and he understood the tech. There was nothing else he could do, other than to sit, wait, see what the President wanted, and try to keep his family alive. He had an ally, somebody knew he was alive. That was security which he might rely on later.

He escorted Matt across the Sector 1 grid and took him as far as the exit.

The two men shook hands and parted. Matt wasn't at all sure about Jacob's take on Delman, but he believed him to be a good person. In The City they all had to do things they weren't comfortable with. You could speak up and take the consequences or you could stay quiet and keep your family safe. Most chose the latter. Matt certainly had. It's what had kept his boys alive and his wife safe.

He headed down in the elevator, calmer now but in urgent need of medical attention. He craved rest, he just wanted the torment to stop for a while. The door opened, and as instructed he ran across to the Sector 2 elevator. He waited outside the door until the Transporter area activated. Three armed guards were there. They weren't Centuria, they seemed defensive rather than hostile.

Matt held up his hands to show that he was unarmed and not a threat. There was somebody else standing behind the guards, he hadn't seen him at first. He stepped forward.

'Welcome to The TriPlex. My name is Philip Schaelles.'

The Address

Wiz was delighted with his new tech rig. He wished he'd had all of the equipment earlier. It almost made it worthwhile having to dangle from the scaffolding and risk his life in the elevator. He'd finally been able to do what he'd set out to do.

The tech teams had re-established the signal from the sewers, across The Climbs to the rebel base. The Centuria had located the mast at Harry's apartment and torn it off the side of the tower block. That was a nuisance, but not an insurmountable problem. They hopped the signal via a nearby high-rise, it was probably better that way. The Centuria would struggle to track the path that had been created across from the other buildings.

Wiz made a few adjustments and confirmed that everything was in place. He'd got direct access to Matt's data on the Fortrillium servers and he'd got the feed Delman was using to communicate beyond the walls of The City. He'd been allocated assistants, a tech team of three rebels who knew the equipment well. They were from Silk Road and, like Joe and his family, they'd been sent to The Climbs for one reason or another. Each had a grudge to bear, they were perfect members of a resistance movement. They had specialist tech skills from their former lives on Silk Road, fused with a hatred of Damien Hunter and all things Fortrillium. It was the perfect combination.

Wiz needed to prioritize. There were people in The Grid depending on him. Dillon was doing well, and he felt relieved that at least he'd managed to keep Joe's brother alive. He'd accomplished something. He intended to do his best to improve on his results. That was not going to be the only thing he achieved, he was determined about that.

Talya was ready to make her address. He needed to locate the holographic message from Matt. He got his team to interrogate Matt's data files. There was a lot of information in there, they would be able to work through it much faster than he could on his own. It was a case of sifting through notes, images and diary entries – it was time-consuming but should be productive too.

Everything worked better and ran faster in the rebel base. It was a help that Wiz didn't have to monitor the power levels continually. Eventually he was ready and called Leo over so that he could talk discreetly.

'I want to show Talya this message alone at first. I think she's going to find it quite a shock.'

'That's okay, use the briefing room, Wiz. Send your data to console 3c, you'll be able to access it from there.'

Talya had been checking in on Dillon. She was quite clearly nervous. Wiz had always known her as confident and assured when he'd seen her taking part in debates and news items on the screens, he wasn't used to her being like that.

'I want you to see this alone for the first time, Talya. We need to decide if we're going to show this during your address. It's explosive stuff, and it may put people in danger.'

Wiz accompanied Talya to the briefing room and began

a replay of Matt's video message. Talya watched quietly until the end, hanging onto Matt's every word.

'I'm still alive, Joe, and you need to come to me now ...'

He spoke his last words and the holographic message ended. There was silence for a moment.

'Do you think it's a trick, Wiz? Was it recorded before Matt died?'

Talya was looking for explanations and reasons for it not to be true. The implications were too great. She'd never seen Matt's final moments, Tom's body had never been recovered. Could her own husband still be alive?

'I'm sure it's for real, Talya. I've done some checking and this message was placed on Matt's server area just after he was supposed to have died in The Grid. It makes sense. If Matt had handed Joe his data card it would be the ideal way of getting a message through to him – if Matt could still access Fortrillium, that is.'

'What if Joe hadn't managed to access the data? It's a bit of a risk to take, isn't it?'

'What other options did Matt have, Talya? He was arrested by the Centuria without warning. Although he was so young, even then he knew his tech, and Matt wanted to pass the data over into safe hands. If he thought he was about to perish in The Grid, what other choice did he have?'

'And what about this more recent message? Where might it have come from?'

'I just don't know, Talya, but it makes sense that if Matt were alive and wanted to get a secure message to Joe, that's where he'd place it. He'd set up a secure area already and had managed to give Joe the key to access it. If you were in a place where you were unable to get a message directly to Joe, what would you do?'

Talya considered this for a moment. Wiz was right. It

was the ideal way to try to get a message to Joe. It was a long shot for Matt, but what other way did he have to communicate with Joe from wherever he was? Talya thought about Tom. Was it possible that he too could still be alive? It seemed incomprehensible. She and Lucy had gone through the grieving and the nagging sense of loss, they'd rebuilt their lives without him. Might he be alive too?

Talya reined in her thoughts. There was no evidence to suggest that her own husband could be living. She needed to focus on the facts. It seemed to make sense that Matt might be alive. His disappearance had been very similar to that of Joe and Lucy, a sudden interruption to the screen feeds. No evidence of death. And then there was the most recent development, the use of clones of Joe and Lucy in The Grid.

She'd had to slip off quietly into a room to get to grips with that development. At first she'd thought her daughter was back in The Grid, in much better health, clean, clothed and armed. Joe was the same, he seemed to have had some time to recover from his previous battles, he appeared much stronger and alert. Then Fortrillium began to play a new show reel explaining that these were just clones sent in to trick the Justice Seekers. They looked so real. She could swear she was looking directly at Lucy. After composing herself, she'd checked in on Dillon. She had to remember she was responsible for more than just Lucy. There were Joe and Jena to think about, Max, Mitchell and Hannah. The lives of so many were hanging in the balance. And now, alongside the resistance, she could finally fight back. It would no longer be with words alone, she would now be able to back things up with force. For the first time in the history of The City, or certainly during her lifetime, they were capable of striking back.

'Let's use this video, Wiz. The citizens of The Climbs are going to need something more than just hate to get them to take action. We need to give them hope, hope that something else is out there. Let's get ready for broadcast, I want to do this now.'

The address was put together at great speed but its impact was dramatic. Talya and Leo wanted the message to be released as soon as it was ready.

The broadcast area was set up. Wiz's tech team located several damning images of Damien Hunter from Matt's files. Wiz prepared the holographic image for replay. They were ready.

'Okay, Talya. Standby, we're breaking into the screen feeds now. There'll be a short delay. I'll give you a signal when you're on.'

Leo controlled events with assurance in the makeshift broadcast room. Talya had had enough experience on the end of a TV camera to know exactly what to do. She was calm and ready. She'd rejected writing a script, she wanted her message to be spontaneous and straight from her heart.

'You're on, Talya!'

Talya waited a moment, looking at the camera. This was being broadcast across all the screens in The Climbs. It was possibly being seen on some screens on Silk Road, they couldn't be sure. Thousands would be watching this. How many would it take to begin a revolution? It was in the early hours of the morning – who would even be watching at that time?

'Many of you will know me already. My name is Talya Slater. You will be aware that my daughter is currently fighting for her life in The Grid. You will also know that I was recently made a Law Lord, at President Josh Delman's request. One of my first duties was to pass sentence over my own daughter. I'm sure you will understand how that felt.'

Talya paused. The crowds watching the screens throughout The Climbs had fallen silent. Images of Damien Hunter committing atrocities in The Climbs were being shown on a screen behind her. They needed no words, they spoke clearly enough for themselves. Those watching did not know what was going on, but they sensed immediately that it was unauthorized and important. There was a charged atmosphere in The Climbs. Those who were in their apartments felt the sudden change in mood on the streets below, and many looked out of their windows to see what was going on. It was the middle of the night, yet The Climbs was alive with activity.

'We've all known loss in The City. The loss of my own daughter to the justice system is just one story. Many of you will have lost family members in The Grid. Others will have disappeared. It's rumoured they go to a place called The Soak, but even I as a Law Lord was denied access to this facility. People of The City, we've been fed nothing but lies!'

A murmur rippled through the entire city, from one screen audience to the next, along the streets and throughout the tower blocks. Talya had kindled a spark.

The Centuria became unsettled. Those who were part of the increased street patrols had been drawn to what was happening on the screens, they'd felt the mood beginning to change among the crowds. There was silence, everybody waited for Talya to continue.

'Like you, I have been terrified to raise my voice in The City. Where I saw injustice, I protested meekly, then I was silent. I was scared for my own life, but even more fearful for the life of my daughter. I have been privileged to live a life on Silk Road. My friend, Jena Parsons, was thrown into The Climbs six years ago. She and her family were left to fend for themselves. Jena's son, Joe, has fought to keep my daughter alive. Jena is now incarcerated in The Grid and her youngest son, Dillon, is safe with me after being hunted like a criminal. He is still a child.'

Another pause from Talya. She'd learned many tricks during her time making appearances on the screens. She wanted what she was saying to have time to percolate. It was important that her words created an impact. The Centuria teams began to seek guidance from their command centres. They could sense that the mood was beginning to change.

'We are all mothers, fathers, brothers, sisters and children. Whichever side of the gates we live on, we are all trying to survive and protect those we love. But we do it in fear. It does not matter if you live on Silk Road or in The Climbs, we all live in fear for our lives. We dare not speak openly for fear of punishment. We dare not protest for fear of repercussions. The shadow of fear was cast over our lives a hundred years ago and it has stayed with us ever since.'

People watching in the crowds began to shout out in agreement.

'That's right, Talya!'

'Yes! Keep talking, Talya!'

The calls were tentative at first, then they became more frequent and confident. The Centuria quietly and unobtrusively began to form offensive positions around the gathering crowds. Many people were running down the staircases in their tower blocks, anxious to see for themselves what was being said.

'You will have heard about an explosion in The Climbs today. The news reports are claiming it was an accident.

The truth is it was caused by a resistance group which has been operating in The Climbs secretly for many years. I am with that group now and I have agreed to be their spokesperson. The explosion was caused by their soldiers rescuing two young people who had been trying to save my daughter and Joe Parsons from their fate in The Grid. They were trying to do what any of you with loved ones would do if they had been thrown into that terrible place.'

The mood of the crowds had changed from interest, to surprise, then on to acknowledgement and finally to increasing anger. The Centuria sensed it, fingers tightened on triggers. Their instructions were not to fire unless it became absolutely necessary.

'Many of you will remember that I lost my husband, Tom, six years ago. I lost a husband and my daughter lost her father. He'd been working with Matt Parsons, who we all believed had perished in The Grid. Today I have been handed this holographic message from Matt which was sent securely to his son.'

Wiz played Matt's message. The holographic projection was placed just to the right of Talya. Her eyes filled with tears as she thought about Tom and the possibility he was alive. Everything was seen by the people watching the screens.

'I believe we have been lied to. If this message is true, Matt Parsons is still alive and he is safe somewhere outside The City's walls. That means there is life beyond these walls and we are being held in a prison which is run by Fortrillium.'

Talya steeled herself. She had to take care, she was rousing the crowds to action. The Centuria were often innocent too, their hands had been forced in different ways. She didn't want a bloodbath on her hands.

'I have no doubt that, as I have been speaking, the Centuria in your streets and in your squares have become increasingly restless. Many of them will be gripping their weapons right now, wondering what is going to happen next.'

The crowds looked around, suddenly becoming aware of the armed presence on the streets. There was a growing sense of unease. Revolution had consequences after all.

'Two of the Centuria have helped to rescue my friends. One of their own friends, also a Centuria, is currently incarcerated in The Grid where she may perish alongside all of the other Justice Seekers. It will be hard for many of you to sympathise, but the Centuria are people just like us. They also live in the shadow of fear, but I have learned today that the Centuria can be compassionate human beings too.'

Had Talya been addressing the crowds directly, she would have sensed confusion. The message she had seemed to be giving was changing. They'd assumed Fortrillium was their enemy.

'We have been lied to and our families have lived in fear and danger for a hundred years. We came here to escape the plague, but we became prisoners of a different scourge — the disease of fear. I do not know what lies ahead, but I know there has never been a better moment to seize the opportunity for change. That time is now. Centuria, I ask you to lay down your weapons. Citizens of The City, I ask you to reclaim this city.'

Talya had not been certain of what she was going to say, but as she had worked through her address, the enemy had become clear to her. She had known it all along, but she had always hoped a deal might be forged.

'The enemy here is Damien Hunter, Fortrillium's head. You have seen the images behind me. They were gathered by my husband, Tom, and his friend, Matt Parsons, before they disappeared. They had discovered what Damien Hunter was doing and had collected the evidence. You can see with your own eyes who has been holding us to ransom. I urge you to reclaim our city and reclaim justice. There has never been a better time to take action. If we fail now, we may never get our chance again. Stand together citizens of The City, it is time to banish the fear!'

Talya finished her message and the screens went blank before the Justice Trial feed reappeared. There was a tense silence. Somewhere in The Climbs a man and a woman emerged from the crowd and walked up to a group of Centuria. Weapons were lifted, aimed directly at them. They continued to move forward.

They were the parents of a man called Chris. He'd been taken away from them and placed in the Institute. He'd later appeared in The Grid, dazed and confused by what was happening to him. Lucy Slater had cared for their son and shown him kindness and compassion. The Justice Seekers had fought to protect him and keep him alive. Their son had been so moved by Lucy Slater's kindness that he'd repaid the debt by saving her from Schälen. He'd died, not as a victim but as a warrior, surrounded by a group of supposed villains he would have been proud to call his friends.

Lucy Slater's mother had just spoken. She had asked for their help. They were going to give it.

As Chris's parents walked up to the Centuria, they gently took their weapons and placed them on the ground. The crowds watched on, terrified the gunfire would begin at any moment.

Rebellion

Damien Hunter's face was bright red. He had clumsily interpreted the events of the day, and his complacency was coming back to bite him. He'd had to sit through Talya Slater's address and there was absolutely nothing he could do to stop it.

He'd tried. He was immediately on his WristCom demanding the feed be taken down. The tech teams did their best, but the rebels had circumnavigated Fortrillium systems. The only consolation seemed to be that it was the ring main which served the screens in The Climbs that had been hijacked, so residents on Silk Road were not seeing Talya's feed. Hunter was getting his feed directly from the ring main, and his internal feed continued to show what was going on in The Grid.

Hunter had established within five minutes that there was nothing he could do to prevent the sabotage. Sitting in anger and frustration, he listened to what Talya Slater had to say.

It wasn't so long ago that he'd seen her himself. How had she gone from leaving the Fortrillium building to leading a rebellion in a space of a few hours? Had she been involved all along? He called up her Gen-ID data, looking specifically for her crossings into The Climbs. There were several over the years, but it had all seemed to be above board and connected to her legal activities. Had he been blind to what was going on? There had been no sign of organized resistance in The City for many years. The explosion earlier that day had been the start of things.

Hunter's brain made a connection. Law Lord Sivil hadn't been present for the beginning of Mode 3. Sivil was always there. Was he connected too? Hunter cursed the deception and lies.

His only sense of relief came when Talya avoided making a call to arms. Her misplaced sense of justice meant she still couldn't make herself place the order for death and vengeance. Hunter actually laughed at that and shouted at his feed.

'You can't win a rebellion without spilling blood. It won't all be sorted with a hug!'

Reports began to cascade in via the Centuria teams which were placed in The Climbs. The crowds were becoming agitated. People were beginning to shout their agreement with Talya. They were getting more confident and brazen.

Damien Hunter ordered the Centuria teams to open fire at the first sign of unrest. The reports continued, the tension was growing. Then they stopped. There was no news of shooting or riots. The feed of information suddenly broke off.

Hunter understood that he would have to seize control. The President would be chasing him soon for a full briefing. He held the upper hand as far as the Centuria were concerned, and he'd be able to turn events quickly and halt any rebellion.

First, he ordered the complete lockdown of all of the security gates allowing passage from The Climbs to Silk Road. The vast iron doors which had remained open for decades were closed, their aged ironwork creaking and groaning in protest. The Climbs was contained, and groups of Centuria at the gates were withdrawn to Silk Road before they got wind of what was going on and joined in the rebellion.

The next thing Hunter did was to make his own

impromptu address via the screens. He didn't send his message to the Silk Road residents, he didn't want them to know what was going on. The Fortrillium building was safe against attack, but if any effort at rebellion spread to the Silk Road side, the facility would be vulnerable.

'Citizens of The Climbs, it is with a heavy heart that I make this address. Talya Slater has made some serious and deeply damaging claims to you this evening. This is a woman who was due to be scrutinized by the Law Lord panel for her level of competence and ability to perform her duties. Today she has stood up before you and made certain claims about my leadership and the functions of Fortrillium. The images you have seen are fabrications, those events did not take place. The claims that there is life beyond the walls of this city are ludicrous. There is no life out there, this is our home and our sanctuary.'

He borrowed one of Talya's speaking techniques. He thought her pauses had been a particularly useful device.

'Talya Slater's sanity and judgement have been under scrutiny from her peers. Her daughter had been plotting against The City and it's likely that her husband was murdered six years ago because he was involved in dubious activities too. This is a family which is working against Fortrillium, the organization which has fought to protect you and your families for a hundred years.'

Another pause. He looked directly into his Console-Cam. He liked to use the screens to broadcast direct messages from his office, and he preferred not to have to go through the nuisance of studios, lighting and camera crews to do that.

'I ask you now, in sadness and genuine concern, if this is a woman that you wish to follow. You must question her sanity and her motives. She is unreliable, unstable and she will stop at nothing to see her daughter rescued from our justice system in The Grid. Fortrillium has fought to protect you all from the ravages of the plague for a hundred years. I am your guardian, I am here to preserve all life in The City.'

Damien Hunter felt he'd done his bit as far as diplomacy was concerned and it was time to start on the threats. These were always best framed against a background of rationality and legality, but when there was no alternative, he was prepared to slaughter anybody who stood in his way.

'I need to remind you that your Gen-ID chips allow me – us – to ensure that order is maintained at all times. You will not be able to cross the boundaries of The City onto Silk Road. This is for the benefit of everybody in our community. I understand that a number of Centuria will be deciding whether or not to believe Talya Slater's lies. I remind those servants of Fortrillium: think of your families and your own lives. Reflect on the allegiance you pledged when you first took up your role.'

This was Hunter's direct threat to the Centuria. He understood how it would be in The Climbs in the heat of the moment. The Centuria would be terrified of being overrun by the crowds, they'd also find Talya earnest and convincing. They'd probably forget what he could do to them. No problem, he'd remind them.

Hunter's camera feed continued as he turned his back to his audience and typed at his console. He made no apology for this and gave no explanation. He pulled up the list of every member of his Centuria army. He polled Gen-ID chips to isolate those who were in The Climbs at that moment. He then terminated twenty of them at random by invoking the terms of the contracts they'd signed when they joined the service. Not that that would have mattered. The contract was what gave him legitimacy, but he would have killed them anyway.

He sneered as he thought of what would be happening in the squares and streets of The Climbs. The Centuria would have watched as some of their colleagues dropped on the streets in front of them. No warning, no chance to surrender, just randomized terror. They'd wonder if they were next. He'd rule them with fear, they just had to be reminded who they answered to. He could do the same to their families too. He'd save that for later if things escalated. Damien Hunter understood the requirements of information flow. He did not want Silk Road to know about any rebellion if it could be helped.

He turned back to his screen. He looked directly into the camera and thought carefully about his next words.

'Some of you may be standing close to Centuria who have dropped to the ground and appear to be dead. They are dead, and their families may follow. If you are one of the Centuria, your duty is to pick up your weapon and to protect the interests of Fortrillium. Fortrillium is here to guard The City, that is our primary objective. It saddens me to have to remind you of this, and you should consider it carefully when you decide what to do next.'

It always came back to fear. You could inflict many injustices and grievances upon human beings, it would take a lot to force them beyond their fears. Hunter understood this better than most people. Whatever the crowds thought about Talya Slater, even if they believed everything she said to be true, they would still be paralysed by the fear of what might happen. He was relying on that. He needed to finish, he had things to do, he wasn't going to get caught unawares twice.

'Centuria within The Climbs, the gates are lowered,

there is no way to cross onto Silk Road until they are opened again. They will be opened when you present me with Talya Slater's dead body. I wish also to see the bodies of Leo Bachus and Jody Carn. I will accept, dead or alive, the fugitives, Shen Li, who is also known as Wiz, and Dillon Parsons, the brother of the traitor, Joe Parsons. I will terminate ten Centuria at random each hour until this is done and order is restored in The Climbs. I expect this to be completed by 06:00, the end of Segregation.'

Hunter shut off his camera. He was confident his broadcast would immediately put an end to the unrest in The Climbs. It was contained within the walls anyway, and he'd leave them to fight it out until it was over. He then put his final plans into motion.

First, he instructed the Fortrillium buildings to be placed on full alert. All staff were forbidden to leave the building, full fortifications were enabled, and guards were deployed to defensive positions around the perimeter and at the security gates separating The Climbs and Silk Road. That would protect the main vulnerabilities. He deployed armoured vehicles on the streets too, but their teams were under instructions to position themselves at key vantage points, they were not to cause panic or alarm on Silk Road.

Next, he gave firm guidance to those operating the screens output that absolutely no indication should be given about what was going on in The Climbs. He demanded a full information lockdown.

Finally, he instructed the Gridders to prolong the trial and to make sure it was good. He wanted there to be a distraction on the screens. He would look for opportunities to throw in rebels and make an example of them. He'd have to sacrifice Talya and the two Centuria as soon as possible, they were too capable and influential, but Wiz and Dillon would make excellent fodder for the screens.

Damien Hunter took a moment to think things through. Had he done everything he could? He was still expecting Delman to contact him for an update. It seemed unusual that the President had not yet requested a security briefing. He would certainly know what was going on, security protocols ensured he was kept constantly updated on Fortrillium developments. That excluded, of course, the events Hunter made sure were hushed up.

He needed to examine the Psyche-Evals, it was going to be a long night. There would be no sleep for him, that was for certain. He hoped that by 06:00 he'd have the bodies of the key rebels and the temper tantrum experienced in The Climbs would be over.

When Hunter was under particular stress, he would either go to shoot off some rounds in The Climbs or visit his family in the Umbilica. The Climbs option was closed to him, though if ever there was a good reason for shooting its filthy, disgusting citizens, he figured this was certainly the night for it. He'd have to abandon that course of action until the gates were opened and the rebellion over. Instead, he went to visit his family in the Umbilica. They calmed him and reminded him of a simpler life before the responsibility of running Fortrillium had been placed on his shoulders.

Hunter was alerted the moment he entered the area. There was a persistent buzzing sound as soon as he went into his family's chamber. He assumed it was just the machinery at first, calibration perhaps, or going through some routine maintenance.

He held out his hand, stroking his son on his head, touching his daughter's hand and whispering to his wife through the thin membrane that kept them apart. He was sure they moved when he came to them. In his imagination, he believed they knew he was there.

'Soon, darlings, soon. We'll be together again very soon.'

The buzzing persisted, it was beginning to annoy him. He became quickly agitated when things annoyed him, but he did not want to feel angry in this of all places. It was his personal sanctuary, the place where he came to feel human again.

Hunter walked round to the control panels. This was not his area of expertise, but he understood it showed life signs, health, brain patterns and so on. As long as the screens were active, his family were alive and well.

He'd checked several years ago that there were fail-safes in place. He understood what would happen if there were power failures, and he'd confirmed maintenance routines and health checks. He was not going to leave the welfare of his family to chance. Delman might have the final say on whether they lived or died, but while they lived he would do everything he could to care for them.

He studied the screen which was emitting the buzzing he had heard when he came in. He scanned the dials and readings. There was a red bar forming at the bottom of the screen, red bars were never good. What was it? He couldn't see what it was monitoring.

He hurried to the door, keyed in his access code and shouted to the operative outside.

'Come in here, take a look at this data. I think there's something wrong!'

The operative didn't need to be told twice. She jumped up and followed Hunter into the chamber. She scanned the information on the screen and it was clear she didn't want to deliver the news.

'This unit is being switched off, sir,' she began. 'It's been done on an override setting, there's nothing I can do to fix it.'

She looked at Hunter, waiting for his reaction. She did not want to have to be the one who delivered that news. He looked at her calmly.

'Are you certain there's nothing you can do?'

'No, sir, it must have been activated at a senior level, the order must have come from the President's office. I'm sorry, sir.'

'How long until the situation becomes critical? Are my family in immediate danger?'

The operative studied the data once again.

'The command was initiated a few hours ago, it will take some time to reach a critical status. Your family can continue to live for a short time, even when the system is entirely shut down. You need to speak to the President's office as a matter of urgency, sir. There must be some mistake here.'

'Oh, I'm sure it's no mistake. I think President Delman knows exactly what he's doing.'

The operative had not expected Hunter to take the news quite so well. He was calm and measured, there was no shouting. She began to make her excuses so she could leave the chamber.

'One moment!' Hunter commanded, seeing that she was edging towards the door.

'Is there anything you can do to alleviate this situation or am I entirely in the hands of the President? I just need to be absolutely clear on this.'

'Of course, sir. The President has a full override on these chambers, as you know, and there is nothing I can do to reverse the situation. You need to deal directly with the President's office.'

'In which case you are no use whatsoever to me.'

Hunter hadn't expected to be able to get a kill in that night, but here was his opportunity. However, he did not want to sully his family's chamber with something as unsightly as a dead body.

He put his hands around the operative's throat and began to squeeze hard. She was taken aback by the shock and the force. She looked into his eyes, but he was calm and in control as if this was a routine task for him.

She was not dead when he pushed her out of his family's chamber, but her neck was broken shortly afterwards. Hunter waited for her body to go limp in his grip, then he let her fall to the ground by her workstation.

So Delman had begun to make his move, the endgame had started. It was the perfect time as far as Hunter was concerned. It would be easy to overthrow Delman while the rebellion was being extinguished. He could even apportion blame to him, he'd have to think that one through. But with the disruption in The Climbs came an opportunity. A chance to remove the President and take control of The City.

As Hunter let go of the operative's neck, his attention was drawn by her console. She'd been monitoring events in The Grid and the feed was playing out with muted audio on her second screen. It was the way of moving that had drawn his attention. Justice Seekers usually looked cowed and scared. This person was confident and assured. He was also very old and accompanied by a younger woman.

President Josh Delman had just entered The Grid. The President was finally making his play.

Error

'We need to leave now, Teanna. I hope you dealt with the Umbilica.'

Teanna looked at the President's face on her console. It was top-level encryption, he didn't want anybody to monitor this message.

Delman had just seen Talya Slater's address on his own console. He'd known the woman was clever, that's why he had made her a Law Lord in the first place. But a rebel? He'd missed that completely, it seemed unlikely in spite of the evidence.

Delman had known his time was up when he'd watched the scrolling images of Damien Hunter's atrocities in The Climbs. Delman had been no part of that, but he immediately knew them to be true. Hunter was an animal, it made perfect sense.

The combination of Talya Slater's words and Damien Hunter's atrocities would spark dissent in The Climbs. Besides, Hunter would be on the defensive, he'd be protecting his own back, things would get nasty.

With Catharsis almost upon them, Delman had to act immediately. He'd secured Clay as his escort through The Grid and Teanna had begun the process of shutting down the Umbilica. The timing was far from perfect but he had to move. They'd all die in a matter of hours if he didn't get out of there. He'd have to leave behind whatever unrest was brewing in The City.

The holographic image of Matt Parsons had been the final blow. Here was proof there was something beyond The City's walls. Could Fortrillium kill that rumour? They could claim it was fabricated by the rebels and try to quash it before things got out of control, but they'd never succeed.

Life beyond the walls was the impossible dream. If the citizens believed there was even a remote possibility of life outside, the idea would quickly gather a life of its own.

It was the time to act. He called Teanna and told her to meet him at the Fortrillium buildings. They'd both need to be armed.

He then made a call to Reevil96. He'd noticed that his contact was getting jittery – there was something in the air, everybody could feel that change was coming. Reevil96 responded immediately. After all, he had nothing else to do, there were no distractions where he was.

'I want you to clear me a way through!' Delman demanded. 'This is your last mission now. You get me through this and you're free. You get to see your family again, it's all over. But you must get me through The Grid safely.'

'Understood, sir, but Fortrillium is on complete lockdown. The Gridders are under massive scrutiny. I'm going to have to tread very carefully. If they detect me now, they'll close me off and you'll be at the mercy of Fortrillium.'

'You have to make it work or you will never see your family again. You understand that, don't you? If I come to any harm in there, I will activate the death codes, it will be the last thing I do. You have to get me through there, and you have to make sure the man Clay is unharmed, he will escort us through. Once we exit, finish him.'

'Understood.'

Reevil96 thought through the options. As usual, there was no way out. Either he did as he was told or he'd never see his family again. The President had assured him he was protecting them all, that his actions were for the greater good. Reevil96 had believed that for many years, even though he'd seen plenty of evidence to the contrary. Block the exits to The Grid, assist the President, keep The City safe from plague, see his family again. It seemed simple enough, but nothing in The City was ever that simple.

'This is the last time we speak, next time we'll meet in person,' Delman continued. 'You get me through this and it's all over for you, just as I promised.'

Delman seemed uncertain as to whether he was pleading or threatening, but he held the upper hand, all of the power was his. Reevil96 still believed the President's actions were for the greater good, in spite of his way of going about things.

'There's one thing ...' Reevil96 began to speak just at the wrong moment. The feed was terminated, that was it, Reevil96 was on his own. This feed had been his only company for six years. He hoped he would soon be free to see his family and friends again. His sentence would be over.

Josh Delman made sure he was armed. He took two firearms and a knife. President's privileges, he would not be without some form of self-defence. You could never be too certain.

He opened his safe and pushed the pages he'd torn out of Hunter's copy of The Pact into his pocket. He left the rest of it, he wouldn't be needing that. In his rush, he left the safe half-open. A car was summoned and Delman was driven to Fortrillium's HQ. As he made the short drive to Hunter's domain, he observed the presence of armoured vehicles and was not surprised to see the fortifications on the gates. He passed through them and saw Teanna standing by a wire fence, awaiting his arrival. It wouldn't be long before Hunter came for him. A rebellion in motion, a lockdown on the Fortrillium facility, it was the perfect time for Hunter to make his move.

'We're going into The Grid. You know this is the end now, Teanna, don't you? We get through this alive and you get to see your father again. We'll put it all right.'

Teanna looked at the President. She knew she had no choice in the matter, but she still didn't trust him. What had her father said? Not to trust Delman. They'd been his last words. Why would a father's final words to his daughter carry a warning?

She'd got insurance: the Umbilica had been tampered with, she was armed, and she had her WristCom so she'd be able to access Hunter if she needed to. Hunter would be her guarantee, he'd do anything to be reunited with his family.

Delman and Teanna made their way through the corridors of Fortrillium. The Centuria were tense but they passed through without challenge. Delman was the President after all, ranking higher than Hunter, there was no reason to block his access.

They passed through many of the areas which Talya had seen on her tour of the Fortrillium penal facilities, but she had never got anywhere close to the heart which was where the President was heading.

He and Teanna moved closer and closer to the entrance to The Soak and the holding cells for the Justice Seekers. They passed the cell where, only days before, Joe, Lucy, Clay and the others had awaited trial. The guards acknowledged Delman with the respect a President commanded, but Teanna could sense their inquisitiveness. Why was the President visiting the heart of the penal areas? What business did he have there?

Delman strode into the Prep-Room.

'Check our implants!' he commanded the medics. There were three of them, a doctor and two assistants. They leapt out of their chairs, they had not been expecting a visit from the President.

Delman took out his weapon and shot one of the assistants through the head. He'd seen the look of enquiry in their eyes, he hadn't got much time, he needed to get into The Grid and begin his final journey.

There was shock, stunned silence, then the doctor started to move. Teanna was startled. She'd seen that Hunter was capable of this irrational behaviour, but Delman had always seemed more calculating. He certainly got the reaction he was looking for.

The doctor ran a scan on both of them.

'Both implants are fully operational, sir. Yours is a unique model of course—'

'Give me an extractor!' Delman demanded.

The assistant rushed to a safe in the wall, entered the codes and authorization, and handed Delman the unit. It could be held easily in the hand, it fitted in his pocket. Delman raised his weapon and shot the doctor and the assistant. Teanna gasped.

'What did you think would happen, Teanna? You know what's required here. We'll need to get these cursed implants out as soon as we reach Centrum.'

Teanna did, of course, understand that in matters of security sometimes extreme action had to be taken. She knew they were in a rush, they had to start making their way to The Core, but had the deaths really been necessary? He was the President, they would have done whatever he wanted.

She kept quiet, not wanting to betray her disgust at what had just happened. She was going to need a stronger stomach whichever man she finally aligned herself to, Hunter or Delman.

She followed the President through the corridors to an area she had not been before. He went through the authentication protocols and they entered. It was empty, there were just electro-cuffs and shackles waiting for the next inmates. This was the transportation area where Justice Seekers moved from Fortrillium to The Grid.

It was bothering Delman that he'd cut off Reevil96 before he'd finished what he was going to say. He'd been in such a rush – he had to hurry, Hunter could begin to close things down at any time. He hoped it was something trivial. They had to move, he had to get to The Core.

'Stand on the platform,' he motioned to Teanna. 'Draw your weapon, you might need it. Ask questions later, and any sign of threat, you eliminate it, alright?'

Teanna nodded and reached for her weapon. Delman touched his WristCom. He was trying to reach Clay inside The Grid. There was no response.

'Damn him!' Delman cursed. 'Be ready for anything, Teanna!'

He went to the control panel at the side of the transportation area and keyed in the commands. It was a single function area, there was only one place to go. This transporter was taking them to The Grid.

The platform began to activate, and Delman stepped alongside Teanna and drew his weapon once again. It was bloodied from its recent use, he'd been close when he'd shot the doctor.

The transportation process was completed. They were in The Grid. Their implants had ensured they got in there safely, but whether they would survive was another matter entirely. They were in a cityscape – it looked very much like The Climbs. Delman was familiar with it, Teanna much less so.

Delman tried his WristCom again, cursing when he couldn't raise a response.

'We need to locate the Justice Seeker named Clay Hillman, he's our guide through this place.'

As his words trailed off, Delman got the answer to two of his most recent questions. He'd been concerned about what Reevil96 wanted to say to him and also Clay's whereabouts. The answer came in the form of two drones which came out of nowhere from among the rubble and high-rise buildings.

Teanna and Delman split off in different directions, both tracked by drones. Delman ran and fired his weapon. The drone dodged and weaved but kept on its target. Teanna tried to take cover. She ducked into an alleyway just as her drone shot out its needle. It hit the side of the wall, shattering and dropping to the ground. She thought she'd dodged it, pointed her weapon and took aim to shoot the drone. It flew over her head, came up fast from behind and shot a second needle into her neck. She was paralysed.

Delman was tiring quickly, he didn't have the strength he'd had the first time he'd entered that terrible place. He shot several times, but his first weapon was empty, he had no time to stop and reload. It was only a matter of time. The device shot its needle. It missed and entered Delman's leg. He gave a shriek of pain as he fell to the ground. The drone circled around him at a low level, trying to get a clear shot at his neck. It took a few moments until Delman tired, but it found its opportunity and shot the dart into his neck. He froze, unable to move.

Reevil96 had been trying to warn him about the Psyche-Mode that had been activated in The Grid. With implants fitted to allow them to get in and out of the arena, Delman and Teanna were subject to the same conditions as the other Justice Seekers, there was no seniority or special treatment. Delman had an implant too, it was different to the rest, it gave him all the access privileges President James Morgan had enjoyed. But it also gave direct access to his mind, something that should never have occurred for a man in such a senior position.

Delman had just made his darkest secrets available via his implant and there was one man in particular who was very keen to find out what those secrets were. He was sitting in his office at Fortrillium HQ wondering what to do next – and he'd just got his answer.

CHAPTER ELEVEN

Action

Talya's address drew an enthusiastic round of applause from the rebels crowding round to watch and monitor the output on their screen feeds. After so many years in hiding, planning and waiting for their moment, it was amazing to be fighting back.

Talya was more anxious. She wanted reports back from the screens. She'd been playing with fire, she knew, and she didn't want to turn The Climbs into a bloodbath. Already reports were coming in from the rebels who were based around the screening areas. The situation was tense. Some of the Centuria had been killed, seemingly by a form of remote access. They had fallen to the ground without warning, their hearts stopped by a sudden violent shock.

Many of the citizens had stepped up to the Centuria teams in a gesture of peace, and the majority had removed their helmets as a sign of solidarity.

But some had fired on the crowds, choosing to fight for Fortrillium. They'd regrouped and tried to make for the exits, but Fortrillium had closed the rusty iron gates which separated Silk Road and The Climbs. Nobody in living memory had seen them shut, it was assumed they were no longer functioning. It was a measure of how defenceless they all felt: the gates of their minds had kept them in their place as well as anything that Fortrillium could put in their way.

'Do we have anything we can use to blast them open?' Talya asked.

There was surprise in the room. So many years of plotting and planning, and now here it was. They were attacking. Finally they were fighting back.

'I don't know how strong they are,' Leo began, 'but we have one armoured missile launcher and two missiles. That's it. The resistance has had the launcher since it was first procured by two former engineers ten years ago. It had been abandoned over here by Fortrillium and they renovated it and fixed it up. The missiles were recreated from empty shells. We don't know if they'll work, but there's one way to find out.'

'Let's do it!' Talya replied. 'What level of resistance can we expect on the other side of the wall, Leo? Jody? Do you think the Centuria will work with us or against us?'

'Difficult to tell. It all depends on how much threatening Hunter does. Our Gen-ID shield devices have kept our whereabouts concealed so at least he can't take us down – for now.'

'He'll save that for a special occasion. If I were Hunter, I'd want to make the most of your capture,' said Talya. 'He'll want to make a spectacle of it. Let's get those missiles ready and assemble teams to head for the gates. We need to target the gate that's closest to Fortrillium. I want the shortest distance for us to have to travel when we cross over.'

All around her, teams mobilized, grabbed weaponry and headed for the exits. She was aware that Wiz had been trying to get her attention. He'd been left with his tech team as silence descended on the ops area.

'You did well with the hologram, Wiz, thank you.'

'No problem, Talya. What's the plan now?'

'I need you to gather as much evidence and information as you can on Damien Hunter and President Delman. I want them put on trial after this, if we get that far. They need to answer for what they've done.'

'We don't have anything on the President, Talya. This all points to Hunter. There are just folders and folders of images, video feeds and documentation. Delman doesn't figure anywhere.'

'Okay, create a file on Hunter. What about the outside source? Do we have any idea yet where that's coming from?'

'I need to tell you something about Delman,' Wiz began, 'although I'm not sure it's going to help us. He's planning to enter The Grid, he's going somewhere. Whoever is helping him is doing it under duress, he's been threatening their family. I can't find out what his plan is, but I think he's in there already. Look!'

Wiz pointed to his console screen which was showing a looped replay of the feed from The Grid. It was only a short clip, but Talya could see what it was straight away.

'That's Teanna Schaelles, isn't it? What's she doing in there with Delman?'

'They pulled the camera feed on them immediately, but if you ask me, all routes lead to The Grid, that's where you're going to find your answers. You need to get to Fortrillium and get inside The Grid.'

Talya looked at the clip again and thought a moment.

'You're right, Wiz. Everything we need is in The Grid,

with the exception of Damien Hunter. He'll be holed up at Fortrillium. We need to take our fight there. Is it possible to hack into that Comms line? Can you talk to our mystery friend who's been chatting to Delman? If we can find their location, I think it's going to move things on significantly.'

Wiz considered the problem and surveyed his new tech team. They were good, they knew Fortrillium's systems and protocols.

'We'll give it a shot, Talya. There's also the WristCom we managed to place inside The Grid – it would be a good idea to try to locate it. We can find Tom's ID in the Fortrillium archives, and we may be able to poll the WristCom directly if we can get through The Grid firewalls.'

'Okay, Wiz. Do it. I want you to stay in constant contact with me and keep me up to date with everything that's going on here. We're going to try to get inside Fortrillium. If we fail, it's up to you to get everybody out of The Grid.'

Talya was on her way, joining the rebels who'd been swiftly mobilized for the attack on the security barricade. She watched the battered missile launcher making its way out of the underground parking area which housed the few vehicles the resistance had managed to salvage. She was unsure about the good sense of this attack. Was she sending people to their deaths? There had been enough of that in The City. But if they could overthrow Fortrillium and replace Hunter and Delman with some form of elected government, perhaps there really could be a more just world within the walls of The City.

They were committed – Hunter knew who they were. He was killing Centuria. This battle would end in victory or defeat. If it was defeat, it could end any thought of rebellion for another hundred years. If it was victory? Who could tell what future awaited them?

There was something beyond The City, a place where Matt Parsons had found some sort of sanctuary, if the holographic image was for real. They had to push on, to discover the truth about their lives within the walls. The citizens were galvanized at last. There was no retreat for Talya, she'd committed them to action.

The rebels made their way through the streets of The Climbs, moving in small groups to prevent an attack. There were sporadic attempts at combat, but the Centuria were split up and divided into small groups. Within The Climbs they were outnumbered, but on Silk Road they'd have superior firepower and would be waiting for the rebels.

Talya was handed a weapon by Leo. The only time she'd ever used violence was with Max Penner. He was an innocent man and she'd tortured him. The Centuria were all coerced in one way or another – she wasn't sure if she'd be able to kill them when it came to it. They were all guilty of turning a blind eye, they'd followed terrible orders and done things which terrified everybody living in The City. Yet they were caught up in a trap from which there seemed no escape, and underneath the uniforms they were still human beings, Leo and Jody had shown her that. Talya resolved to press on with the mission. They had to try, at least. If they were beaten, so be it, she would take the consequences.

It took some time to reach the security gate Talya wanted to attack. If they were able to break through that huge iron gate, they'd be able to get into Silk Road and move quickly on to Fortrillium.

Talya ran through her plan as the small groups of armed rebels came together at the gates. There were huge crowds gathering – civilians and Centuria without helmets. The mood was for rebellion, but there seemed to be little taste for blood so far.

The chances of there not being bloodshed on the other side of that gate were remote. Talya reflected on the wisdom of a full-on attack. She was no military strategist. She'd inspired the people to gather there, but she might have been leading them directly to their slaughter.

She beckoned to Jody and Leo.

'Is there another way we could do this without a huge battle? What if we were to focus our attack on this gate as a distraction? Wouldn't it make more sense to go in as a small group and take a surgical approach to Fortrillium? I can't help feeling that we're going to lose a lot of lives here. Can The Climbs residents even cross these gates without Gen-ID issues?'

Jody nodded. They hadn't thought it through very carefully.

'We'll be able to cross over, as will you, Talya. Our Gen-IDs will not mark us as Climbs residents. We can use the screening devices too – we used one on you when we brought you over here, and Wiz and Dillon have them too. We're all wanted people anyway, it's not as if they don't know who we are.'

'I think it's unusual that Damien Hunter hasn't come for us already,' Leo picked up. 'Maybe he's decided it might make martyrs of us if he takes us out without a fight.'

'Whatever his plan, he'll have thought it through,' said Talya. 'I'm beginning to think he wants me at Fortrillium. If he takes me alive, he can make a spectacle of my death.'

'I think you're right though, Talya,' Jody agreed. 'There's a lot of sense in us going in undercover rather than risking all those lives.'

'Here's my plan then,' Talya continued. 'I want us to

make attacks on this gate, but I don't want the missile launcher used. Deploy smaller explosives, let's not bring the gates down. That will give the crowds something to focus on, but keep them safe. Leo and Jody, we're going to go through another gate.'

Leo looked doubtful.

'How do you expect to do that?'

We're going to use some of the Centuria. They're going to claim they've captured us. Hunter will not waste that opportunity, he'll let us through. So long as the assault continues at the other gate, he'll believe it to be true. He'll want to hang us out to dry on the screens before they break through.'

'Okay, it's a big risk, Talya, but I agree. It's us that Hunter wants, we have bargaining power now even if it all goes wrong.'

Leo moved away and gave orders to key rebel members to prepare to attack the gate. Jody moved among the Centuria who'd remove their helmets to join the resistance. They'd seen for themselves how loyal Damien Hunter was to them when he'd locked them into The Climbs to fend for themselves.

It was quickly arranged. Leo, Talya and Jody concealed their weapons and got ready to be escorted to the next security gate by four volunteer Centuria. Brad Sivil walked up to the group, sensing that something important was going on.

'I want to come with you, Talya. I'm locked in here now like everybody else. Hunter knows I'm a traitor. I'm more use to you as a captive – my Gen-ID will let me through the gates. If we succeed, I might be able to work with the other Law Lords – we're going to have to re-establish law and order as soon as we can.'

Talya nodded. He was right. Law Lord Sivil would be an asset. The Law Lords despised her, but they might see more sense if Sivil were among them. She'd been sure he was loyal to Fortrillium, and it had taken her by surprise to see him at the rebel base. He had the respect and friendship of the other Law Lords, he might be able to turn things in their favour. A bloodless coup was preferable to a firefight.

The group made their way along the perimeter of the wall to the next security checkpoint. They'd been placed in electro-cuffs though the clasps were open and they could free themselves at any time. As they moved along the concrete barrier to the next iron gate, they heard the explosions begin behind them.

'Make it look good. If we don't convince them this is real, we're never getting inside that building,' whispered Talya.

The leading Centuria touched his WristCom.

'Request temporary gate release. Rebel leaders captured and required for processing.'

Talya was aware of the cameras moving to focus on them. She feigned a struggle and attempted to make a run for it. One of the colluding Centuria struck her with his weapon butt and she fell to the ground. It looked worse than it was, but they needed this to look good, there was no way they were getting through that gate if it didn't look convincing.

There was no response. There was an immediate tension within the group, they'd expected more excitement about the captures. After a long delay, a voice came over the Centuria's WristCom.

'Kill them there and record the footage.'

Inside The Grid

Throughout The Climbs and Silk Road, the screening of the Justice Trial continued. On the Silk Road side, it was still the main focus of attention. The scenes depicted were dramatic and gripping. Each of the Justice Seekers was being put through their own mental torture, the images of their greatest fears and horrors playing out for everybody to see.

The drones had placed a direct link into the Psyche-Eval implants, allowing thoughts and feelings to be depicted as real-life events. A release of a finely tuned narcotic via the needles that had been shot into the necks of the Justice Seekers ensured there was nothing trivial to see. These were the terrors lurking in the consciousness that sometimes human beings can't articulate.

For Max Penner, it was the fear of being eaten alive by the bots at Fortrillium. He pictured himself being slowly consumed by the serrated metal grinders, his body being pulled through the teeth while he was aware of every moment. The machines spewed his own guts into the disposal pipes, but he was conscious throughout. All Max could feel through the slow horror of the nightmare was that he should have done more to stand up to the injustice and cruelty of Fortrillium.

Mitchell's nightmares were more recent. He was forced to watch as Lucy was peeled, strip by strip, by Schälen. With every scream she made through her agonizing ordeal, she looked him directly in the eyes as if to ask 'What have you done?' He saw Joe tossed on the tusks of the creatures in the labyrinth, never killed just pierced, scraped, gouged and wounded, but he would not die. As Mitchell was forced to watch, Joe stared at him throughout, asking the same question as Lucy. 'What have you done?' To make matters worse, as the terrifying scenarios continued, Mitchell was joined by Talya, Jena and Dillon. They looked on as Joe and Lucy were tortured, their screams echoing across The Climbs, and all the while their accusatory looks demanding an explanation.

For Jena, the torment was a different one. She saw Joe, Dillon and Matt. They were being hunted by Centuria in The Climbs but they didn't know they were going to be caught. She kept trying to scream at them, to warn them, but she had no voice, they couldn't hear her. She felt a terrible sense of impending doom, but there was nothing she could do. She had to look on in silence as, time and time again, they were captured, tortured and killed.

In The Grid, all that could be seen were Justice Seekers flinching and jumping as if in a fitful sleep, but in their minds the horrors were real, as if they were actually happening. But unlike a dream, the terror did not end, it continued and repeated as the narcotic was released slowly via the needles.

Julia suffered a different type of dream but it was still no relief for her. It fed into her darkest moments and the hideous silences that all humans have to conquer in their own minds.

She saw a baby. It was in a field, crawling along in the grass. There wasn't a lot of grass on Silk Road and there was none in The Climbs, so to Julia it was a symbol of life and freedom. She'd joined the Centuria because she realized that there was no normal life for her, everything in The City turned to dust in the end. As the baby crawled forward, the grass beneath it became black and the clouds above it turned grey. The baby's hands began to burn in the grass, its flesh started to blister and redden, but still it kept crawling. The grass rotted away, the baby began to crawl through filth and rubbish. It became covered with maggots and lice and slowly started to decay. Still the baby kept crawling forward. Its flesh rotted, its eyes dropped out, it began to struggle to move, but still it continued, slowly crawling forward. Eventually, there was not enough flesh to keep the bones together, and the baby decayed into the putrid ground as the dream began again. Julia felt a crushing sense of loss, a sadness for what might have been. It took her breath away.

In spite of his physical strength, Clay too was tormented. What humans can fight off with their hands cannot be so easily subdued in the mind.

Clay's terrors were not of the real world. He conjured up the living dead chasing him through the decaying streets of The Climbs. There were hundreds of them – thousands even – and their grey, rotting hands all reached out for him, trying to pull him down and suffocate him. He ran and fought, he killed the half-dead and repelled them, but still they came. In his dream he had endless energy, he didn't seem to tire, but the battle never ended. He was stuck in a continual fight which had no conclusion. Every moment he felt the adrenalin rush of his struggle for survival, a terrible cocktail of fear and violence.

Every second of their nightmares played out in slow motion in their minds, and on the screens everything could be seen, every detail, every death, every reaction. Heart rates and life-signs data were shown at the bottom of each screen – the hallucinations were placing the Justice Seekers under extreme stress.

For Joe, the dream fed directly into his greatest fears for his family. It captured everything he felt at that moment: the euphoria at seeing his father again after thinking him dead; his love for his mother and extreme frustration with her behaviour – his desire that she'd been stronger when Matt was taken away; his concern for Dillon who wasn't strong enough, fast enough. It tormented him, slowly, surely, methodically.

In his mind, Joe was running up the stairs of his tower block. He was trying to save his family from some unknown event, he had to get to them as soon as possible. He was desperate to stop for a few seconds to catch his breath, but he knew he was running too slowly, he had to force himself forward. He'd never managed the fifty-two flights of stairs in anything less than eleven minutes before, now he had just ten minutes to reach the apartment and get them out of there.

He'd started out of breath, his lungs wanted to explode with exertion. He willed his legs to move faster, but he could not force any more out of his bruised and battered body.

They'd got so far, so many lives had been lost and they were so close. Now everything was going to be destroyed because of him, because he was unable to summon the resources he needed to rise to this challenge.

They should have suspected that the Psych-Evals would be used to manipulate them. Fortrillium had managed to access the deepest secrets of their souls and was now going to use their own fears and weaknesses to destroy them.

Joe counted off the levels one at a time: thirty, thirty-one, thirty-two ... he should have reached thirty-eight by that stage, there was no way he could make it.

Everything in Joe's body screamed at him to stop and give up. He knew he could never make it. Fortrillium had stacked events against him, they'd done this to punish him, he should never have dared to challenge their authority.

As he reached the forty-second floor, the stench of scorched flesh began to permeate the stairwell. The smoke became black and overwhelming as he neared the fiftieth floor, the place where his friend Zach had lived. Another friend who'd lost his life in The Grid.

Joe knew it was over as he reached the floor that had once offered sanctuary to him and his family. He knew what he was going to see when he walked through what was left of the burnt door.

On the floor, with hands and feet bound by wire, were the charred bodies of Jena, Dillon and Matt. They'd punished him for daring to rise against the might of Fortrillium by taking away from him the only thing he had left.

Just as he'd had his family within his grasp and everything he'd always wanted had almost been there for the taking, Fortrillium tore it away from him, dashing his hopes and bludgeoning them on a hard concrete floor.

On the screens, the watching crowds saw that Joe's heart rate had rocketed, reaching dangerous levels. Not only did he experience the real physical exhaustion of running up the stairs in his hallucination, he also felt every moment of fear and despair as his family slipped away from him.

Every moment was shared on the screens. The purpose of The Grid was to scare the residents of The City, to make them fearful of speaking out and to ensure they never raised a hand against Fortrillium. However, the effect of seeing these dreams was very different. Throughout Silk Road, and for those still paying attention in The Climbs, it was the humanity of the Justice Seekers that shone through. Here were people just like them, haunted by fears for their loved ones, too terrified to dream of a better life, exhausted by the perpetual struggle to survive. What they were seeing on the screens reflected their own lives. It was their own fears and nightmares they were watching through the eyes of others.

The people being tormented inside The Grid were not evil. They were not the monsters that had been depicted in the promo films and video bursts. They were regular citizens, taking each day at a time, fighting to stay alive and looking out for their loved ones. Their struggle was one and the same. As the scenarios played out on the screens, many on Silk Road turned away, switching off the feeds and preferring instead to spend time with their own families or alone with their thoughts.

Some became aware of more activity on the streets than usual. With the booming of the screen commentaries switched off, the world outside became more visible. There was definitely a sense that something was going on, a tension, a different atmosphere. Some turned their screens back on waiting for an announcement from Fortrillium, an update perhaps. They wondered if there was something going on, events which might interrupt their comfortable lives on Silk Road.

As the scenes played over and over on the screens, they were studied by a lone man sitting in his office. He'd watched the feeds of Joe Parsons and Lucy Slater with interest, but there was nothing much there for him to hold on to. Matt Parsons was still alive, there was a place beyond The Grid – he'd worked that out already. They were all up to speed on that information now.

It was the feeds from President Josh Delman and Teanna Schaelles that were proving far more interesting to him. He'd suppressed them on the main screens minutes after they'd appeared in The Grid. There was no way he could let the people of The City see the truth about their President.

He'd got a feed patched directly through from the Gridders and he was studying the Psyche-Evals with great interest. He no longer needed to get his hands on the torn-out pages of The Pact. Damien Hunter had access to everything he needed inside the President's head. In ignoring the final words of Reevil96, President Josh Delman had made his first careless move since entering The City. It was going to give his enemy the upper hand. He was about to reveal his own darkest secrets.

Gridders

It had occurred to Linwood some time before, but he'd dismissed the idea as ridiculous. He hadn't seen his brother in years – he'd been much younger at the time, his memories were getting mixed up. Then the thought had surfaced again, then again, until he was unable to reject it.

The hidden opponent, the person who'd been interfering, the one who was not inside the Fortrillium building – whoever he or she was – he recognized them. He or she didn't have a face, a name or a gender, but did have a style of gameplay. He and his brother Jacob had played together when he was very young. Jacob had patiently coached him, inspired him, and shown him how to use the code systems. But then he'd changed, suddenly and unexpectedly.

As Linwood felt his brother growing more distant, he'd continually reached out to him, desperately trying to reconnect. But his brother was long gone, firstly by becoming withdrawn and distant, then by disappearing altogether.

It had come as a huge blow to Linwood – he'd always looked up to his brother and aspired to follow in his footsteps. He would play games on his own and create lines of code for gameplay environments to try to recapture what they'd had, but it was gone.

That sense of loss turned into a desire to find answers, to discover what had happened to his brother. Linwood had found some of his answers. He'd discovered the same self-loathing and hatred for the trap he was caught up in. Linwood had seen that clearly for himself.

But from a flame he thought had died, the embers began to glow. Linwood had noticed it some time ago, but it was more forceful now. That flame had begun to flicker. The fire was now beginning to roar.

There was something about the gameplay style of this mystery Gridder that was familiar to Linwood. It had all the signs of Reevil96 – Jacob Carley. Linwood had played a move his brother had created, the amazing idea he'd had to win his own Gridder Games all those years ago. Nobody had thought to play it since, but Linwood had deployed it in the current trial. Not just because he thought it would buy some time for his friends but also because he wanted to leave a trail.

Linwood believed the person who was interfering with the trials was his brother. If it wasn't his brother, then whoever it was must have studied his gameplay history very well. Either way, there was a connection across The Grid. They were linked by a respect for, or a knowledge of, his brother. By playing the Psyche-Eval scenario in exactly the same way Jacob had done, whoever was controlling The Grid from afar would see the message. But would they reach out?

Linwood had done the best he could to protect his friends, given that he could feel Damien Hunter's breath on his neck. The Psyche-Eval Mode created terrifying images for those watching the screens. They were conjured up from worst nightmares, it was the Justice Seekers' own minds that created the most terrible scenarios of them all. However, it also kept them safer, even though to be immersed in a constant flow of hallucinations would put a huge strain on their hearts. There could be deaths too, but it was more unlikely this way. Damien Hunter would get his great gameplay, and Linwood could try to keep Hannah and the others alive.

Linwood felt that things were coming to a crisis point inside The Grid. He'd had a very agitated Damien Hunter chasing him several times already and he was completely intrigued by the re-entry into The Grid of Hannah's friends, Joe and Lucy. They were followed shortly afterwards by another two unscheduled entries. There were no announcements from the Law Lords, no profiles, no warnings even. Just two new Justice Seekers, a man and a woman, their identities as yet unknown to the Gridders.

The drones had found them immediately, firing their needles directly into their spinal columns and accessing the cervical vertebrae. A direct line to the Psyche-Eval implants – he'd get an idea who they were soon enough.

Linwood was distracted. Somebody had created a neutral area in The Grid. This was the same sort of zone that had been created to conceal the bot earlier. It was unseen and inaccessible by the Justice Seekers, but Linwood saw it.

He surveyed his fellow Gridders. They were too terrified to do anything, they were just happy that as Head Gridder he'd taken the initiative and created the Psyche-Eval Mode. They were beginning to make preparations for the final part of the trial, Ascension. This would follow directly after the end of the third Mode.

Linwood zoomed in on the area and took a look around. It was empty except for a rose. A pressed red rose. Linwood's mother had worn a red rose at her joining. They were very hard to come by – flowers were seen as a vanity in The City, anything that grew in the ground was supposed to feed mouths, either human or animal. Linwood's dad had managed to procure a red rose, and she'd always talked about it to them as children. She'd pressed it and would take it out on their anniversary.

This either had to be a sick trick or it had to be Jacob. There was one way of checking. Linwood created a small object-rendering environment. He grabbed a framework for a book from his presets. He made the book brown leather, created some fading pages and placed the pressed rose inside.

As children, Linwood and Jacob had found an old leather-bound notebook on the outskirts of Silk Road. They'd never seen books before, and their mother had been anxious to conceal it. She was angry with the boys at first, but when they got home she held it in her hands as if it were the most valuable thing inside The City.

She placed her pressed rose in the book, and there it lived, carefully hidden, the Carley family's secret.

Linwood placed the book into the neutral area. Moments later, the image on his console refreshed. The book had a large stain spread across half of the cover. It had been damaged and soaked while lying in the wasteland on the border of Silk Road. Only Jacob could have known that. His brother had to be living. His brother was a good man, he knew that to be true, in spite of what he'd seen in The Grid. Whatever he was doing had to be under duress or for the good of The City. His brother was alive. They could communicate through The Grid. There had to be a way to work together to get them both out alive.

Secrets

Damien Hunter could not have dreamed of a better opportunity. President Josh Delman had just walked into the perfect trap. He'd been so caught up with his own escape plan, he hadn't bothered to find out what he would be walking into in The Grid. He thought he'd had it all worked out but the minute he stepped in there, expecting Clay's help, and assistance from Reevil96, he was caught by the drones and plugged directly into the Psyche-Eval units.

When Hunter saw what had happened, he contacted the Gridder team immediately.

'I don't want this shown on the screens. Delman is kept off the screen feeds entirely, understood?'

'Yes, sir. He's not been seen on any public feeds. As Gridders we did not know it was the President. Might I ask who is his companion?'

'That's another traitor, Teanna Schaelles. She may be shown on the public screens so long as it is never with the President. You are forbidden to show the President under any circumstances.'

'Understood, sir. What about their involvement in the Justice Trial? We can protect them from the events in The Grid if that is required.'

'No, I want them to be subjected to the same conditions as everybody else. He knows what he's doing in there, he wouldn't have entered if not. I want him left to do as he pleases, but if he gets to the centre he must be blocked. I don't know what's there, but that's where he's heading, I'm certain. I should add, 97TRaider, that I am now invoking clause 6b of your contractual agreements. You are now working under military conditions, which means that failure to follow direct orders will result in instant court martial and is punishable by death. In addition, full confidentiality protocols are applied. You must not impart this knowledge to any of your team, but you must ensure my orders are followed without question.'

'Understood, Mr Hunter.'

'One final thing. I want you to send the direct feeds of Delman and Schaelles to the private port on my console. Do it now!'

Hunter terminated the connection and waited for the data to be routed directly to him. At last he'd been handed the perfect opportunity. He'd been trying to work out what was going on in Delman's head for many years. Now he would know. He had a direct link to the President's thoughts. How could the man have been so careless?

He sat at his desk waiting for the secure feeds to come through. Teanna's was established first. He was anxious to know why she had betrayed him. Granted, they had a loose alliance but it was mutually advantageous. He scanned her thought clusters, looking first at those which indicated strong emotional reactions. On his screen they appeared as folders, simple units of storage for a lifetime of memories. Millions of electronic patterns had been scanned and assembled to achieve this simple interface which permitted him to dive in and out of her thoughts like a thief raiding in the night.

Each folder was fronted by a visual thumbnail recreated from images that had passed through the retina. Often they were too vague, like the retelling of a dream which never quite conveys the emotion or engagement of the person who'd been immersed in it.

Three folders were clear. One folder had an image of Delman on it, on another was a picture of himself and the last folder used a thumbnail of a middle-aged man. Hunter had never seen him before. He looked like Teanna, and he guessed it was her father or brother.

Vanity took him to his own folder first. Emotional response readings showed hate, revulsion and discomfort as the key variables in Teanna's relationship with him. Prime motivators were shown to be self-interest, self-preservation and strategic planning. In simple terms, she hated Damien Hunter and she was using him. The anger began to burn stronger in him as he cursed placing any trust in her. His own feelings had been exactly the same. He'd been using her for the same reasons, but he preferred not to be played, he liked to be in charge.

Her pivotal images were dominated by Mitchell Cranshaw's torture and her initial meeting with Hunter himself several years before. She'd immediately targeted him as a potential ally, but the torture of Mitchell was what had pushed her away from him. Hunter was angry with Teanna but not surprised. He was about to close that folder and move on to her knowledge of Delman when his eye was caught by a thumbnail of the Umbilica. He opened up the memory cluster to take a closer look. The folder had a date stamp of that day.

She'd been at the Umbilica. It was she who had begun the process of destroying his family. She'd broken her bond with him and made the final betrayal. This pushed Hunter's anger over the edge. He looked around the room for a weapon. His instinct was to go The Climbs and shoot it out. He stopped. That wasn't possible, The Climbs was on lockdown.

He went back to the file, struggling to calm his mind.

There was a heightened emotional response to what she'd done at the Umbilica, and it was also highly ranked with strategic planning. She'd set it up so he could reverse the process. She'd intended to use it as a bargaining chip. Hunter could save his family, she hadn't fully betrayed him, she'd kept her options open. He was torn between rushing over to the Umbilica to reverse the process of decline or to continue looking at Teanna's thought clusters. He chose his family and routed the data from his console to his tablet.

He ran over to the Umbilica. The security guard was still undiscovered behind the desk where he'd left her. He rushed into his family's room and started to follow the process he could see on his tablet. It was as easy as that. With direct access to Teanna's mind, Hunter had all the information he needed. He could not revive his family entirely without Delman, but at least they were safe, he no longer had a loaded gun held to his head.

He held his wife's hand through the protective film and watched as the life-signs units began to return to normal. He was relieved but still anxious to close the circle. If he could access enough of Delman's thoughts, he might have his family back with him before the night was out.

As he scanned through the files, his impulse was to look at everything. How could he tell where the most useful information was stored? He'd seen another recent folder with a strong adrenalin rating connected to it. He figured these recent files would be linked with what was going on in The Grid. That made sense to him. He opened the file. He was astonished at what he saw. Teanna had got her hands on The Pact, she'd actually seen the final pages. She'd even broken into Delman's safe to get hold of them. And she had images stored on Fortrillium servers.

'I want a download of all files saved to Teanna

Schaelles' private encrypted area which have been saved in the past forty-eight hours.'

Hunter had connected immediately with Fortrillium's Head of Data. As Fortrillium's leader, he could access these files and unlock them for viewing. Only he and Delman had that facility, it was passed on with the post. If he had suspected Teanna was hiding something like this, he could have got in there earlier.

Delman's file access arrived as Hunter finished running through Teanna's key thought clusters. He was torn on whether to take a look through her other two primary folders or to move on to Delman. He decided on Delman, even though he was anxious for The Pact files to arrive. He didn't know where to look first. He had so much information at his fingertips. Hunter was also mindful that these were live feeds and if the connections were broken in The Grid they would be lost. There had never been a man-made server built that could store all the complexity of the mind as the brain did. This was simply a feed of it, a visual representation. The storage system was the brain and his console merely interpreted it and assembled it in a way that was meaningful.

He opened Delman's files and was immediately confused. Within the single brain cluster, there were two primary folders. One was labelled 'Josh Delman' the other 'James Morgan'. The second folder was completely locked, like a sealed box. There was no way in.

Hunter was intrigued. He knew the rumours about Delman's appearance in The Grid. Could this be a clue as to how it had happened?

He opened the folder marked 'Josh Delman' and began to scan the memory clusters inside. The core clusters held the secrets. Everything he had ever wanted was there.

The pivotal folders related to Damien Hunter, Teanna Schaelles, James Morgan, The Pact, Jacob Carley and something called Centrum. Some of this was what Hunter had expected, but there were other things there that were completely alien to him. What struck him most was that the key emotional readings for Delman were regret, guilt and resolution. That didn't ring true at all. The Delman he knew was not like that. He looked at the prime motivators: restitution, justice and closure. He almost laughed aloud at 'justice'. This was not Delman as he knew him, he'd thought him to be a controlling and obstructive man.

Hunter began to work through the files. As he did so, he began to piece together Delman's story. Everywhere the name Schaelles came up. He'd completely missed what was really going on. He'd thought they were fighting for control of The City, but the real battle had been bigger than he could ever have imagined. This was a battle for the human race.

He scoured the files, hungry for the information which would give him the answers he craved. He pieced it together quickly.

The man he'd known as Delman was not Delman. It was his mind, his memories, his thoughts, but he was in James Morgan's body. He'd transferred bodies. Hunter hadn't known this technology existed, it was almost unthinkable. Yet scientists could keep his own family alive in suspended animation in the Umbilica, so perhaps it was possible to transplant minds too.

This technology was not of their world. There *was* something beyond The City, other life based around Centrum. Hunter struggled to comprehend the enormity of what he was seeing. They had all been deceived, every single citizen within The City had been deluded. And he had presided over all of it.

While he had maintained the fabric which determined how life played out for the citizens every day, all the time Delman had had his eyes on the bigger goal. Survival.

But there was guilt too. Delman's motivation was not greed and power, as Hunter had always believed. His driving force was guilt and a need for atonement. Hunter struggled with the data to work out what had happened. The answers were contained in a huge file in which guilt and remorse were the dominating emotions.

Delman had been driven by regret. He'd been implicated in a tragic error as a young man in the heat of the plague years, and it had resulted in the deaths of millions. He occupied his body of birth at that time. He'd been hunted down and punished by President James Morgan, but he was still driven by guilt and a burning desire to put things right. For a moment, Damien Hunter almost felt sympathy for his tormentor. But how could he ever forgive Delman for what he'd done to his family? He'd been denied years of access to his wife and children, and for what purpose? To keep him loyal? To ensure he did not overthrow the President?

The story was gradually coming together – how Delman had made some discovery about President James Morgan and the true purpose of the cities. There were three of them. It took his breath away. *Three* cities? All built around a place called The TriPlex. How could that be true? He'd been born in The City, it was all he'd ever known. There were rumours and theories about what was beyond the walls, but they'd always believed they were the only ones. They'd felt lucky to live in The City, they'd never questioned if what was beyond the walls was better than what was inside.

Hunter had perpetuated these ideas himself. He'd believed them. If that's all you knew, why would you question it? Life worked in The City, the hierarchy kept them alive. He'd accepted his obligations to rid it of remnants of the old world. They created unrest and dissatisfaction, it was right that books and other relics were removed.

But who was this President James Morgan? Why was Delman using his body? Hunter could barely comprehend that it was even possible but he had the facts before him. If Delman had told him to his face, he would have laughed. But there was no way this thought cloud could be cheated, it was a direct feed of his memories. It was the truth as Delman saw it.

He saw how being in Morgan's body had given Delman access to The City. He'd been on the run, he needed to hide. That made sense. But why had he colluded with the Schaelles family? What had driven him to The City?

Hunter could see that President Josh Delman was well over 120 years old in his chronological age, but he could also see that he'd only been conscious for a fraction of that period. He'd spent a lot of time in Cryo before Edward Schaelles had activated the body transfer. That technology looked similar to the Umbilica, keeping people alive without any degradation of their brain or body. One day his own family would emerge from the Umbilica as if nothing had happened. The only question was, would he still be alive to greet them?

Hunter wanted to know what was going on. It was difficult to believe, but he could accept that there was a place called The TriPlex. It accounted for how Delman had managed to exit from The Grid and it explained where

Parsons and Slater had gone – maybe they were in on the President's plot too? It was a struggle, but he could also see how there might be another two cities. Why not? They'd accepted the walls that contained them without question. The fear was that the plague was out there, and they were safe in The City.

The secret seemed to lie in the motivations of the President. Delman had taken Morgan's body for a reason. Two generations of the Schaelles family – three if you counted Teanna – had colluded to make it happen. What was Delman's motivation? What was he trying to put right?

There was a sound on his console. The files he'd requested from The Pact had arrived. He entered his private encryption codes and ran the DNA confirmation. He'd been after this information for years. Delman had always denied it. Damn him! He opened up Teanna's files, making straight for the recently dated images of pages from The Pact.

Hunter saw immediately they were the pages that had been torn from his own manual. Delman had ripped them out and kept them concealed. He rapidly scanned the words to get a sense of what was going on.

Catharsis had begun. That's why Delman was running. Teanna had to be part of some kind of a deal, she was crucial to it all. The City was going to be destroyed. Damien Hunter had thought he'd saved his family in the Umbilica, but they were all going to die anyway. Delman was abandoning them to their fate and seeking refuge in The TriPlex. Catharsis could happen at any time. When it began, the population of The City would be destroyed and the walls and tower blocks would collapse in on themselves. There would be nothing left of their world. The Pact had promised the preservation of humanity in a post-plague world. This would result in total destruction.

It would be preceded by The Cleanse. This was the removal of all organic matter from The Grid. In other words, all humans would be cleared from the area. The only way out of The City was through the centre of The Grid, it had always been set up that way. One way out, controlled by – who knew? The Pact did not reveal that information. The exit would be closed. If Catharsis had begun and the President was making his escape, there would be no way for Hunter to flee when The Cleanse began. He had to get to Delman before he got out. He had to enter The Grid for the sake of his family. Delman would have to release his wife and children and let him take them safely through The Core to whatever protection there was beyond The City.

His purpose was clear now. He had to save his family. The rebels would head for Fortrillium first since it was the seat of control in The City. It had to be protected at all costs if he was to make his safe exit. He would stop Delman making his escape and force him to release his family. He would then take them through The Core to whatever life was out there. They would go where Delman was going – to safety.

Hunter could see what was happening, but he didn't understand why. Why was Delman doing what he was doing? What had President James Morgan done that meant he had to be removed? And why was Delman so driven by a need for atonement? What was he trying to put right that meant it was better to destroy an entire city?

There was an urgent poll on Hunter's WristCom, a top-level alert, one he couldn't ignore. It was the rebels. He had a more immediate problem to deal with. Her name was Talya Slater.

CHAPTER TWELVE

Captured

'Wait!' shouted Talya as the Centuria began to look at each other, wondering how to respond to the command to shoot their prisoners. Talya stepped forward, looking directly at the cameras.

'Is that on Damien Hunter's command? He will want to see these prisoners, and he will want to speak to me too. You have a rebellion on your hands, if you hadn't noticed. I suggest you run this by Hunter.'

There was silence. They waited.

'Stay as you are,' Leo whispered to the group. 'We're still your captives, remember.'

'Make sure your cuffs are locked now,' Talya said in a low voice. 'They need to see us properly secured.'

Leo didn't want the Fortrillium officials to suspect that the small band of Centuria had already thrown in their lot with the rebels. In any case, he wasn't entirely sure about the rest of the group – they would probably do whatever it took to stay alive. And that meant switching sides once again if the going got tough.

The silence seemed to last forever. It was broken by the scraping of the iron gates opening. Talya was relieved that she'd instructed the rebels not to break through the gates further along the wall, as awaiting them on the other side were three of the biggest machine guns she'd ever seen. Where did Fortrillium keep this equipment? Their patched up rocket launcher would be no match for these weapons which were capable of mowing down hundreds of people in minutes. She'd made the correct decisions so far. It was right that they were risking their own lives instead of sacrificing hundreds or thousands of innocent people.

Their treatment was rough and contemptuous. Talya wondered what the Centuria knew about the rebellion. Many of them would not have seen her address on the screens if they were on the Silk Road side – they'd only managed to broadcast in The Grid. She should have set Wiz and his team onto that task. They needed to be perceived as a force for positive change, not the enemy.

Leo and Jody fared particularly badly. They were struck with gun butts and knocked to the ground. The Chief Centuria was the initiator of this assault. He would be ensuring that discipline remained strong, he would not want his teams to believe that treason did not have severe consequences. He kicked them both in the ribs when they were down on the floor, and they groaned with the pain of the blows from his heavy boots.

He drew his weapon and held it to Jody's head. She looked directly into his eyes throughout, struggling through the pain of a cracked rib, defying him to pull the trigger.

'Kill us now and you'll make martyrs of us!' Leo shouted, attempting to stand. He'd done this intentionally to draw the Chief Centuria away from Jody. He struck Leo again, and spat on him as he lay on the ground. That last blow had hurt him badly, he was in a lot of pain.

'Take them away!' the Chief Centuria commanded. Talya noted the reticence from his team. There was a fraction of a second when they looked at each other before moving. That would be her opportunity. Rebellions were best fought in the mind, not through violence, and these Centuria were already halfway there. They just needed the push to stand up and be counted. They understood that they were a mistake away from ending up like Leo and Jody. They were ruled by terror.

Leo and Jody were thrown into a truck. Their bodies were bruised and battered, but they were alive. Talya had to trust that they could take care of themselves. The Centuria defectors who had accompanied them through the gates were led towards the same truck, supposedly for a debriefing. She hoped they could survive together and their change of allegiance to the side of the rebels remain undiscovered.

At last Talya and Brad Sivil had been recognized as the assets that they were: two Law Lord defectors, one of them the rebel leader. The Chief Centuria had given Leo and Jody such a hard time because he'd been humiliated by Damien Hunter. Hunter had berated him for thinking it might be a good idea to execute the traitors on the spot.

'You damn idiot!' he'd shrieked via the WristCom. The Centuria under the Chief Centuria's command had nervously shuffled, they could hear everything.

'Why would you think that would be a good idea? And you're in command of a team? I'm taking your name and I'll review your position later. In the meantime, debrief the two Centuria traitors and bring Slater and Sivil to me.'

Leo and Jody had borne the brunt of that admonishment. The Chief Centuria's team would also pick up the aftermath of his temper. Evil ripples were sweeping through The City and at their epicentre was Damien Hunter.

Talya and Sivil were given marginally better treatment. They were rough-handled into a military vehicle, but nothing was done to bruise or damage the assets. That would be Damien Hunter's job. Their cuffs were checked and they were blindfolded. The vehicle drew off and made a ten-minute journey. Talya tried to work out roughly where they were. It had to be Fortrillium, there was no other place for Hunter to take them.

She finally caught some thinking time. Perhaps this wasn't such a good strategy after all. She hadn't thought things through beyond getting past the gates. Hunter would want to use her as propaganda. She was reasonably sure he wouldn't kill her, that would be a waste of a good show trial. He'd put her in The Grid, as he'd want to draw out her demise for as long as possible. That would give her time. Time to manoeuvre, time for the rebels to gain a stronger foothold, time for the news of the rebellion to spread to Silk Road. Would it be long enough for Lucy and Joe? Could Wiz and his team make a breakthrough in that time? There were too many events in play. She had to keep pressing onward, her main target was Hunter. She would have to deal with their most immediate problem.

They were kept blindfolded. Talya thought they were at Fortrillium but she wasn't certain. It had a military feel about it, there was no doubt about that. She heard his voice first.

'Talya, what a pleasure to see you again!'

It was Damien Hunter, of course. His presence turned her stomach.

'And Law Lord Sivil too, what a surprise to see you

both. Remove their blindfolds and sit them on the chairs in front of the camera.'

Talya and Sivil were moved into place as instructed, and all of the Centuria left the room. One staff member remained behind the camera – Damien Hunter had set up his spectacle already. Talya supposed they were in his office, she'd never seen it before.

'You know that this is the end of your little rebellion, Talya? You don't hand your opponent the main players. Did they never teach you that in Law School? Of course they wouldn't. You think that everything can be solved by negotiation and rules. Sometimes, Talya, those things don't work and you have to be a little more proactive.'

Talya thought he was deranged. He was raving, his eyes were wild. She'd never seen him like that. Certainly there had been hints of it in the past but never this extreme.

'Time to make a broadcast on the screens. By the way, Talya, you're probably not up to date with what's going on in The Grid. Your daughter is currently being tormented by some rather unpleasant nightmares. She gets to live through every blow and wound – she's being peeled alive by that nice fellow, Schälen. Not for real, of course, that would be too easy. Much more fun if she gets to live through it time and time again.'

Hunter faced the camera, standing in front of Talya and Sivil. This broadcast was for The Climbs only, it would be a disaster if it was seen by those on Silk Road.

'Citizens of The Climbs, good evening! As you can see, your little tantrum is over. Your two leaders have been captured and, to be honest with you, there really isn't a lot of point carrying on. You need to return to your homes now. You should stay there until you get the signal that lockdown is over. I will personally ensure that extra supplies are delivered to all areas—'

'Nothing will change if you listen to him! We need to rise up against Fortrill—'

Sivil had stood up behind Damien Hunter and started to shout towards the camera. Before he'd finished his second sentence, Hunter had taken a gun from his belt and shot him through the head. Everything was on camera. Pieces of his exploded brain spattered across Talya's face. She retched, her eyes wide with terror.

'As I was saying before that rude interruption, do as I say and we'll all be back to normal in a couple of days. Continue with this futile resistance and you'll find out what it's like to be Law Lord Sivil. You have until 06:00 to comply with this request. Fortrillium thanks you for your attention.'

Talya didn't know what to do next. Sivil's limp, bloody body was slumped next to her. The red light at the top of the camera went out indicating that the broadcast was over. She gasped for air, trying to catch her breath.

'So, Talya, as you can see, things really aren't working out how you'd expected. Looks like we now have two vacancies on the Law Lord panel. Such a shame. Law Lord Sivil was a valuable member of our little team. Did you know he'd accepted a larger house to help me press through the trial of Matt Parsons?'

Talya was distracted, just for a moment. Her eye had been caught by the red light at the top of the camera. It had been activated again. The operator gave her a stern look indicating that she should look away. She complied, realizing what was going on. Another frightened person was helping with the resistance. He couldn't fight Damien Hunter or challenge the Centuria but he could switch on the camera feed so that The Climbs was treated to Hunter's private conversation with Talya. Talya held Hunter's gaze, she wanted him looking directly at her.

'It's all over anyway. Delman has betrayed all of us. You're wasting your time, it's too late for a rebellion. The whole of The City is about to be destroyed and you're too busy throwing a tantrum!'

He laughed loudly. Talya was sure he was losing his mind. He'd always seemed so calm and calculating, but he had become manic and unstable.

'What do you mean? Why is The City going to be destroyed?'

He was pacing the room now. She did not want him to see the red light on the camera.

'What do you mean, Damien? I want to know what's happening to The City?'

'Didn't you know, Talya? It's all been one big lie. A hundred years in here, our supposed sanctuary, and the danger was always somewhere else. I've seen it for myself now, and Delman knew all along. He's killing my family too. He wouldn't even give me my family back before he stole everything!'

Talya couldn't make any sense of what he was saying, but she could see that something very serious had tipped the balance of power.

'You're not making any sense, Damien. I came to you in friendship before. We can still resolve this, we don't need to lose any more lives.'

'That man has tormented me for years. He incarcerated my family and stopped me watching my children grow up. And now he's going to finish us all off, Talya. This rebellion of yours, it's a waste of time. We've been fighting the wrong enemy!'

Damien Hunter stopped suddenly. He stared directly at the camera, seeing that the broadcast light was on. He raised his gun and pointed it at the operator.

'Was that broadcast? How long was that broadcasting?'

He didn't let the camera operator speak. He shot him directly between the eyes, then he shot the camera. The red light went out.

'That decides it now, Talya. You're coming with me. We're going to finish this thing together. It's time to end it.'

Hunter grabbed Talya's arm, pulled her up out of the chair and held his gun to her back. She tried to control her shaking, she had to hold steady. How had Joe and Lucy survived living in constant fear in The Grid?

'You're going to get your tour of Fortrillium, Talya, the parts of the complex you weren't allowed to see.'

'Where are you taking me, Damien? We need to start evacuating The City, don't we? You have to tell me what's going on. We can work together. We should have worked together before.'

'Just come with me and don't make a fuss. We're all on borrowed time now, but there's one way we can stop it. We have to get to President Delman before he gets out of The Grid. We're going into The Grid, Talya!'

Breakthrough

The combination of the rebel tech team and the break-throughs Joe, Lucy, Mitchell and Wiz had made facilitated progress at a remarkable speed. A full dossier of Damien Hunter's atrocities was soon assembled. They had just skimmed the surface with the images they'd shown during Talya's address.

They'd discovered something that none of them had

known: Damien Hunter had a family which had mysteriously disappeared at the time he'd got the job as Head of Fortrillium. The atrocities in The Climbs began shortly afterwards. There had been a cover-up on a massive scale. Powerful people within the Centuria had protected him and concealed the trail of carnage he left in his wake.

There were records of payments made to certain individuals within the Centuria: the greater the atrocity, the higher the payment. It appeared that a group of senior personnel within the Centuria and Fortrillium had helped to sustain Hunter's activities. They had been well rewarded for their efforts.

The evidence trail had dried up six years previously when Tom and Matt were stopped dead in their tracks. But the personnel were still in post, there was enough information in those files to damn Damien Hunter in hell for several lifetimes. He'd be accompanied by some very senior people too, Leianna Richwald included.

What provided the greatest breakthrough was the work they'd done on accessing Matt's secure server area. From there, the tech team managed to reach the Fortrillium mainframe, piggy-backing in via Matt's old profile. They'd reverse engineered the protocols and were able to penetrate several other secure locations.

'We can bring down Fortrillium from here,' one of the team had announced. 'We can switch the power off and take over the Comms.'

'Can we power down The Grid?' Wiz asked hopefully.

'Not a chance. It has a separate power supply, I can't get to it from here. But we can throw everything into disarray.'

'Hold it for now. We might mess things up for Talya, Jody and Leo. Let's focus on this external source, see if we can see what's out there.'

There was more tapping at keyboards. They were doing ten times the work Wiz had been able to achieve, in a fraction of the time. Great tech, reliable power and skilled people. If they'd known about the rebels a long time ago, they could have achieved so much. They'd all been working in isolation, but when they came together like this they finally regained control. They monitored the line. There was no sign of Delman or his mystery contact, but Wiz noticed a slight reverberation on the line, not audio, but something electronic.

'Can you scan for data rather than audio?'

'No problem.'

A short delay, a few buttons pressed.

'Look at the screen, Wiz. They're communicating by text. It's the same source from the external location, but they're talking to somebody different. They're hooked directly into Fortrillium.'

Contact

Linwood felt that every move he made on his console was being scrutinized by the Centuria. It was only his sense of fear and guilt, of course, but he was nervous as he typed the messages onto his screen. He was concerned too about how long to run the Psyche-Eval Mode. He was pushing his luck, he knew, but at least the Justice Seekers weren't killing each other while they were trapped in their own minds. Some of the heart rates were being pushed to the extremes – Joe and Max in particular looked under strain and at risk. Linwood didn't want to chance any heart attacks, but to a certain degree the Justice Seekers determined their own demons in this round. He hoped it would be over soon. He was making his own move now, taking his own risks. It only takes small actions by a few brave individuals to create change, and Linwood had seen his opportunity and was ready to grasp it.

For Linwood, it had always been about finding his brother. Jacob had inspired him as a child, and he'd been heartbroken when he saw him pulling away from the family and becoming more distant. When his brother had disappeared, he'd been distraught. His sadness turned to rage and then became focused on finding out what had happened. That had taken him to his present position as a Gridder at Fortrillium. If he didn't act now, when would he?

He could see what Jacob was doing, if indeed it was Jacob. He had opened a Comms socket in their private area within The Grid. Linwood had to reciprocate. It had to be secure. Was this a trap? Was Damien Hunter luring him to his death? Hunter would not have known those details about their family. Nobody knew about the book. It was forbidden to keep it, Jacob would never have shared that information – it would have placed his family in immediate danger. Looking around to make sure nobody could see his screens, Linwood opened his own secure socket in the virtual space. He waited. He wanted the person at the other end to make the first contact. A text message appeared on his screen, and he had barely enough time to read it before it disappeared. It had to be Jacob. Only someone as capable as he was would think to send self-destruct text messages so as not to draw attention. Linwood typed some lines of code, emulating Jacob's idea in his own way.

J: *Linwood?*

L: *Jacob?*

J: *07:41 Marlene 29iK02.*

Linwood recognized the data immediately. It was the

hour of Linwood's birth, his mother's middle name and the key code for their door lock.

He typed in his reply.

L: *7DFt4kl David 22:43.*

Linwood typed the key code for the family's data storage, his father's middle name and Jacob's time of birth. None of this was completely secure information, but with all the other clues it had to be Jacob. If it was a trick, it was worth taking the risk for.

J: *It's me. I'm safe. I'm not in The City. There are other cities.*

The text messages flashed up on the screen, moving to different locations then disappearing without a trace.

L: *I'm at Fortrillium. In charge of The Grid. Need some help!*

J: *I know. Delman is up to something. Thought I could trust him. Not sure now.*

L: *Need to keep Justice Seekers alive. Friends. Fortrillium breathing down my neck.*

J: *Missed you brother.*

L: *Missed you too.*

Linwood continued to scan the room. He felt that a hand might land on his shoulder at any moment, but they'd been careful, nobody would know what they were doing. There were no more texts for a moment or two then Linwood's screen gave a momentary flicker.

W: *Hi. I'm Wiz. You don't know me, but you know my friend Hannah.*

Was this the trap he'd been waiting for? There was no movement in the room, the Centuria remained in their positions.

W: *I know you're afraid. It's okay. I'm friends with Joe*

Parsons and Lucy Slater. Talya Slater too. I see what you're doing. I need your help. Hannah needs our help.

Linwood waited for his older brother to make the first move. Should they play dead. Disconnect quickly? Linwood didn't know what to do. He checked the safe area. Somebody had created a third, secure socket. How could they do that? They'd have to have access to both Fortrillium and Jacob's networks. He took a leap of faith.

L: *Where are you?*

W: *The Climbs. Working with rebels. Talya Slater too.*

L: *Rebels?*

W: *You're on Silk Road side, you won't know. Hack into security gate feeds. The Climbs is on lockdown.*

There was no sign of Jacob, he'd gone quiet. Linwood patched through a feed of the security gates. He saw heavily armed teams of Centuria, military vehicles and closed iron gates. They hadn't been told, but something was going on out there. He'd never seen anything like it. Had there been a riot?

L: *?*

W: *There's a rebellion in The Climbs. They've locked them in. Can you keep a secret? Very important! Must trust you on this.*

L: *Of course.*

W: *Delman making a run for it through Grid. Have you seen? He's going to exit. Need help to get him out. Will you work with me? If we succeed, I can come home.*

That piqued Jacob's interest. He joined the conversation, three faceless people connected by a hidden and illegal link.

J: *?*

L: *Have seen Delman. He's caught in Psyche-Eval. Your*

idea originally! Justice Seekers may attack him when they see him.

J: Exactly! We need to get him out of there. He's trying to help.

W: Really? Delman? Help?

L: What, Delman?

J: I have to trust him. I believe him. Don't have much choice!

There was a pause. Jacob had just seen something incredible on his console. He knew Linwood would only see the pixelated version.

J: Have you seen what happened in The Grid?

L: Two new people just stepped in. How? I can't see. Just figures on my console.

J: It's Damien Hunter and Talya Slater. What is going on in there? He's come armed too. I'll bet he's come for Delman.

Release

Clay Hillman was a man on the edge. For the past hour he'd been tormented over and over again by the sight of the half-dead trying to bring him into their world of death and decay. He'd fought furiously but he was beginning to get agitated, his strong mental resilience was floundering. He was starting to crack up. On the screens he thrashed around, jumping violently, getting dangerously close to the other Justice Seekers who were fighting their own demons.

Joe Parsons was beginning to look more and more uncomfortable. He was sweating heavily, his breaths were shallow and he'd vomited. To the watching public he looked like a man who was incredibly ill. He'd been pushed too far. Joe would never have known it, living in The Climbs, but his heart was weak. Without medical check-ups it had passed unnoticed and had never caused him problems in his daily life. But it was a volcano waiting to erupt. Every time he'd run up the stairs of the tower blocks, he'd put it under strain. In The Grid he'd been subjected to more strain than he could cope with. Joe dropped to the ground. He'd gone into cardiac arrest.

As Joe fell, the thud of his body hitting the hard surface of The Grid made its way into Clay's head. He started to confuse his hallucination with what was happening right in front of him in The Grid. Still clutching a weapon, he began to thrust at Joe, seeing a vile, faceless undead monster instead of his friend. Joe was defenceless. He was fighting for his life, with only minutes left to live.

There was one Justice Seeker who had already confronted his nightmares. Where the others fought and struggled, trapped in the most horrific ordeals their minds could create, Mitchell had already stared his worst fears directly in the eye – and survived.

The Psyche-Eval Mode had confronted him with his biggest fear – that he simply wasn't good enough. But he was. He'd already saved Lucy once, he could do so again. He'd made a mistake, he'd been stupid, vain and conceited. He'd cowered and been too terrified to act. When he had stepped up, he'd saved her life. He understood that Lucy would only ever be a friend. But her friendship – and that of Joe and Wiz – was the most important thing in the world to him. When he'd killed the Schälen clone, he'd seen that nightmares can be conquered, terrors must be overcome. He'd had to find that small reserve which resides in all humans, sometimes very deeply hidden, which forces us to act when we absolutely have to.

Caught up in his hallucination, Mitchell's conscious

mind fought with his unconscious, battling with the Psyche-Eval implant, forcing it into submission and finally defeat. Mitchell's consciousness began to return. The image of Lucy's torture subsided, his accusers walked away and he was on his own. The real world began to make demands on his senses.

Mitchell saw the cityscape first. He saw Jena, Max and Julia shaking violently as if possessed by devils. Each had a needle implanted into their neck. He placed his hand on his own neck, found the needle and pulled it out of his flesh. It had burrowed into the top of his spine. He groaned with the pain as he tore it out. His senses sharpened immediately.

Joe was on the floor, still, deathly still. Clay was thrusting his weapon at him. He'd lanced Joe's protective clothing and begun to draw blood.

Mitchell pushed Clay away from Joe, creating as much distance as he could. He tore the needle from Lucy's neck as she was close by, but decided that his priority was lying on the ground in front of him. Clay's weapon had fallen to the ground. Mitchell made directly for Joe. He'd seen this done before on Silk Road. It had to be Joe's heart, but surely he was too young?

Mitchell had seen it happen to an older man once. Somebody had rushed up, felt his pulse, then beat his chest until he came round. Mitchell couldn't remember the details. How long had Joe been on the floor? He wondered if he was too late already. Mitchell felt Joe's pulse. It was very weak but still there.

He couldn't remember what to do. Something about blowing into the mouth – that had to be for oxygen – then pounding the chest – that had to be to get the heart going. Mitchell opened Joe's mouth and blew into it. He needed to hold his nose shut, he remembered that bit. He tried again. Joe's chest moved upwards as his lungs filled with air.

Mitchell pounded on Joe's chest. He couldn't remember what he was supposed to do. Did it matter? He breathed into Joe's mouth again. His lungs raised and Mitchell began to push on his chest once more. There was no sign of life. Mitchell was trying frantically to save his friend – if only he could begin to make up for the damage he'd done.

Mitchell had his back to Clay and didn't see that he was picking up the discarded weapon. Disoriented by what was going on in his mind and the push he'd received from Mitchell in real life, Clay was struggling to identify his enemy. He picked up a discarded spear and ran at Mitchell, thrusting it into his back so it exited through his chest. As Clay pulled out the spear, seeing in his mind a hideous, faceless monster, Mitchell saw the circle of blood form on his chest then felt the pain of the spear straight afterwards. His head swam, his surroundings began to swirl, but still he could only think of saving Joe.

Using the last of his fading strength, he gave his friend his final gift. Mitchell made a determined push down onto Joe's chest. As Mitchell slumped on the ground at the side of Joe, Joe took a gasp for life. As one lived, the other died.

Lucy had been slowly coming back to reality, fighting to remember who she was and what was going on. Her mind had sharpened as Clay had lunged at Mitchell. They were in The Grid. Joe was on the ground, hurt or ill. Clay had just killed Mitchell. Was it real or imagined? She was struggling to make sense of it. She ran at Clay, taking his spear and pushing him away. There was a needle in his neck, instinctively she pulled it out. Jena, Julia and Max were there too, they also had needles. She pulled them out, crushing them underfoot.

Her friends took some time to adjust, flinching and calling out as they struggled to leave their dream world and rejoin reality.

Lucy saw it first. She shook Mitchell and shouted his name, desperately hoping this corpse was just her imagination. It was not. Mitchell was dead. Her friend was dead. Clay had been driven by the demons in his mind to kill one of his own. Clay, who'd helped keep so many of them alive, had now turned killer. How would he live with himself?

But Joe needed help too. He was breathing and in great pain. Lucy moved over to him and tried to make him more comfortable. He was starting to talk, rambling incoherently. Lucy checked the needle was no longer in his neck. He was clear of whatever had poisoned their minds, but he didn't look good, he'd sustained a shattering blow.

All around her, the other Justice Seekers were adjusting to reality. They were trying to work out what was real and what was imaginary, exhausted from the mental torture they'd been experiencing. Lucy too felt sapped of all strength. She'd already learned that you had to keep a reserve all the time in The Grid, you never knew what was coming at you next.

There was Mitchell. Another death. This time a friend killed by another friend, Clay. She wouldn't tell Clay what he'd done, she would make up some lie about how Mitchell had died. How could she tell him? They needed him strong, he'd helped to keep so many alive, it would destroy him to know that he'd killed Mitchell.

She could see what Mitchell had done. Not only had he saved her from the attack of the Schälen clone, he'd also fought to save Joe, who would have died without Mitchell's intervention. Mitchell had died as a victor. Whatever he'd done in the past, it was forgotten now. He'd stepped up and become a hero. She'd always believed he was a good person. His crime was to have been weak, if only for a moment. He'd shown himself capable of immense strength, yet his life had been struck down unfairly, and not even in the heat of a battle.

One more death to avenge. There was a trail of bodies behind them. For those deaths to count for anything, they had to press on. They had to find Delman and take him back to Centrum.

'Lucy ...'

Joe was beginning to speak, still weak but struggling to force himself into full awareness.

'What happened?'

'Mitchell is dead, Joe. He saved your life. Whatever was going on in our minds, he was killed by it. Maybe he even killed himself, I didn't see.'

She committed to the lie and resolved to take it with her to the grave, whatever it cost her. How could she possibly tell the truth?

Joe was distraught. Jena rushed over, she'd got a grip on what was real and what was unreal and could see that Joe needed help. Clay seemed dazed. Julia and Max were helping each other, locating the water supplies to share around. They were despondent that Mitchell had lost his life, but full of admiration for what he'd done to save Joe.

The question of how he had died soon faded. They'd all seen how things worked in The Grid – anything might have happened to Mitchell while they were experiencing their hallucinations.

Clay joined the group. The mood was dark, another life lost, another step closer to the brink for all of them. What would be next?

They didn't have to wait long to find out. Out of the

shadows stepped Damien Hunter with Talya Slater. He was holding a gun to Talya's head.

'I want all of you to stand by that wall. We're going to have a question and answer session. Answer incorrectly and you'll be joining your dead friend!'

Ascension

Joe saw that the drones had become deactivated. It was an unusual thing to notice as he lay on the floor, struggling desperately to overcome the utter exhaustion inflicted upon him by his ordeal. He was shocked too by the sight of his friend, Mitchell, lying dead beside him. Had he found peace now? Joe hoped so. In The Grid it was a close call which was better – life or death. At least the terror had stopped for Mitchell, maybe it would be a blessed relief when death came to all of them. He could see that his friends were fighting to overcome their own experiences, but the drones seemed to have deactivated and that meant the final Mode was over. All he could think of was what was coming next.

Three Modes, then Ascension. If any of them were still alive when Ascension came, they'd die. Nobody got out of The Grid. Whoever was left would be cleared up. He had to force himself to stand up. He had to be ready for when Ascension came or he'd die on that spot. He didn't want to die lying down. If it happened, he wanted to be on two feet.

For a moment he thought that the dreams had begun again. He felt vague and detached. He could hear Lucy and his mum worrying about him, but it was in the background, it didn't seem to be entirely real. Then he saw Damien Hunter and Talya Slater. He almost laughed. It was like the cast of thousands in a bad nightmare. Now it was Damien

Hunter's turn to torment him. But Talya was there, Talya was not a source of nightmares.

Then Hunter spoke. Everybody jumped and moved. He was pointing a weapon, he'd come heavily armed. He was shouting at Joe, indicating that he should stand with the others.

'We have to help him, you stupid man!' Lucy was screaming at him. She seemed to have lost any fear for her life.

Talya was clearly overjoyed to see Lucy again, in spite of this peril, but Hunter would not let mother and daughter have their reunion. He forced Talya to her knees and placed his gun at her head.

'Any sudden moves and the rebellion is over!'

Joe stumbled, and Lucy and Jena moved to support him. He'd received a devastating blow, he was fighting hard to recover. They didn't need this. Catharsis was almost upon them and their mission was to recover Josh Delman. This was a delay. Ascension would begin at any time now the final Mode had ended. Joe couldn't afford to be in this state.

Then something happened which convinced Joe that this had to be a dream. President Delman, looking very distressed and flustered, was approaching Damien Hunter from behind, with another woman alongside him. He thought it was Teanna Schaelles, he'd seen her on the screens from time to time but had no knowledge of her personally.

That was good news. They needed Delman, they had to get him to Centrum. He'd come to them and that solved a huge problem. But what was going on? Why were the two most senior people in The City trapped in the centre of The Grid? He looked for some information to confirm that this was not part of the hallucination. He felt his neck, there was no needle.

Delman and Teanna had been released from their own nightmares when Mode 3 had completed and the needles dropped from their necks. It had been long enough to give Damien Hunter all of the information he needed, enough to force him into The Grid to apprehend the President. As Delman and Teanna had worked their way through The Grid, looking for Clay to escort them safely, they'd chanced upon Hunter. He was in the middle of more threats and imminent violence.

Everybody was gathered at the centre of The Grid. The final solution lay here, in this group. But Catharsis was about to begin, and it would preceded by The Cleanse. They would escape Ascension, only to be subjected to a more unimaginable horror. That process had been set in stone a hundred years previously. It was always to have been this way.

'Damien, enough!' Delman shouted. 'Put down your weapon.'

For a moment, Hunter hesitated, automatically deferring to the President's voice. But he stopped himself, swung to the side and pointed his weapon at Delman and Teanna, making sure his back was covered to prevent an attack from the Justice Seekers.

'You have no authority here!' Damien Hunter shouted back. He wondered for a moment if this would be playing out on the screens. Without his authorization, would 97TRaider show the President now? He hoped so, he wanted this conversation to be witnessed by everybody in The City.

'Why are you abandoning The City, President Delman? Perhaps you'd like to explain what brings The

City's most senior official into the heart of the justice system where thieves and murderers are sent to die?'

President Delman kept his weapon trained on Damien Hunter, meeting his opponent's stare directly. Teanna looked uneasy. She was standing between two dangerous men, she'd colluded with both.

'You don't understand anything, Damien. You're too caught up in your power games and dreams of the presidency. You need to let me pass, you'll have to trust me!'

'That's not going to happen Mr President – or should I call you President James Morgan?'

Delman's face went white. All of the Justice Seekers saw it. Clay and Lucy were looking for an opportunity to strike, waiting and watching. There would be a moment of distraction, a chink of light. When it came, they would take their chance.

'Damien, it doesn't have to be this way. Do I need to remind you about your lovely family?'

'I know exactly what you did to my family, President Morgan, and I've reversed the process. My family are alive. I discovered what you were up to.'

Delman looked to Teanna who was checking her WristCom data. She gave Delman a small nod. Inside she cursed, that had been her bargaining chip if she got into a tight spot with Damien Hunter. This was exactly the crisis she'd been dreading.

'What's the thing you want most, Damien? You want your family back, don't you? If you allow me to pass through, I will release your family. Teanna, open up the control console. Let me pass, Damien, and you will get your family back.'

Hunter searched his face, looking for an indication of

deception. Delman didn't flinch. He was certain this was for real.

'But what about Catharsis and the destruction of The City? I think you knew about it all along,' said Hunter, looking at Joe and Lucy. Clay observed the opportunity. If they could draw his glance from left to right, they'd get their distraction.

'I promise you, Damien, that if you let me pass on my way, I will release your family and you can all follow me to The Core.'

Clay wondered if Hunter would meet the same fate as Miron. Was Delman setting a trap? There was no way Clay was going through that elevator door, not after what had happened to his fellow Justice Seeker.

It was obvious that Hunter was tempted by this offer, he was quite clearly thinking it through.

'Let me see you activate the release codes, as an act of faith.'

'You must let me pass you and wait by The Core, then I'll activate the codes,' replied Delman.

Damien Hunter nodded. He was running out of places to cover his back.

'Join your friends!' He motioned to Talya who got up and rushed straight to Lucy. She held her daughter tightly in her arms, she never wanted to let her go.

Delman moved towards the area which he believed to be masking the exit to The Grid. There was no visible way out, but he seemed to know roughly where he needed to be.

'Okay, now activate the release codes.'

Teanna sent some commands from her WristCom. President Delman handed her the weapon and he entered his data, performing a retinal scan and a DNA confirmation.

'It's completed, Damien, your family will be released

from the Umbilica. You should go and fetch them now, they'll want to see you when they wake up.'

'I want a feed of their life signs and a two-way video link to their chamber. Can you do that? You try to trick me, Delman, and I swear you'll be taken out of this place in tiny pieces.'

'There's no trickery, Damien. I promise. Your family will begin their awakening now. Teanna, give him the feed and pass the override controls to Damien. I want him to have full access now.'

Damien Hunter's WristCom buzzed. He looked at the screen, glancing from his device to Delman, to the Justice Seekers, distrustful of all of them. He saw a video feed of his family. The awakening process had been activated. They were kicking and jolting in the liquid of the Umbilica which had begun to drain. Their conscious minds were being restored. If he rushed back, he'd be able to see them once again. He would be there when they awoke. But how could he exit The Grid?

Damien Hunter had blindly followed President Delman into the arena, that was simple enough. He had followed the painful path which had been taken by so many Justice Seekers before him. Inserting the implant had been excruciatingly painful, he'd made Talya go first, to make sure he carried out the process correctly. He was doing it for his family, it didn't matter how much it hurt. He was their guardian, without him they were dead.

Hunter hadn't thought beyond apprehending Delman. In his anger, he'd followed his nemesis into hell with little thought as to how he'd get out again. He'd assumed Delman would know the way. He'd done it before, after all.

For a moment he panicked. He was in reach of what he'd always wanted, yet suddenly it had taken another leap away from him. He needed Delman still. He couldn't let him leave The Grid without knowing that his family was safe. Hunter raised his gun and shot Teanna in the leg.

'That's for deceiving me, Teanna. Delman, walk away from the exit!'

That had taken Delman by surprise. Teanna dropped to the floor, the bone in her leg shattered by the shot.

'Don't shoot her you fool!' Delman screamed at him. 'Without Teanna we're all dead. She has to come back alive!'

Seeing his chance at last, Clay ran at Damien Hunter, managing to deflect his second shot at Teanna. The concrete walls to the side of them began to pixelate and the door to the elevator re-emerged.

Joe saw it first. It wasn't just the entrance area that was changing, the entire Grid was transforming. Surely not now? Was this Ascension? They would be finished off in no time. Whatever followed their final Mode would be fast and violent.

Joe was half correct. This was to be the most brutal challenge they'd face, but it was not Ascension. Ascension was the final stage of The Grid when, if the Justice Seekers survived, the entrance would open before them and The Justice Walk would be their gateway to freedom. Nobody had ever seen that – only Delman had walked out of there alive.

This was The Cleanse. It had been preordained a hundred years beforehand. When Catharsis finally began, the citizens of each city would be locked in and anybody trying to exit The City via The Core would be cleansed. This was as brutal and violent as Ascension. The difference was, there was no way out. It was there to clear all life forms from The Grid prior to Catharsis.

The sound of huge grinding machines could be heard in the distance. There were several of them. The city ruins pixelated all around them and vast iron walls replaced the ruins and tower blocks that had stood there before. The Core was gone, the door was no longer there.

Everyone froze. This was The Grid, they all knew that something terrible could happen next. They got the answer they were looking for in seconds.

'Run!' shouted Joe. This was the endgame, this was how he was going to die. It was how they were all going to perish.

A giant metallic machine, with a sloped front and enormous, grinding teeth roared towards the centre of the Justice Seekers. Joe pushed Jena and Lucy out of the way, feeling a sharp pain in his heart as he did so. Max and Hannah saw the approaching object and ducked to one side, but it ran straight into Julia who never saw it coming. As she fell against its shining metal blades, her arms were caught in the grinders which lay behind them. The machine pulled her in, arms, head, body and legs. It ground her up and spat her out, taking less than a minute to complete its terrible task.

'Spread out!' Clay called. He was still looking out for the group. There was no time to mourn in The Grid, survival was the only option.

There were several iron-clad corridors to run down, each one completely clear and offering no shelter and no weaponry. It was a funnel, a way to contain and kill them. Everybody spread out as Clay had commanded, but it was obvious that this was the end. Three more machines emerged, as if from nowhere, their cogs, blades and wheels grinding away ominously, ready to take a life.

Joe ended up in a tunnel with President Delman and Clay. Delman had picked up Teanna, but was struggling to carry her so Clay had taken over. The three of them took the nearest corridor and ran as fast as they could. Joe's heart throbbed painfully in his chest, he was weak and faint, but he had to press on, they had to get Delman out, if they could. If he died in the process, fine. He had to push his aching body as hard as he could.

Hannah, Lucy and Jena ran in a different direction. Damien Hunter took yet another corridor and, for a moment, Talya considered whether to follow her daughter or to pursue him. She chose Hunter, and Max followed her too. They'd come this far, there was no way he was getting out of there without facing justice. Preferably, it would be a trial by the citizens, but if not they'd settle for the judgement of the grinders.

Each iron corridor led to another, it was impossible to tell them apart. All around the sound of the grinders could be heard. They were in no hurry. There was nowhere to hide, nothing to fight with, it was simply a process of clearing The Grid. All life would be eliminated by The Cleanse.

This is how it had been conceived a hundred years previously. It had never been anticipated that there might be some way of escaping The Cleanse. But outside The Grid a small group was watching, and they were going to do everything they could to get those people out alive. When the end came, it was Wiz, Linwood and Jacob who would signal its beginning.

The Cleanse

When the end came, it was fast. Wiz, Jacob and Linwood had been monitoring developments on their live feeds. Linwood had hesitated for a moment when he saw that

Damien Hunter had entered The Grid. He didn't know it was Hunter, his pixelated view concealed that to him, but Wiz and Jacob did not have the same limitations, they could see exactly what was going on.

In any conflict, there is always a moment as you stand on the precipice when you know it is time to jump. It was Linwood's moment to jump. When he allowed the images of Damien Hunter on the screen with President Delman – as had been expressly forbidden by Hunter – he knew he had signed his own death warrant.

The entire live feed was being streamed directly to The Climbs and Silk Road. Every Fortrillium employee and every member of the Centuria could access it.

News spread across The City fast. Their leaders had been seen threatening each other in The Grid. Delman was trying to escape and there was some terrible event looming which threatened the destruction of The City. Delman had imprisoned Damien Hunter's family, denying him access to them for several years. The men who were supposed to be in charge of their city were no better than the rats which infested their homes. And there was Talya Slater, the woman who had promised to bring them freedom and real justice, at the mercy of Hunter.

There was a stir on both sides of The City. Those in The Climbs, inspired already by Talya's words, strength-ened in their resolve to overthrow Fortrillium. On Silk Road, where the rebellion had remained a secret, the expla-nation for increased Centuria activity on their streets instantly became apparent. They were all now fighting for their lives.

Many stayed glued to the screens, watching with horror as Julia's mangled body had spattered across the camera lens. Others began to grow restless, wondering what could be done to save the city. It all seemed to be in the hands of the Justice Seekers. The last battle would take place in The Grid.

Wiz, Linwood and Jacob watched in disbelief as events unfurled. They understood that they were the only chance that anybody had of making it out alive. Jacob could partially control The Grid, and Wiz was accessing it via his link, but Linwood was cut off now, he had no ability to influence events. Jacob and Wiz worked fast to reroute access to Linwood. It went from Jacob to Wiz, and Wiz was then able to form the bridge between the two.

W: *They have a WristCom in there, they have Tom Slater's WristCom.*

L: *Get a message to them, tell them we're going to help.*

J: *We must get Delman out of there. We have to take a leap here, I'm not betting on Hunter, that's for sure!*

L: *Jacob, open up the exit if you can. Wiz, you and me, we keep them safe and steer them to the centre.*

W: *Agreed.*

J: *Will do.*

And so began a race against a program that had been created a century beforehand, its sole purpose to destroy every living thing that entered The Grid. Wiz and Linwood worked at a furious pace. As the Justice Seekers ran blindly through the iron corridors, they opened new exits and placed concrete blocks in the way of the grinders.

W: *It's adaptive, it's learning as we challenge it.*

L: *We need to work faster, get them towards the centre. I'll deflect the grinders, you create the corridors.*

J: *Got the exit cleared. Get them there asap. I'll work on the WristCom.*

The grinders adapted quickly to the concrete blocks. As Joe, Delman and Clay paused to draw breath, the nearest grinder stopped in its tracks. Its wheels retracted and it began to hover above the floor. The front blades parted to become aerofoils, revealing an open mouth packed with sharp, rotating cutters. Julia's clothing could still be seen caught in the jaws which were dripping with her blood.

Joe was exhausted. He felt as if his heart would give way any moment, but he had to press on. As the grinder began to move towards them, a corridor opened to their left. They ran through it, pursued by the airborne device.

'The elevator exit is up ahead. It's open, run for it!' shouted Clay.

'Are you an Immune? ... you can't get in if you're not ... you'll die on entry.'

Delman was an old man. He puffed through the sentence, trying his best to warn Clay.

'What's an Immune? I don't know,' Clay replied, startled by the question.

They ran as fast as they could along the corridor. There were no side turnings, no diversions. There was now a single path, one way only, directly to the exit. Joe could barely move himself forward, Delman's aged body was struggling to keep up. Only Clay still fought with a fury, carrying Teanna and determined to save one more life before the grinder took his own.

Clay arrived at the exit first. He placed Teanna at the door, not daring to cross the threshold as Miron had attempted earlier. Joe and Delman reached the elevator, the BioSweep scanned their bodies and they climbed inside, pulling Teanna close as the grinder made its rapid approach towards them.

'Thank you, Clay, thank you,' Joe said. They were the only words that came as the grinder raced up the corridor directly towards Clay's head. It was moments away, the elevator doors were about to close. His WristCom beeped, followed by Wiz's voice.

'You're an Immune, Clay. Get in!'

Clay didn't know who was calling him on the WristCom he'd been carrying. It had once belonged to Tom Slater, it had been procured by Josh Delman, hidden inside Jay, discovered by Max, and discarded in The Grid. It saved Clay's life. He took his chance. He ducked through the narrow gap in the doors, just as the BioSweep completed its scan. The elevator began to descend as they heard the crash of the grinder above. The machine had not stopped in time and had hurtled into the roof above in an attempt to avoid the exit. The explosion was the last thing Joe heard as his heart finally gave way and he slipped into oblivion.

CHAPTER THIRTEEN

Escape From The Grid

The events in The Grid were seen by everybody on the screens. If anybody was in any doubt about who the real leaders should be, it was evident from those final moments. Working together at great speed, Wiz, Linwood and Jacob had managed to create the environment which allowed the crucial elements to be put in place.

Wiz had heard Delman remark to Clay that he might not be an Immune – it had been fed through the audio feed in The Grid. He'd immediately checked Clay's personal data in the Fortrillium files to discover his plague status record. Clay *was* Immune. He'd thought there'd be no way to get that information to Clay in sufficient time to save his life, but then he remembered the WristCom they'd spent so much time trying to get to Joe and Lucy. It had paid off in the end, giving Clay the information he needed at precisely the right time. Without it, he'd have perished, another victim in the direct path of the grinder.

As the elevator made its way below ground, Clay looked

at Delman and his friend Joe, who was still and lifeless on the floor next to a wounded Teanna.

'You've got until those doors open to convince me not to strangle you right now!' Clay seethed at the President.

Sixty seconds later the elevator doors opened, and Delman was still alive.

'You make sure Joe gets help straight away, then do what you have to do!' Clay shouted.

'Where are you going?' asked Delman.

'There are still people alive up there. I'm going to do what I can to help them. You just make sure that these two live!'

Clay helped Delman move Joe and Teanna out of the elevator, then headed back up to The Grid.

Linwood had been steering the others to the exit all along. By the time the elevator doors opened, Clay could see Hannah, Lucy and Max running up the long, iron corridor, pursued by a wheeled grinder. They stood more chance with the wheeled machines. The airborne devices were much harder to beat.

Wiz's voice came back on the WristCom.

'Thank God, Clay. I thought we were going to lose our Comms. Lucy and Talya are clear, Max is not, Hannah I'm checking. As for Damien Hunter, I can't get into his files, they're not open like everybody else's.'

'Get in, get in,' Clay motioned to Lucy. Max, you can't cross over the threshold, it'll kill you, you're a plague carrier. I'm sorry. I'll help you. We'll survive it together. We'll work with whoever it is at the end of this WristCom.'

'It's Wiz, he's good. Wiz, thank you! What about Hannah?' Lucy spoke breathlessly. She was safely inside the elevator, she'd made it through the BioSweep. Hannah was outside, the grinder was getting closer and closer.

'I can't get into her files, they've been given an additional security level because she's been working as a Gridder.'

The grinder got closer.

'Max, we need to draw it away from Hannah. Help me. Stay there, Hannah. If you're clear, get inside the elevator straight away.'

Max and Clay stood in front of the machine until it was almost upon them, then they went separate ways, confusing it for a moment. It chased Clay.

'Hannah, what's your GEN-ID code?' Clay asked, running as fast as he was able to. Shout it to me!'

'HjKKl'

Clay relayed the code back to Wiz.

'You're clear!' Clay shouted. Hannah stepped forward and with the BioSweep completed, she entered the elevator, embracing Lucy, but terrified for her friends.

'Mum is still out there with Damien Hunter. We can't leave her,' Lucy screamed.

The grinder began to work Clay into a corner, Max watched as his new friend ran out of places to go. At the same time, Hunter came running up the corridor, followed by Talya who'd been in pursuit. Behind them were the remaining two grinders, both airborne.

'Mum, run!' Lucy shouted. 'Clay, it's Damien Hunter and Mum.'

Clay was distracted for a moment. He'd been walking backwards, his eyes fixed on the grinder. He stumbled and fell. The grinder moved forward. Clay knew it was over for him. If he could only see Talya out safely, he'd be content to die.

Realizing there was no way he was getting out alive, Max ran towards the grinder.

'Make it better in The City, Talya!' he called out to his former torturer, before he ran directly into the path of the machine's jaws. It scooped him up by the legs, crunching its way through the bones, then shredding and spitting out his bloody remains. He'd ended up the same way as the Justice Seekers he'd cleaned up in The Grid. Only his death would count for more.

Clay screamed in frustration as he saw Max minced alive, but he knew he had to move on fast. Talya Slater had to go down in that elevator, even if he lost his own life making it happen. He'd been reconciled to death for some time, it wouldn't matter if he died, but Talya had to get out.

The two airborne grinders were close to Talya. She was tired and fading fast. As she ran up the corridor, Clay could see that her eyes were losing hope. She could feel the fans on the grinders blowing on her neck, they were almost upon her.

Without warning, a massive iron bar appeared from the ceiling. Talya just had time to dodge it. One of the grinders did not. It struck the bar and exploded, Talya felt the blast on her back. It had been placed there by Jacob, he was trying to keep her alive.

'Keep running, Talya!' Clay shouted. He was standing in front of the open elevator doors watching the grinder that had just consumed Max. It had completed the process, bought Clay some time, and was about to seek its next victim.

Damien Hunter was going to reach the elevator first. He was running and looking at his own WristCom. His family had begun to emerge from the Umbilica, first waking, then stepping out from the protective film that had sustained their lives for so many years. He was running straight for the elevator, half looking ahead, half watching the resurrection of his family on the WristCom.

'Cassie, children, at last you're awake. I'll be with you soon, I'm coming my darlings, I'll be with you soon ...'

Behind him, Jacob had intercepted the final airborne grinder with a second iron bar. He was taking risks, he had to hope Talya would dodge in time. She was dead anyway if he couldn't stop the grinders. As that device exploded, pushing Talya forward with the force of the blast, two more devices materialized and began to power up.

Damien Hunter was almost upon the elevator. Clay could see that he was going to make it, but Talya might not. The wheeled grinder was making its way back towards Talya now. She was sandwiched between that and the two airborne devices.

Clay was torn. Talya had to survive. He would do what Max had done if he had to.

'Wiz, is Damien clear? Is he Immune?'

'Trying to find out, can't get into his files ...'

It was over in seconds.

Hunter reached the elevator, the BioSweep scanning him as he pushed Clay away from the doors to secure his own safety. His body exploded as Miron's had done when he'd attempted to do the same thing. Talya, summoning every last drop of energy she could muster, used her momentum to jump over the blades of the grinder, onto its top, then back to the ground. She fell through Damien Hunter's bloody remains onto the floor of the elevator as the BioSweep let her pass and the doors began to close. Clay ducked in after her. The descent began. Behind them the two remaining grinders sensed Hunter's bloody remains, and chewed up the severed body parts in mid-air, spewing them back out into The Grid.

There was silence in the arena of death. All that could be heard were the voices of Damien Hunter's family from his WristCom which was lying on the floor, attached to his severed hand.

'I don't know where Daddy is darling, I'm sure somebody will help us to find him soon ...'

60 Seconds

It took fewer than sixty seconds for the elevator to make its descent. President Josh Delman had been given very little time to convince Clay that he was worthy of being kept alive. What he said in those vital seconds forever changed the fortunes of The City.

'I thought I'd made the plague worse in the first place. I never meant to, I was trying to find the cure. President Morgan used me as the fall guy. They substituted NiVac3, but we'd told them it wasn't ready. I was young, I didn't know what to do. I kept the evidence, but I didn't speak up. The world was turning to hell anyway. Millions more died because of NiVac3. I had the cure, I could have saved lives. I was captured and held in Centrum – it's where we're heading now. Morgan tortured me, he wanted to be sure the truth wouldn't leak out. They couldn't kill me because I held all that information about the plague in my head, so they froze me for nearly fifty years. They put me in Cryo. Morgan was going to take my body when his wore out.

'A man called Edward Schaelles discovered that we were part of a conspiracy to use our country as lab rats, and he woke me from Cryo. He knew I'd worked with Morgan before the plague, and I told him how Morgan had released NiVac3. We live in a contained area which used to be a key centre of commerce: an alliance of governments used us.

Our cities are just big laboratories, they took advantage of how the plague had almost wiped out our entire country. Morgan had sent us to hell with NiVac3, then he'd engineered his way out of it by making a deal with those other countries. They tested cures on us, we were lab rats. Sectors 1 and 3 are dead, we're the only ones remaining.'

'What do you mean, the only ones?' Clay asked.

'The only ones on the planet. We're all that's left. When our city dies, we all die. They repeated the mistakes of NiVac3 and wiped everybody out. Our cage became our protection, we survived.

'Morgan put himself in Cryo forty-nine years after the cities were created, he was the only one who was ever going to walk away from this. He could start or stop Catharsis. His deal was to walk out after Catharsis, take my body and live out his days in a secure location. I beat him to it with Schaelles' help. I have taken over Morgan's body so that I can save The City. It has to be now, at the last moment. If I don't stop Catharsis, we all die. Morgan was the only one ever getting out of here, he and some of his cronies in Cryo. His own family are being held for ransom, they're in an Umbilica facility, I think. I can't access his memories. If you kill me now, Clay, we all die. I've been trying to stay alive all this time, this is the only way I can put things right. If we don't survive this, we all perish today.'

Clay made his decision at that moment. He'd seen incredible things since he'd entered The City's justice system but all of the evil seemed to rest at the feet of Damien Hunter, President Delman had always been detached. He was not without guilt, that was for certain. But Clay took a leap of faith. In the end, it saved the lives of millions.

The Dead Cities

There had been three Sectors when the cities were created. Their city was Sector 2, Sectors 1 and 3 had died decades before.

Sector 1 had been destroyed by a cure that was inadequately tested. It had been deployed at scale to the entire population, but it was not ready. It killed everybody within its walls, Immunes as well. They died terrible deaths, their final moments were spent in agonizing pain. That was seventeen years after the Sectors were created. This so-called cure would have wiped humanity off the face of the Earth if it hadn't been contained in that Sector. Aircraft from other countries had flown over the city, distributing the airborne vaccine. It had failed and within twenty-eight days the entire population was annihilated.

Sector 3 had perished thirty-two years afterwards. Another failed test. They'd forgotten the lessons of NiVac3. It had appeared to work at first, life in Sector 3 had gone on, the residents were testing clear of their strain of plague. Everything looked good in the lab tests. The cure was deployed to the world beyond the walls of Sector 3. Confidence was absolute that they'd got to the heart of the disease and could finally rid the world of all three strains.

It was then that President James Morgan had gone into Cryo, confident that a new plague-free world would be waiting for him when he emerged. He had just one pre-determined action to perform when the Centurial came and his new life in a different country would be waiting for him. It was to be his reward for turning his own people into lab rats.

But the virus had been incubating and mutating. The plague was not cured, it had just been dormant. Released worldwide as the final solution to the pandemic, it was that which almost wiped human beings from the surface of the Earth. Those in Sector 3 died, just as the rest of the Earth's inhabitants had perished. Sector 2 and Centrum hosted the only remaining life on the planet. Sector 2 was saved by a last-minute suggestion from a junior scientist who'd thought it would be a useful idea to preserve a population in one self-contained sector so that further live tests could be carried out in secrecy. Meanwhile, the man who was ultimately responsible for the carnage slumbered peacefully in his Cryo chamber.

Caught in The City, completely unaware of life beyond their walls, the citizens had continued to live while the rest of humanity perished. The very walls that imprisoned them had become their protection. Only President Josh Delman knew what had gone on, only he could prevent the annihilation of the last humans on Earth. He'd learned the truth from Edward Schaelles, a man he'd called his ally before he killed him with his own hands in a moment of vanity and greed. Schaelles had overheard Morgan's private conversations while preparing him for Cryo. He'd been horrified to learn what the President had set in motion and that he'd colluded with other countries in order to use his own people as lab rats.

With Schaelles' help, Delman hijacked Morgan's body and fled to the relative safety of Sector 2. There he fought with successive Fortrillium heads to preserve his position. He was the one human who had to survive at all costs, but only he knew it. He needed to stay alive for fifty years until the Centurial. Only then could he finally put things right.

President James Morgan had forged a treacherous deal. After a hundred years he'd planned to emerge from his Cryogenic sleep and destroy Centrum and any surviving cities. The evidence of the live tests would be eradicated. He and his team were destined to emerge in a world that had been cured of plague. He would destroy whichever cities were still standing, banishing the planet of all remaining contamination, then claim his prize along with the other officials who'd plotted and colluded in this scheme. They would be reunited with their families, who'd been held as collateral in Umbilica units based elsewhere, and they would live out the rest of their lives in a plague-free Utopia, their bodies still youthful and healthy, their former identities completely forgotten.

Only, there was no Utopia to emerge into, and the only life left on the planet was destined to be destroyed by a timed destruction sequence which had been activated by Morgan in the certainty that a cure had finally been found.

Now those citizens would inherit what was left of the world, their walls no longer needed to contain them. And with the death of Damien Hunter and the revelations about Josh Delman, a new society could be created without the divisions and horrors of the old ways.

But Josh Delman had one more secret to reveal. He'd carried it alone for several years. It was a sign of the cowardice that had led to his downfall in the first place. It was why he'd killed Edward Schaelles, to keep his secret safe.

Morgan's body was failing and Delman required a new vessel to travel in. He would need to make a final transference once Catharsis was averted. Like Morgan, Delman was vain enough to believe that he'd earned his place in Utopia. Seizing an opportunity and taking his final risk in The Grid, Delman positioned Reevil96 safely in Sector 1, an ally to help him navigate The Grid when the time came. He also took Tom Slater, who was destined to die in The Grid alongside his friend Matt Parsons. Delman had got to Slater before Damien Hunter, but he would need one final favour from the Schaelles family. He coerced Philip Schaelles to move Tom Slater into Cryo where he'd remain healthy and sleeping until it was time for Delman to transfer to his body. Delman would take over Slater's form, the strong body of a man in his forties, and banish his thoughts and memories to a small electronic archive stored in an unused area of the brain. To all intents and purposes, Tom Slater would be dead, but Delman would continue to live, discarding Morgan's spent body.

His security was Teanna Schaelles. He took Philip Schaelles' precious daughter as his guarantee, to make sure that Schaelles would complete the transfer in secrecy when Catharsis was aborted. Philip Schaelles had had no option but to comply, though he'd warned his daughter not to trust Delman, before she left Centrum. His own father, Edward, had told him about Delman, and how they'd colluded to stop Morgan destroying them all. He'd carried that terrible knowledge for almost fifty years, it had worn him down.

When President Josh Delman exited the elevator, he was met by Matt Parsons and The TriPlex guards. Delman didn't know about Matt Parsons, he'd always thought he would be able to pass through The TriPlex undetected. But they were expecting him. Although Schaelles had kept his secret, Matt had shared as much as he knew as his trust of the Centrum team grew, still keeping his word to protect Jacob in Sector 1. Delman understood immediately that it was over for him, he knew exactly where to go and what to do. If he didn't deactivate Catharsis, they would all perish, there would be no more life for anybody. He would get to live, but he'd lost his leverage, there would be no new body for him to transfer to now.

As he placed his hand on the panels of the console and registered his retina ID, the program that had been set up a hundred years ago booted up. He entered the codes he'd so meticulously committed to memory and it was switched off in a moment – the entire future of humanity held in a single electronic process. Had the real President James Morgan been allowed to execute his treacherous plan, he would have entered the death codes and set in motion the destruction of millions of his own people, oblivious to the knowledge that there was nobody coming to rescue him and reunite him with his family. They were all dead, he'd set those events in motion before he took his place in the Cryo-Labs.

As Catharsis was averted, The Grid powered down, leaving only a vast open hangar and the bodies of those who had died there.

Teanna and Joe were taken to the Med-Centre. Matt was in a state of panic about Joe, his son was pale and lifeless. President Delman was given medical attention, then placed in a holding cell pending further investigations. Sector 2 was safe, Centrum was protected, Catharsis was over.

In the Med-Centre, a medic desperately fought to revive Joe Parsons whose heart had stopped beating fourteen minutes beforehand ...

Final Wish

Harry got her final wish. She wanted to be buried in the way that had been customary when she was a child. It was fitting that she should be the first to be buried. Talya had suggested it. It would mark the coming together of the world that Harry had known, the past hundred years in The City, and the future – whatever that held for them.

With The Grid deactivated, those living in Centrum had reunited with the citizens of The City. The standoff at the gates of The Climbs had resolved peacefully, as Talya had hoped it would. The dividing gates were opened and the residents of The Climbs poured out onto Silk Road. There was no violence. Those who'd lived on Silk Road took their first steps into The Climbs, they were horrified at what they saw. Many on Silk Road welcomed families from The Climbs into their homes. The Centuria who had defended Fortrillium until the end removed their helmets and lay down their weapons in peace. Jacob Carley was finally relieved of his isolation in Sector 1 and there was a period of fourteen days when everybody got used to each other and to the removal of the barriers.

It was clear there would have to be new leadership, there was no doubt that Talya Slater should head any transitional government. She was acceptable to all parties. Representatives from The Climbs met with Talya and others from Silk Road and the way ahead was agreed upon.

Firstly, there would be no more divisions. All citizens would be equal in terms of rights and opportunities. Secondly, the justice system would be abolished, The Grid would be destroyed so that it could never be used again.

It was a huge mess. Some who had lived in The Climbs or on Silk Road would need to answer for their crimes. There were Centuria and Law Lords who would have to account for themselves.

There were several graves alongside Harry's. It was thought to be a fitting tribute to those who had laid down their lives in the name of The City. For some of the Justice Seekers, there was no grave, just a headstone – there was nothing left of them to retrieve from The Grid. The holes in the ground had been dug outside The City's walls. Some explosives had been taken from Fortrillium's armoury to blow an opening through the vast concrete wall leading to the outside world. It had taken many days to break through the wall, hence the delay to the funerals, but Talya wanted the burials to mark the beginning of the new era. The funerals were shown on the screens and the entire city came to a standstill as a mark of respect for those who had fallen.

Each had a headstone, their name inscribed into small concrete fragments of the fallen wall.

Talya read the names.

'Harriet, known only as Harry, last name unknown, Julia Levett, Mitchell Cranshaw, Max Penner, Marjani Dimka, Miron Panko, Ross Donaldson, Brad Sivil, Chris Farley ...'

Talya looked over to Chris's parents. They nodded at her through their tears. They were grateful for the humanity that had been shown to their son inside The Grid and they had repaid that kindness by helping Talya in her own time of need, by taking the first tentative steps towards peace in The City.

Talya continued.

'Rick Stokley, Grace Makins.'

Talya hesitated, bracing herself for the next name she would have to say. It would be difficult for Jena and Dillon to hear the words.

'Zach Fuller, who was the first to fall in the final battle for freedom.

'We owe an immense debt of gratitude to Wiz, or Shen Li, Leo Bachus, Jody Carn, Clay Hillman, Hannah James and my own daughter Lucy as well as her good friend, Joe

Parsons. Joe cannot be with us today, he is still confined to the Med-Centre, but I know he's watching on the screen feed, alongside his father, Matt Parsons. Thank you, Joe, for everything you have done with your friends, we owe you a great debt.

'We face a new and challenging future. I am determined that the new world we build will be based upon fairness and integrity. We owe it to the millions who have died. We are the survivors. Because of the work of former President Josh Delman, we are finally freed from the terror of the plague.

'There will be huge challenges as we move on with our new lives. Families will be reunited. Those prisoners incarcerated because of minor crimes will be released from The Soak. Prisoners who were charged with more serious crimes will be held humanely and given a fair trial. Families will be reunited, others will find that loved ones have perished. My own family is lucky to have been reunited. My husband, Tom, who we'd thought had died six years ago, is with us today. Like many others, our family must adjust. We will learn to live again. We will be able to love.

'Finally, before we start to build this new world of ours, we have to put new systems in place so that this can never happen again. Former President Josh Delman will be restored to his original body, then tried in a fair court for the crimes he has committed. He will answer for what he has done in his body of birth. President James Morgan will be relieved of his office and he too will face trial once his consciousness has been fully restored. There are many others, such as Philip Schaelles and Jacob Carley, who will have to account for their actions. There will be many trials to come, but in memory of these brave people who lost their lives fighting for The City, I swear to you today that we will no longer subject our citizens to punishment by death. Furthermore, judgement will be passed by a group of citizens rather than an elite and corrupt group of privileged officials. The Law Lords will be abolished, The Grid destroyed and every man, woman and child will begin life anew with a basic right to freedom and justice. Today the walls to our prisons have fallen, never again will we build them back up again.'

There were cheers and celebrations throughout The City. Everybody knew there was a long and difficult haul ahead, but with freedom and equality they were prepared for the challenge. They would work side-by-side, free and without the fear of Fortrillium.

Joe looked on at the video feed from his bed in the Med-Centre. He'd told his friends to go to the burials. He'd desperately wanted to be there himself, but it would take some time for him to regain his strength. The Centrum medics had fitted a small device into his chest which would give his heart the help it needed. He would regain his strength and take his place alongside Lucy and his friends in their challenge to create a new life.

He thought of Zach, Mitchell, Chris and Ross ... so many friends who'd lost their lives fighting to save The City. They'd all been confined within the walls of their own fear. Life beyond the walls would be just as terrifying, but it would be the fear of their own choosing. It was the fear and risk which comes with living a life spent in freedom.

If you enjoyed reading The Grid Trilogy, you'll love The Secret Bunker Trilogy, available in e-book & paperback formats now.

ABOUT THE AUTHOR

Hi, I'm Paul Teague, the author of The Secret Bunker Trilogy and The Grid Trilogy as well as several other psychological thrillers and non-fiction titles.

I'm a former broadcaster and journalist with the BBC, but I have also worked as a primary school teacher, a disc jockey, a shopkeeper, a waiter and a sales rep.

I've loved sci-fi all of my life, starting with the Danny Dunn books and progressing to the huge franchises such as Terminator, Star Trek, Babylon 5, The Hunger Games and The Maze Runner series.

Be first to hear about new books and special offers:
https://paulteague.net

Copyright © 2018 by Paul Teague

All rights reserved.

No part of this book may be reproduced in any form or by any electronic or mechanical means, including information storage and retrieval systems, without written permission from the author, except for the use of brief quotations in a book review.

www.ingramcontent.com/pod-product-compliance
Lightning Source LLC
Chambersburg PA
CBHW021303190726
48288CB00003B/672